RiGHT DOES NOT ASK PERMiSSiON...

Garda Nua Part 3

PALADiN SHADOWS SERiES, BOOK I2

A Novel by **Aidan Red**

To my wife for her patience, tolerance and encouragement. Many thanks to my family and friends for their past and continued encouragement and assistance.

Right Does Not Ask Permission...

Bullies are still bullies, but this time it is Shara's girls, Sedona and Sierra's fingers on the trigger. With the help of the other talented children, Sedona and Sierra approach the problem like any eleven year olds would... head on and with unexpected twists...

Chapters

One Thirty   1

One Thirty-One   27

One Thirty-Two   47

One Thirty-Three   69

One Thirty-Four   91

One thirty-Five   111

One Thirty-Six   131

One Thirty-Seven   151

One Thirty-Eight   177

One Thirty-Nine   191

Riggin Town Map   211

Riggs Valley Map   212

Glossary   213

Books by Aidan Red   235

More Books by Aidan Red   236

About the Author   237

One Thirty
C.3486.748

Knobaal's Prince Regent Wilmet Kiese Lukré sat straight in the high-backed cushion chair behind his semi-circular conference table in his private conference room adjoining his private suite. Before him, the directors of his Intelligence and of his Information Security Departments sat rigid across the table.

"As I explained earlier," Prince Lukré continued, "I have been thinking about the rumored secret communications those within the Peace Force seem to possess. My late cousin, Prince Kiese, seemed to believe the rumors were true to the point that he even tried to arrange a marriage with one expected to be strong in the capability of *hearing* those of the Traders blood and those of the Peace Force blood."

The director of intelligence nodded without speaking.

"When the humanoid woman was reported as having been accidentally terminated, I understand another woman, maybe slightly less desirable than the first, was found and substituted." The prince ran his fingers over his bearded chin. "Which means, there are likely others that possess the talents he was seeking." He held them with a fixed stare, his expression hard. "I want those talents! You have three turns to bring me a plan and a schedule to locate and collect the rest of that talent pool."

Tuesday, December 12

After introducing Neila to the conveniences of her en suite bath and hanging towels out for her, Cheral suggested that a warm shower or bath would help her relax. She hung the robe that Shara had picked out on the hook beside the door and left

1

Neila to bathe. Cheral had just finished bathing herself, dried, and had donned her nightgown and robe when she heard Kiile's sudden "Oh my, Neila!"

Cheral stepped quickly out of their bath and saw a red-faced Kiile standing with his back to their bedroom door. He quickly looked at Cheral. "Please give her a hand, Cheral."

Cheral went to the door and found a naked Neila standing in the hallway holding a bra. "I just wanted to know what this is. Am I supposed to do something with it?"

"Come on, Neila," Cheral said softly, and guided her back to her room.

"Is Kiile all right?" Neila asked. "I didn't mean to do anything wrong."

"I know, love. But we need to get some clothes on you before you go wandering around," Cheral said, and started looking through the clothes Shara had put into the clothespress. She selected appropriate sleepwear and handed the items to Neila. "Here, love. Put these on." Then she collected her robe from the bath.

Neila dressed and picked up the bra and looked at Cheral.

"I just assumed, that as mature as you are becoming, you were acquainted with support clothing," Cheral said, and patiently helped her try it on. "ST12 made an estimate on your sizes, and if this isn't correct we will get correct ones tomorrow. You'll find you'll feel better wearing one during the day as you grow. Trust me."

"Why was Kiile upset?" Neila asked when they finished and she had settled in her flannel sleep pants and top and her warm robe. "Did I do something wrong?"

"Not wrong, Neila," Cheral said, and sat down on the edge of the cot beside her. "Just very unexpected. You are quickly becoming a young woman, and it isn't appropriate for you to be around men or boys without clothes on."

"Sorry. At home no one worried about that sort of thing," Neila said softly. "Clothes were only for protection from the sun. Not often worn inside or at night."

"Were girls your age sexually active on Nevar?" Cheral asked, suddenly thinking she knew what had enticed Kiile—a young, unattached marine home on Leave—to become involved with Neila's mother.

"Most of the boys and girls were, but it wasn't an age thing," Neila said. "Bdor wanted me to eat sora root, but Mother would not let me."

"Sora root?" Cheral asked.

"It is a plant we grew to keep girls from becoming fertile," Neila said. "But Mother would not let Bdor have his way with me. If I ate sora root, he could do as he wished with me and Mother might not know."

"Well, I'm glad for that," Cheral said. "Your mother was wise in that regard. Here, there are too many people that take a pill, our version of your sora root, and are way too promiscuous, if you ask me. You'll probably hear talk about who slept with who and more, but just remember that's an activity that should not be for young women. When you have any questions about a man's intentions, please come and ask Kiile or me. We want you to have a happier and pleasant life without undue worry, and certainly without the burden of an accidental child."

"Thank you, Cheral," Neila said. "I don't want that burden either. Mother said I should wait on sex for the one I mate. I want to learn to be happy and for you and Kiile to be proud of me."

"We are proud of you and we're very glad you want us to be. That's more than half the battle," Cheral said, and smiled. "Now, do you want to try to sleep or would you like to sit up and visit for a while?"

"Visit," Neila said, and stood up. "Do I look okay now?"

"You look beautiful, Neila," Cheral said, "and very proper for a quiet evening before we retire." Cheral stood up and took Neila's hand, and together they walked down the hall to the living room.

⚐

"Come and sit," Kiile said, and shifted to the end of the

three-cushion sofa. He patted the space in the middle. "If you want. Or there's a chair you can curl up in."

"This will be okay," Neila said, and took the spot he suggested.

"Mind if I sit too?" Cheral asked, and gestured to the space next to her, putting Neila between her and Kiile.

"No, I don't mind," Neila said, and patted the space beside her like Kiile had done.

Kiile put his arm on the back of the sofa and gently felt the strands of her long, still damp hair. "Did you happen to bring a brush?"

"No," Neila said.

"But I did," Cheral said. "I was going to brush her hair, unless you want to."

Kiile took the brush and leaned Neila forward so he could catch her locks. "Cheral's hair is too short for me to brush, so I guess I'll have to learn how by brushing your hair."

"I don't mind," Neila said. "I like having it brushed."

"You'll have to show me how you like it fixed," Kiile continued, "so I can learn how to do that too."

Neila giggled and then Cheral saw her expression turn serious.

"Kiile?" Neila asked as he stroked her hair. "Do you like my name?"

"Of course, I do," Kiile said, surprised by her question. "Why would you think I don't like your name?"

"Mother chose it," Neila said, "and you didn't have a say in the choosing. I thought maybe you didn't like what she chose and that was why you never came to see me."

Startled, Kiile put the brush down and leaned forward. He gently turned her toward him, and without asking, drew her into a firm hug. "Neila, I would have come to see you, but I didn't know your mother had you. I only found out that you existed when your *gpada* sent word after the attack. I swear, love, I didn't know about you until then." He squeezed her again and then relaxed, setting her upright and holding her eyes. "I am very glad to know you are, that you do exist, and I certainly wish meeting you was under better circumstances. But please, don't ever think I don't like you or your name."

"When Gpada told me you were coming," Neila said softly, "I was so afraid you wouldn't like me, and then I worried that I wouldn't like you and would have nowhere to go."

"I worried about that as well. We both did," Kiile said, and smiled, running his fingers through her hair. "And I hope that you do like me, and us. We both like you very much and will do everything we possibly can to always be here for you."

Neila smiled and glanced around at Cheral. She leaned to Kiile and hugged him. "I like you too," she said, and quickly turned to hug Cheral. "And you too." Then she sat back upright and turned her back to Kiile. "Will you brush my hair some more?"

Kiile chuckled. "Certainly, love." And he picked the brush up and continued where he had left off.

▲

Kiile woke with a start, suddenly feeling that something was wrong. He looked around their dim bedroom and saw the ambient lighting was still at its lowest intensity, suggesting it was still very early in the morning. He confirmed the time and wondered what woke him.

Then he heard Neila in her bedroom and he slowly got up, hoping he would not wake Cheral. At Neila's door he could hear her soft sobs more clearly, and he walked over and sat down on the edge of her bed.

In the dim light he could see her wipe her eyes with the corner of the blanket, and he turned and leaned back against the wall at the head of the cot, stretching his legs out on the blanket beside her. He was surprised when she crawled up and lay beside him with her head on his chest.

"I'm here, Neila," he said softly, and rubbed her back, holding her against him.

She pushed herself tight against his side, pushed one arm

behind him and the other around his waist, and Kiile suddenly realized she had not had anyone to hold her and to share her sorrow and grief with since the attack. Anthor slept in his reclining chair and was too feeble to give her the tangible comfort she needed. He was extremely impressed with her courage and fortitude, bearing the changes in her world bravely and keeping her grief private and to herself.

Kiile held her tight and ran his fingers gently through her hair, feeling her tears as they wet his nightshirt. He held her fast and let her cry herself out. When she finally fell asleep, he closed his eyes and thought about how they could make the days ahead better for her.

Wednesday, December 13

"Thanks for meeting with me on your day off," Greg said as Kiile entered the small briefing room off the main flight ops briefing room.

"Glad you could wait on us a bit," Kiile said, and sat down at the small table. "I should have asked if you wanted any coffee or anything from the Mess."

"Not necessary," Greg said. "Did your sortie go well?"

"Yes, sir. It really did," Kiile chuckled. "Shara went with us and we started at Sally's Casuals for the pretty girl clothes, then the General Store for the daily essentials, and finally Buck's for jeans and some warm everyday shirts. Sorry, blouses, I'm told." He chuckled again. "I know you know all about it, but Neila's bubbling excitement at seeing all of the choices and her reaction to seeing town was something I'm very glad I witnessed. There are times she acts like Cheyenne, all emotions and energy, and yet, in some of the clothes Cheral had her try on, she's calm and looked so poised and so very grown up."

Greg smiled, knowing.

"I had to veto a few of their choices," Kiile continued. "I'm trying to get my head around having a daughter and I certainly don't want to be encouraging the young bucks around here at the same time."

"With Sedona and Sierra starting to fill out, I know exactly what you mean," Greg said. "Shara's had a few talks with them, and they've told us they've been facing the sudden and specific heightened interest from the boys at school."

"It doesn't seem to be any better as the boys get older," Kiile said, and explained what Seventeen told him about Forty-two's experience with two of his men.

"Welcome to fatherhood, Kiile. Trust me, the joys outweigh the trials and worries," Greg said with a smile and a slap on Kiile's shoulder. "But I have something else of importance to discuss with you."

Greg spent the next half an hour going over Franni and Blaire's search for Nikle, what they had found, and that Blaire had figured out why his sensations had become hard to follow.

"I'll pull a squad together and get down to the Niles Reeds' Ranch and see if we can find anything. Then we need to plan a strategy to catch him at his sister's place. Franni and Cheral can keep watch..." Kiile's excitement grew and he pulled his digital pad from his shirt pocket and started making notes. He looked up, thinking, when he caught Greg's calm, steady stare.

"Sorry," Kiile said, and stopped. "You weren't finished, were you?"

"I am for the moment," Greg said in a level tone. "Are you sure one man can see all of the details and plan for all of the requirements?"

"No," Kiile agreed. "One man can't do it all, but..." Suddenly Kiile's expression went pale. "I'm doing it again! Damn! I'm forgetting the one important thing. I promised Neila we'd do everything we could to always be here for her." He looked at Greg, his expression turning to a sheepish smile.

Kiile tapped his earpiece and softly spoke. In a couple minutes, Seventeen hurried into the room, saluted, and took the chair Kiile pointed to.

"Seventeen," Kiile began. "The commander and I have been discussing the latest developments in the Nikle situation. I want to go over the details we know and get your thoughts on how you will proceed."

⌄ ⌄ ⌄ ⌄ ⌄

"Okay," Cheral said as she sat on the edge of the cot and turned Neila around in front of her. "You remember how I described the various uniforms you'll see?"

"Yes. Plain khaki, the light brown color, means cadets or students, both flying and marine. Mottled colored, now because it's winter, it is grays, and light browns on white, means regular marines when they are on duty. The blue-black, Space Blue you called it, means flight crews, cadets, or Shadows when they're on duty or flying." Neila smiled brightly.

"Very good. There may be some differences every now and then, but if you're not sure, ask and they will tell you their rank and position. Just be polite, like you always are. Now," Cheral said, and stopped her turning for a closer look. "Socks and boots."

"Socks are to absorb sweat and keep your feet from smelling, and boots without lining for inside and with lining for outside." Neila repeated what Cheral had told her as she sat down beside Cheral and slipped the heavy socks on her feet.

"I'm thinking clean, pressed jeans and one of these colorful, floral-print blouses," Cheral said, "will do nicely as your daily uniform. That way everyone will recognize you and know you're not a cadet or a marine"—Neila giggled—"or a pilot. I'll make sure you always have a clean set for the next day."

"Thank you," Neila said, and slipped her unlined boots on. "Thank you for taking me into town and for taking me shopping. It seems like a nice town. And I like the trees everywhere and the mountains around the valley."

"You're very welcome, Neila. And we like the valley very much, also. Have you been warm enough?"

"Most of the time. I didn't sleep much last night and I got cold while I was thinking about things." Neila twisted her smile and shrugged.

"Wear socks at night and I'll get an extra blanket for tonight," Cheral said, but knew there was more. "I know you had trouble getting settled last night, but what else, love?"

"I...I've never slept in a room by myself before," she said. "It feels so...lonely. It was better when Kiile came and sat with me and held me. Is it okay if he holds me when I feel depressed or lonely?"

"Oh, love, of course." Cheral pulled Neila close and hugged her. "You should've said something about sleeping alone or how you feel. I didn't think about that, or all that's still bothering you. I am sorry for not realizing what you needed."

"I know I shouldn't feel lonely," Neila said. "Sedona and Sierra showed me their rooms and I asked them why they slept in different rooms."

Cheral waited, still holding Neila.

"They said they're with each other every minute of the day and they needed space the rest of the time. I didn't tell them I didn't know what that meant."

Cheral relaxed and smiled at Neila as she held her eyes.

"They're empaths, and identical twins. They're never alone or apart from each other or their parents," Cheral explained. "Like many of us, they can speak to others mentally, without the aide of equipment. They live with each other's thoughts constantly, except when they are here in training or flying an exercise. Their dad is very strict about anyone communicating during an exercise or a test, especially his daughters and relatives."

"Why 'especially' his daughters?"

"Sedona, Sierra, and Tayn will register with the Force next fall," Cheral said. "They have decided to become Shadows like their parents, but the commander wants them fully trained before they are registered to bypass the need for them to be away in school for four years."

"Four years would be a long time. Almost fifteen hundred terran turns."

"And Cheyenne is a year younger, almost two years away from the normal registration age." Cheral sighed. "She's only ten and a half, but when their talents started developing and the slave traders surfaced again, the commander had no choice but to start training them. Cheyenne has had to prove herself, earn her way by being very good in every step of her training. But enough of that for now. I'll just say that they will be expected to be among the very best in the Force."

Cheral stood up, extended her hand, and Neila took it and stood with her.

"Let's walk down to the supply office and get you a card for the Mess and see about a name tag. After lunch, we'll take a tour of the facility."

'CAPTAIN,' ST12 said as they stepped through the front door.

"One minute, Neila," Cheral said, then to ST12, '*Continue.*'

'*THE FORCE HAS AUTHORIZED NEILA'S IDENTIFICATION CODE. YOU MAY IMPLANT AT YOUR CONVENIENCE. THE SUPPLY TRANSPORT HAS ARRIVED IN EARTH ORBIT. LANDING IN THIRTY-ONE POINT SIX MINUTES.'*

Cheral grinned at Neila. "The supply transport will be landing in about a half an hour."

"You were talking to your ship, weren't you?" Neila asked, tapping her forehead, as they started down the corridor to the supply office.

"Yes, I was."

⋏

Neila patted her magnetic name tag and smiled as she walked beside Cheral back toward the flight training area. She smiled at the many people that took notice as they passed.

"You're making a big hit," Cheral said with a chuckle. "Like I said, there are a few that did not know you were coming and many that did, but either way, you are a beautiful addition to our drab facility."

"Now, I think you are kidding me a little," Neila said.

"Only a little," Cheral laughed. "Kiile's in the Flight Ops Briefing Room with the commander, but I wanted to take you into our training room to show you the maps of the area. It might help you get oriented."

Neila glanced down the corridor from the launch bay and smiled at the red-haired woman coming toward them, wearing her Space Blue flight suit and carrying a helmet like Ani's. Neila stopped and caught Cheral's arm.

"I know who this is," Neila said, and smiled.

Jill stopped and greeted Cheral and then looked at Neila. "This must be the reason for our mission," Jill said.

"I know who you are," Neila said, and extended her hand. "You are Captain Cera Dnar, Keely's mother—sorry, mom. And pilot of Apache Fifteen. I am Neila Beeli. Pleased to meet you."

"I'm very pleased to meet you, Neila," Jill said with a wide, surprised smile. "And how did you figure out who I was?"

"Last night, Keely, or Cheyenne," Neila answered, "told me you, she, and Blaire are the only red-haired females here. And I've met Blaire."

Jill laughed. "That would be my Chy. I take it, then, you have met Tayn and the girls."

"Yes, ma'am. We had dinner at the commander's ranch and he gave cadet Blaire a birthday party. It was very nice."

"Then you know that I'm your Cousin Jill, in a roundabout way?" Jill asked.

Neila nodded. "Cheyenne, Sedona, and Sierra tried to explain the relationships."

"I think it was a little confusing," Cheral said.

"But...Cheral is Shara's cousin," Neila said, thinking out loud, "and by mating, Greg is a cousin, and you're Greg's sister, so you are also a cousin to Cheral. And since Cheral is mated to Kiile, he is a cousin by mating and that makes me a cousin."

"Generally speaking, yes," Jill said. "There is a seemingly infinite list of designations, first cousins, second cousins,

cousins once, twice removed and such, but we don't look that deeply. You're family and I like that. Welcome."

"Thank you, Cousin Jill," Neila said. "We're going to look at maps before the supply transport lands. Do you have a debriefing?"

"Not until Major Glean calls one," Jill said. "May I join you?"

Neila smiled and looked at Cheral's smile and nod.

⋏ ⋏ ⋏ ⋏ ⋏

Forty-Two led his cloaked squad of fifteen to the west of Seventeen's squad as they drifted among the treetops, slowly searching for any signs of transmission or reception equipment as they started their second circle around the Niles Reeds' Ranch. Thirty-two's squad, two men to a remote, covered an arc a little farther out and Q-TTYF8 watched their progress from the east and the Transport from the west.

"I'm not seeing anything obvious," Franni told Seventeen as the vestiges of the afternoon began to give way to the growing evening, the sun sitting nearly atop Chimney Rock from where they slowly wove between the tips of the pines.

"Thank you, Captain," Seventeen said, and focused on each tree as he passed. Half his squad was looking at the treetops and the other half was searching lower, but the telltales were not cooperating, none divulging their presence. "Anything around the seven cabins or the main house?"

"Nothing," Franni replied. "I can't help thinking I'm missing something."

"We'll keep looking," Seventeen said.

⋏

"Okay," Colonel Mooren said as he faced the cadets seated in the Flight Ops Briefing Room. "You all have a Flip-File with today's flight particulars. Same practice area. As usual, Major Iims will conduct today's engagement scenarios. Mount up in ten minutes. Cadets, dismissed."

Blaire stretched as she stood up and looked at the small class. Tayn and the girls had arrived from school moments before the briefing began and they had had to sit behind the rest of the group. Blaire turned and greeted them, asked if they had any new and unusual occurrences in school, and walked through the launch bay to the corridor of steps. At the top, thinking about the search going on east of Hawthorne, she stopped to wish the girls and Tayn good luck in the sessions. She reached out and caught Caiti and Coli's hands and something flashed in her mind, an image of the forest and orange dots coalesced.

"Whoa!" Caiti and Coli said together, jumping at the sudden image in their minds.

"Focus with me," Blaire said, her voice firm yet soft, and she pulled the two girls to her, partially for their physical support.

Blaire felt the girls' thoughts merge with hers and she studied the enhanced image.

'Franni,' Blaire said. 'Link with us.'

'Blaire? Who's with you?'

'Link with us, Franni. We see the equipment. Like at Nikle's sister's place.'

'I see it! How?'

'Luc. Stop!' Blaire said sharply. 'To your right, below your third man. It's one of two small remotes.'

"Seventeen," Franni said through his earpiece. "The shed just north of the feed barn has some of the equipment you're looking for."

'Luc. Southeast of you,' Blaire continued, 'on the same level as the first remote, is a second remote. Seventy-five feet or so in front of you.'

'I see it,' Luc replied. 'Thanks.'

'You're welcome. We're late for a session and have to go now,' Blaire said, and broke the connection.

▲

Blaire released the girls and just stared at them.

13

"What did we just do?" Caiti asked.

"We just *saw* the equipment Seventeen's squads and Franni are searching for," Blaire said. "When we touched, it was like a surge of consciousness! I never thought about doing something like that. Has this happened to you two before?"

Caiti and Coli glanced at each other and Keely, standing close, said, "Yes it has."

"We..." Caiti slowly began, "discovered we could *see* things more clearly and farther away when we join."

"That's not all," Keely said.

"I know," Caiti said. "When the men tried to capture us after school that day..."

"We sort of...turned two of them into vegetables. We scrambled their minds," Coli finished. "We discovered we are a lot more powerful when we touch each other and focus together."

They all looked up at the soft beep from their wrist units, the one-minute reminder.

"Hurry or we'll really be late," Blaire said, and pushed the girls out into the clearing. "We'll talk about this after the debriefing."

▲ ▲ ▲ ▲ ▲

"Kiile?" Neila asked enthusiastically as she and Cheral came back into their quarters. "Are you here?"

"Yes, Neila," he said as he came to the mouth of the hallway, drying his hands with a cloth towel. "I'm here. What has you so excited?"

"Cheral took me to the supply office and I got my name tag," Neila said, and proudly pointed to the tag affixed to her blouse. "We ate lunch and I met Keely's mother, and Cheral showed me the maps of the valley, where all of the ranches are and the towns and of a lot of the country around the valley, and then we came to find you. Cheral says it's time to give me a tour."

Kiile smiled at Cheral and Neila. "The loadmaster notified me earlier when they off-loaded your container, and I just received a message from shipping saying they are bringing your things."

Neila smiled at Cheral and then back at him. "Can we wait? And then do the tour?"

"Certainly," Cheral said. "We should go and get your room ready."

Neila was following Cheral down the hallway when the entry chime sounded and Kiile greeted a corporal and two helpers. The corporal handed Kiile a notepad, and Kiile motioned them in and led them to Neila's bedroom.

After quickly exchanging the necessary formalities, Cheral and Neila stripped the cot and folded the linens and blankets, and the helpers disassembled it and carried the cot out. Neila rolled the rug and cleared the floor as the men returned and collected the nightstand, lamp, and the straight-backed chair.

Inside half an hour, the marines had removed the temporary furnishings and Neila and Cheral had arranged Neila's pieces. They moved her clothes to the clothespress and the armoire and Cheral folded a colorful blanket to make a pad for her Memories Chest.

When Kiile picked up the notepad to sign off the delivery, Neila stepped up to the waiting men.

"Thank you very much for bringing me Gpada's furniture," Neila said to them. "It means so very much to me to have it here and undamaged."

"Our pleasure, Miss Neila," the corporal said. "The shippers and the container did the protecting. We just brought it here from shipping."

Kiile made his notation on the notepad and handed it back to the corporal.

"Thank you for your help, Corporal, men," Kiile said, and followed them to the door.

Neila was standing in the doorway to her room when Kiile

returned. He stepped up behind her and slipped his arms around her shoulders. "You two have made this a very pretty room, Neila. Very pretty indeed. Maybe it won't feel so lonely now."

Neila closed her eyes, smiled, and leaned her head back against Kiile's chest.

"The furniture didn't make it lonely," she said with a sigh.

"I know, love. I know. I miss my family too," he said softly. "But remember them, Neila. Remember all of the good times you had with them, and that way, they are not completely gone."

"Thank you again, Kiile. Both of you," Neila said as Cheral stepped up beside them and slipped her arms around them, "for coming to get me, for helping me, for giving me a new life, and for understanding."

"You are very welcome, Neila," Cheral said. "And thank you, for letting us."

Kiile slowly relaxed his hold and straightened. "I believe we have a tour to give."

"Yes," Neila said, and stepped away from them. "Are you coming too, Cheral?"

"I will have to catch up with you," she said. "I need to see Lieutenant Keli and the Gleans and the Moorens. Then I can join you."

"How will you know where we are?" Neila's expression was full of concern.

"Don't look sad, Neila," Cheral said with a wide smile. "I always know where Kiile is, and now, I always know where you are." Cheral tapped her forehead and Neila smiled.

"Always?"

"Yes, love," Cheral said. "Every second of every day."

"Will I always know where you two are," Neila asked, "after you implant my name tag?"

"Implant? How do you know about that?" Cheral asked.

"Cheyenne and I talked at the party," Neila explained. "She

noticed I didn't have mine yet and ST12 told you it was okay to implant mine now."

Cheral looked at Kiile and chuckled. "You do have very keen hearing, don't you?" She hugged Neila again. "We will definitely talk about what this means after your tour. Now you two scoot and I'll find you as soon as I can."

⋀ ⋀ ⋀ ⋀ ⋀

Blaire's afternoon had been demanding. The exercises were more intense, increased in threat levels as the commander and Major Iims had promised, and Blaire's suspicion that "friendlies" would be slipped into the mix was answered in spades. Each cadet again faced a mix: Caiti faced seven with one friendly, and Coli had two friendlies, and Keely had one. Blaire had three mixed into her eight and she smiled; it was her second *Dance in the Dark*, Tayn's first, Keely's second, and Caiti and Coli's fourth, and each of them had been successful in separating the unfriendlies from the friendlies.

She felt exhausted when she landed and had a hard time staying awake through Major Iims' debriefing, barely made it through the evening Mess, and collapsed on her bed when she got back to her room. She forced herself to get up and shower after an hour's nap. As she dried, she saw Sam's still unopened present, still on her nightstand where she had laid it, still a reminder of the one confusing thing in her life.

She knew she was not looking for a relationship, a special someone. Her choice to become a Shadow and a pilot was the clearest, best choice she had ever made. And it left little time to think about men, but she knew Luc had made an impression on her—a curious one at first, then an angry one when she had misunderstood, and then a contrite one when she had realized she had misunderstood. He was a much more complex man than she had first assumed.

But she still missed the steady, always respectful, always present and caring countenance of Sam. He had been her quiet friend and champion since the first time she had met him. Even when he was mad at her, she knew he was still her friend and that he still thought about her. The gift—and the one he had given her the previous year and the year before—proved that. But it was her personal, unjustified stubbornness keeping her from opening them and she wondered why. She knew she missed him.

Knowing she could not worry about her dilemma now, she straightened her shoulders and wiped away the beginnings of a tear, thinking a glass of wine and a little reading might finish off the evening satisfactorily. She was about to slip into her sleep clothes when her communications console buzzed.

"Cadet Lupis here," she said when she tapped the voice-only key.

"Cadet Lupis, Colonel Mooren," the colonel's voice said. "I'm sorry to impose at this hour, but Commandant Kiile has requested you meet with us in a debriefing of this afternoon's mission to the Niles Reeds Ranch. Can you attend?"

Blaire sighed. "Of course, sir. When?"

"Ten minutes. Briefing Room Charlie," Colonel Mooren said. "Thank you, Blaire."

"Yes, sir."

⋏

Blaire, in her khakis, was surprised the briefing room was almost full when she stepped through the door and Colonel Mooren met her. Everyone associated with the day's mission seemed to be there. He pointed to the empty chairs between the commander and Franni on the far side of the head table.

When they took their seats, Kiile opened the meeting and asked Seventeen to give the overview.

Seventeen explained the objective, to search for and, if possible, find any remote imaging devices located at or around the ranch facilities. He described their arrival and his distribution of the three squads to search in concentric sweeps on remotes, and he described their inability to illuminate any targets or unusual equipment until Captain Mooren was able to place the objects of their quest on their handhelds.

"Forty-two's squad collected two small remotes and deactivated them," Seventeen said. "Thirty-two's squad investigated the outbuilding Captain Mooren identified, and they found a transceiver and two backup units. They also found a small core power unit supplying power to the transceiver. All are of Kyddellan manufacture. I suspect the transceiver was used to link with the remotes and project his presence at the ranch when he wanted to speak with his followers there."

"Were you or your activities discovered?" Kiile asked.

"Not while we were there," Seventeen said. "I left a remote to monitor activity after we left, and it has not reported any discovery."

"Very well done, Seventeen," Kiile said, and turned to Franni. "And a 'very well done' to you, Captain Mooren."

Blaire suddenly felt uneasy, sitting beside Franni when she asked to speak.

"If I may," Franni said, and looked at Kiile and Stran. "I did not find the targets in question. I merely passed the information on, posted their locations."

"If you didn't, then who did?" Kiile asked.

Blaire wanted to shrink and disappear.

"Cadet Lupis asked me to link with her," Franni said, and looked at Blaire, "and she showed me what we were looking for."

"What?" Kiile asked softly. "Cadet Lupis? I thought you were here flying exercises with Major Iims and Colonel Kooich."

Blaire stiffened her shoulders, unable to avoid the questions.

"I was here, sir," Blaire said.

"Please explain," Kiile insisted.

"Yes, sir. I was on my way out to my ship, wondering how the mission was going. That's when I saw the remotes and the equipment and *called* Captain Mooren. They confirmed finding the remotes, and then I had to hurry to my flight." When Kiile seemed satisfied, she glanced at the commander. *'Commander, Casi. I need to speak to you after the briefing. In private, if I may.'*

Stran nodded and Blaire turned her attention back to Kiile

and Seventeen.

The debrief went on for another half an hour, going over the details of the afternoon's activities until Kiile felt the mission log was accurate and the mission properly recorded. When Kiile dismissed the assemblage, Blaire remained quietly seated as the room emptied. Suddenly, she realized she was the only one left and was surprised that neither the commander nor Casi had contacted her.

She slowly got up and stopped at the door. The corridor was empty, and with a sigh she stepped out and started back to her quarters.

'Blaire,' Casi's voice said. '*Small Flight Ops Briefing Room, please.*'

▲

"Sorry I didn't call you sooner," Casi said as she met Blaire at the door. "We were caught in another discussion. Come and sit down."

She followed Casi and sat beside her, across the table from Stran.

"What can we help you with?" Stran asked softly. "You sounded like something might be wrong."

"Maybe not wrong, exactly, sir," Blaire said. "But unusual to say the least."

"What happened?" Casi asked.

"I don't know how to say this, but it's about your girls," Blaire said, and saw both of their expressions become guarded. "When I reached the top of the corridor of steps before our exercise flights, I was thinking about the mission. I knew Luc— sorry, Sergeant Stial was participating, and I was thinking about it when I saw Caiti and Coli. I bent down to wish them good luck, and when our hands connected, theirs and mine, I felt a surge, a connection I've never felt before, and I saw what the troops and Franni were looking for. The girls were as surprised as I was, but afterwards we talked, and they talked about being able to join their talents and focus better when they held hands with each other." Blaire looked at Stran and Casi's confused expressions. "Have either of you experienced this?"

"No," Casi said softly. "When we're together, we've never tried to join our focus on something."

"They told me," Blaire continued, "about the men that tried to capture the five of them after school one day. How they linked and scrambled the minds of two of the men. They said they made them 'vegetables.'"

"They did do that," Casi said. "The men almost couldn't walk and haven't improved any since."

"Well, I wanted to tell you," Blaire said, "because by myself I didn't see what I saw when we joined our talents and all focused on one thing. It was surprising—a little scary, but extremely wonderful to know we can enhance our abilities by linking together. I think you both need to ask Caiti and Coli to help you investigate this new possibility. The girls have already been experimenting, but I think they need your guidance in how to use it. Maybe you'll even discover something more in the trying."

"That is a very good suggestion, Blaire," Casi said, and smiled at the thought.

"Does this linking," Stran asked, "have residual strength, Blaire?"

"Sir? I don't understand your question."

"Today you Danced in the Dark again," he said, and held her eyes. "But with a quick, almost surgical precision. Yesterday, your Dance took nearly twelve minutes from the time you entered the arena until you struck. Today it took three. And you kept the friendlies safe, as if you herded the un-friendlies away first."

"I don't know about any residual qualities," Blaire said, "but today I didn't have to probe for information on the fighters. I knew which was which when I entered the arena." Then she glanced away, rolled her head to one side, and smiled sheepishly. "And I did *push* the un-friendly remotes away from the friendly ones."

"How on earth did—?"

"I can't explain it," Blaire said with a shrug. "I didn't want them close to the friendlies, so I decided where I wanted them to be and they moved there. If they were real ships that probably wouldn't have worked."

Stran smiled at her and then started to chuckle. "I think we overlooked the obvious. Once you know how to guide a remote, you always know how to guide a remote. Knowing the targets are generated by a remote, why not talk to the source and tell it to move? Thank you, Blaire. I don't think that will work much longer."

"I didn't think it would, Commander," Blaire said with a smile. "But I will say that once you've practiced Dancing, I wonder why we should light the targets up at all."

"The only reason I know," Casi said, "is the confusion the 'failed' system causes. In a large engagement, it can sometimes buy you time. But I agree: if the Dance is working well, lighting them up may not be necessary."

"Thank you," Blare said. "I guess you never want to disregard any option. I suspect each engagement has its own set of problems that have to be evaluated."

"Absolutely," Casi agreed. "We will take your comments to heart and see if we can learn something more from the girls."

"Thanks. I just thought that if you didn't know, you ought to know some of the hidden talents the girls have."

"Before you go, Blaire," Stran said. "What is your schedule in the morning?"

"Library time until exercises in the afternoon," she said. "Something you need for me to do?"

"Yes," Stran said, and grinned. "Let me know when you're eating breakfast, and immediately after, come up to the clearing and join us on STSX1."

"Certainly, sir," Blaire agreed. "What do I need to bring?"

"You, wearing your Blues."

"Yes, sir. In my Blues." Smiling, Blaire got up, but suddenly stiffened. "Casi, would you like to test that linking right now?" She extended her hand and closed her eyes. "I *see* three people at the college trying to enter a locked doorway leading..." She hesitated and Casi grasped her hand. "...leading to a tunnel under the building." She looked at Stran. "The tunnels go under the town?" Stran nodded.

"Oh my," Casi said as she *saw* the men. "They're trying to break the door open."

"I am focusing on the one in the center. The one with the pry iron," Blaire said matter-of-factly. "Focus on his mind with me." When she felt Casi's mind join hers, Blaire told WL-One to get Wally or a deputy and have them go to the men, and at the same time she sent a piercing shriek into the man's mind, holding it until she found the right pitch. As Casi *watched*, the man withered and collapsed. Then Blaire focused on a second man that was crouching down to see what had happened to the first. In a matter of seconds, the three lay in an unconscious heap in front of the locked doorway.

Casi released Blaire's hand and sat back in her chair, unsure if she had just seen, done, what she knew she had done.

Blaire inhaled deeply and exhaled very slowly. Then she smiled at Casi. "Deputy Baine and my dad will be there in less than a minute. I just hope I didn't scramble them too much, but wish I could figure out how to just make them sleep instead. Anyway, Casi, that's one of the things your daughters taught me."

🔺🔺🔺🔺🔺

"I could get very used to this," Neila said as she blew the steam and sipped the hot cup of cocoa Cheral had fixed for her. Snuggled between Kiile and Cheral on the couch in their quarters, each in their warm robes and sleepwear, Neila smiled and pondered the surface of the confection and the sugar puffs slowly melting on it. "Gpada didn't have anything like this in his food stores."

"It's from a local bean," Kiile said, "grown here on earth. Not likely found elsewhere."

Neila took another sip and looked at Kiile and smiled. He smiled back at her.

"Are you feeling okay after getting your tag implanted?" Kiile asked.

"I think I am," she replied, and blew the steam wisps again. "I like being able to *feel* your tag, Kiile. And yours, Cheral. It is a different sensation than I expected—similar to hearing you, but you're not speaking."

Cheral smiled. "That's a good way to explain it, Neila."

"ST said the *feeling* should get stronger in the next few seven days, ah, weeks," Neila said.

"Yes, love," Cheral said. "In the process of accepting an implant, your mind has turned on some capabilities, additional talents, to allow you to use the implant and to recognize the implants in others. It enhances your ability to *hear* others." Cheral lightly tapped Neila's forehead.

"I like hearing you clearer," Neila said.

"More clearly," Cheral corrected.

"Yes, more clearly," Neila said, and smiled and looked at Kiile. "Do you *feel* my new tag?"

"Yes, love," Kiile smiled. "I certainly do. It is very nice to be able to."

'Remember what we talked about, Neila,' Cheral said softly in her mind. Neila glanced at her and smiled, then turned back to Kiile.

"Could you *hear* me before?" Neila asked, touching her forehead.

Kiile slowly shook his head. "Not like Cheral can. If I have any talent for *hearing*, it hasn't woken up yet."

"Cheral? Didn't ST say he could enhance one's *hearing*?"

"He did and he can," Cheral admitted. "I lost my *hearing* when I was badly wounded about thirteen years ago. When I started flight school and got my assignment back here as a student, the commander's ship, STSX1, helped me get it back."

"Can ST help Kiile?"

Cheral looked at Kiile and smiled. "You know, he might. But Kiile's never let anyone evaluate him."

"I don't know—" Kiile started to say.

"Please," Neila interrupted, and turned to lay her head on his shoulder without releasing or tipping her cup. "Pleeaase," she said, and repeated the word in her mind, trying to reinforce her plea. Cheral laughed softly. "Don't you want to be able to *hear* me, Kiile?"

"It isn't that, Neila," Kiile said. "It's..."

"What?" Neila asked pointedly.

Cheral cocked her head, smiled, and looked at Kiile. Neila snuggled a little closer to him and he looked at Cheral and sighed.

He lifted his right arm and gently dropped it across Neila's shoulders and pulled her tight. "Okay. I'll let ST see what he sees."

"Thank you, Kiile." Neila smiled and reached out and took Cheral's hand. *'Thank you, Cheral.'*

'You're welcome, love.'

One Thirty-One
Thursday, December 14

"He's coming," Cheral said as she and Neila joined the line at the lunch counter.

"I don't feel him yet," Neila said, and then pointed to a choice in a serving tray. "What's that?"

"You will, Neila. It just takes a little time," Cheral said. "That one is a meat loaf," and she explained what was in it and how it was prepared. "Do you like greens, salads?"

"Yes. And those," Neila continued, "are sliced pork, ham, chicken, and beef. Right?"

Cheral nodded, pleased that Neila remembered things so easily, and then she pointed out the numerous non-Terran dishes the cooks had prepared.

"And the vegetables you said are corn, green beans, carrots, and the white one is potatoes all mashed up," Neila said as she picked a few and the server dished them for her. "And the yellowish ones are boiled and fried issl. I like the issl, especially when they're crispy."

"I think you also like the ham," Cheral said as the server handed Neila her plate.

"I do. It has a sweet flavor," Neila said, and moved to the desserts. "I will try the different choices like you suggested, but today I feel like having more ham. We didn't get meat often while I grew up. It had to be imported, and Mother said it was too expensive for regular eating."

When they collected their drinks and started for a table, Neila saw Kiile enter the Mess. He saw them and quickly crossed the room, stopping beside Cheral. He gave her a quick kiss and then squeezed Neila's shoulders and kissed her forehead. "I'll get a tray and join you two in just a minute."

Cheral picked a table to one side of the dining room and away from the entry. They settled and had started eating before Kiile joined them and sat down next to Cheral.

"How has your morning been?" he asked as he sipped his tea and spread his napkin.

"Quiet," Cheral said, and glanced at Neila. "I think Neila slept good last night. I actually had to wake her this morning."

"I don't even remember going to bed," Neila said, and took a bite of issl.

"I'm not surprised," Kiile said, and smiled. "You fell asleep on the couch and I had to carry you to bed. You didn't wiggle once. I'm glad you slept well."

"Thanks," Neila said. "Are you going to have time after lunch to let ST evaluate you?"

He shook his head absently. "I've got a meeting with the commander right after lunch, and then with Seventeen..." He stopped, seeing Neila's long face. After a moment, he inhaled and smiled. "I'll make time. I can't take too long, but if we go as soon as we've eaten, I can do it and not keep the commander waiting too long."

Neila smiled.

"And I've got a two-hour patrol flight," Cheral said, and cocked her head and looked at Neila. "Are you going to be all right while Kiile's in his meetings and Keli and I are flying?"

"I guess..." Neila said softly.

"No, tell you what," Cheral said. "On second thought, you're coming with Keli and me. I don't think I could concentrate knowing you were suddenly alone in a new place. I'd be listening to you more than I would be to my job."

"Is that okay with you, Kiile?" Neila asked.

"Yes, Neila," Kiile said. "You could come with me, but my meetings are all tactics and missions, trying to figure out where and how to catch a very bad man, an agent of the slavers. I don't think it would be very interesting to you."

"Okay," Neila said. "I like the flying, but will you let me go with you sometimes?"

Kiile looked at her and smiled. "Yes, Neila. I'll figure out how I can do that and it not be too boring for you. Maybe tomorrow." He reached across the table and gestured for her to give him her hand, and he squeezed it. "I'm learning how to do my job differently, letting my men do more of the missions and the daily work. That way I can be here and have more time to spend with you."

"I'd like that, Kiile. A lot." Neila squeezed his hand and smiled. She turned quickly and looked at Cheral. "I like spending time with you also."

"I know, Neila," Cheral said. "But it is right that you'd want to spend time with your father and learn more about what he does. You need to know and understand both of us and our jobs."

"Oh, one more thing," Kiile said without releasing Neila's hand. "We have an invitation for a dinner meeting at the ranch tonight. Business, civilian dress, about six."

"A meeting?" Cheral asked, and glanced at Neila. "And another dinner at the ranch?"

"That's right," Kiile said with a wide grin. "The Beelis were specifically requested. All three of us."

"Any idea what it's about?" Cheral asked.

"None," Kiile said, and shrugged. "The commander seemed in good spirits when he asked."

Cheral smiled back at Kiile and then looked at Neila. She squeezed Neila's other hand. "Please tell the commander that the Beeli women accept his invitation."

⚔ ⚔ ⚔ ⚔ ⚔

"Please take a seat," Stran said as Kiile entered the briefing room. "I'm sorry I had to delay our meeting."

"Afternoon, Commander," Kiile greeted, and pulled a chair

out from the table. "It actually helped me squeeze in some time with Neila."

"Is she settling in okay?" Stran asked.

"Amazingly," Kiile said, and sat down. "Her first night was a little rough—still grieving and she cried through most of it—but last night she seemed to sleep quietly through the night."

Kiile explained a little about Neila's life on Nevar and how much different things were for her here, in her new life.

"We also implanted her tag yesterday and that seems to have made a big difference in how she feels," Kiile continued. "I know I'm reading too much into this, but I think it somehow helps her know she belongs somewhere. Here. And that I—we—both will do all we can to be here with her, to help her any way we can. I know she was very happy when Cheral told her that she could find Neila anytime, anywhere."

"I'm glad she's feeling more comfortable," Stran said. "Did the tagging reveal any other talents?"

Kiile looked at him and smiled. "Cheral had already figured out that she could *hear*, and it looks like her session with ST showed her she can also *speak*."

Stran smiled at Kiile, one eyebrow raised. "And how does Kiile feel about that?"

"I was okay with it," he said quickly, and then saw Stran's knowing look. "Well, not really. I've always known I have some low-level capability because I can *see* people's tags and I know when they are *talking* to others. But I've always been a little afraid to learn why it's just a low-level talent. My folks and my relatives had the ability, but I didn't."

"Is that why you joined the Force and applied yourself so diligently to your assignments? To prove something to yourself? Or to others?" Stran waited.

"Probably," Kiile admitted, and slowly smiled. "You know me, sir. I know I don't always live up to my own standards, but I don't like being inferior." He paused a short moment. "Neila begged me to do an evaluation. She wants me to be able to *hear* her, and..."

"And?"

"I gave in and agreed," Kiile said. "That was the time I spent with Neila when you delayed this meeting."

"I'm very pleased for you, Kiile. When will ST have results?"

"He says later today, maybe tonight. I don't know why he's taking so long. He can analyze the most complex navigational puzzles in a split second and the most complicated firing solutions in half that time."

"I suppose he wants to be certain," Stran said, thinking he could also be considering Kiile's need to settle a bit before hearing whatever the news was. "I'm certain there isn't anything wrong, Kiile. STSX does the same thing in many cases. They consider all aspects of a situation, not just the part we see or the immediate result we've pre-selected."

"I'm learning that," Kiile said. "But since our session, I keep hearing these faint echoes of Neila and Cheral in my head. Like the session is making me remember things they've said, that maybe I missed or something."

"Maybe it is," Stran said, and smiled. "Let me know what ST says."

"I will," Kiile agreed. "Now, I've digressed too long. What did you want to talk about?"

"I'm curious about Seventeen's plans concerning Nikle," Stran said. "Have you discussed the details of his plans or is he still working them out?"

"Shall I have Seventeen join us?" Kiile asked, and tapped his earpiece when Stran nodded.

"What are you looking for?" Neila asked softly from the jump seat as STSX12 leveled just above the atmosphere, heading southeast.

"Anything that isn't as it ought to be," Cheral said, and smiled. "I know that doesn't answer your question, but we never really know what we're looking for until we find it."

"So how will you know if it is something it shouldn't be?"

Cheral chuckled. "That, love, is the hard part. And it is very hard to explain. Can you try the linking ST showed you?"

"I'll try," Neila said, and waited for Cheral.

"I'm *feeling* for the space station," Cheral said, and felt Neila's presence in her mind. "It's on the other side of the planet and I can tell that it is alone. No other ships around it. Can you *see* that too?"

"Yes," Neila said, and smiled. "And there are a lot of other things floating around the planet. Smaller and without people on them."

"Those are the planet's data and communications satellites and a number of military satellites from many different countries." Cheral smiled and explained the number of satellites that were still in use and the growing number of unused remnants, called space trash.

"Too bad you can't just collect all of the unused items," Neila said. "Then they could bring them down for recycling or bundle them and send them into the sun to be disposed of."

"Well, I like how you think," Cheral said with a sigh, "but the cost is too great for any of the countries to pay. And they haven't figured out how to work together for the good of the whole planet."

"Couldn't you do it?" Neila asked. "I mean the Peace Force that you work for?"

"That would be nice," Cheral chuckled again. "But then the people on earth would see all of the debris disappear and they would know someone was here. We can't be seen and do our job. Most of the population doesn't know there are people here from other worlds. In fact, it would scare them beyond belief if they knew. They would not see us as help, but as a threat."

"Why? Why would they see us as a threat?"

"They would see us as being stronger," Cheral said. "Able to take control whenever we wanted to. We have technology they have never seen or even dreamed of. We can cross the galaxy in a couple of their days. We have weapons and defenses they would not understand, and they would focus on how they could be used against them instead of how we use them to protect them."

"So why did the Force come here?" Neila asked, and turned at Keli's chuckle.

"So we can protect them," Keli said.

"But why?"

"To keep them safe from the dangers we know about," Keli said, "even if they do not know we are. The slavers have been stealing people from this planet for more than a hundred of their years. In trying to stop the sale and trading of slaves, we have to protect them as well. And as you can tell, we are related to the Terran humans."

"This can make life here difficult," Neila said, almost to herself.

"Yes," Keli said. "That is why we only visit town now and then and act like visitors, passing through. If we are seen too often, people will begin to ask questions. Whose family are you? Where do you live? Who are you visiting? When did you get here? And things like that."

"What about those that don't live at Shadow Base?" Neila asked, watching Keli.

"I guess I should have ST give you the history lessons," Cheral said. "Those that live outside have a family presence that goes back in the town's and valley's history. My grandfather Paul moved here many, many years ago, with his brother and sister, before this valley was developed. He settled the large ranch I showed you on the maps. He gave part of his land to his brother, Andrew, who was Shara's grandfather, so she has family history in the valley. When Greg came, the first the town knew about him was when they got married, mated. So they accepted that they live together on her ranch.

"Cousin Jill's father came to the valley and got work in town at the lumber mill and established a family, married the boss' daughter, and established a history in town."

"So people think they are like them because they have been here a long time," Neila summarized. "But what about Colonel Kooich? They live outside, at Cousin Shara's ranch."

"They were introduced as friends of the Malones and they live at the ranch and help work with Shara and Greg," Cheral explained. "It's a small lie, but essentially true. Everyone needs a 'purpose' in the people's mind in order to fit in. When Cousin Jill joined the Force, she went back to 'work' at the mill to keep her 'purpose' in town."

"Does that mean we will always have to live at the Base?" Neila asked, and Cheral felt Neila's sudden anxiety.

"I don't know, love," Cheral said. "I hope not. Kiile and I both want to have a place outside and live a more normal-appearing life, especially for you, but we haven't worked out the details. Maybe this is something we can all work together on, and figure out a way we can do it."

Neila smiled. "I like the outdoors. And I like your outdoors, even if it is colder than I've ever been before. The clothes keep me warm, but it is still cold. I would like it if we can someday live in a place outdoors, like the ranch or someplace in the trees. I like the trees."

"Maybe the commander and Cousin Shara can help us figure out a way," Cheral said.

"What about your poor, lowly lieutenant?" Keli asked from the nav-com compartment. "Are you going to leave me at Shadow Base to put up with disorderly pilots and marines by myself?"

Neila glanced at Cheral and caught her thought. "Lieutenant Keli," Neila said, "I think you would have to live with us. You and ST are part of Cheral's other family and that means you have to be close to Cheral."

"Thank you, Neila," Keli said, and chuckled. "If they buy a ranch, I'll just have to learn how to ride and take care of horses."

"Cousin Shara says that part's fun," Neila said. "She said I can learn when I have free time."

Their conversation slowly dwindled and Neila watched the beautiful planet drift under them, thinking about the many places she had researched before coming and the places she had talked to Cheral about when Kiile was away in his meetings. She didn't know how long she had drifted in thought when she felt the tension rise in the ship.

"Keli? Do you *feel* a visitor?" Cheral asked softly, and glanced over her shoulder, past Neila and into the nav-com compartment.

"No. I feel your sudden alertness," Keli answered.

"It's out there," Neila said, and pointed toward the moon, high and behind them.

"ST, contact Shadow Base and the commander," Cheral said, and started turning ST around to face the sensation.

"STSX1 AND APACHE PATROL FIVE ARE EN ROUTE. THEY WILL RENDEZVOUS IN THREE POINT TWO MINUTES."

"How can they be almost here?" Neila asked as Keli made contact with Casi. "You just *felt* it."

"Casi is very keen in *feeling* new presences or sudden changes in the normal sensations, Neila," Cheral said. "Twelve years ago on a Christmas Day patrol, my patrol fighter was destroyed by three enemy mines. They tore my ship open and I was full of shrapnel and hanging out in my harness. My suit was full of holes, losing pressure, and I *called* Casi for help. I was told that Casi and the commander knew before I called, and got to me in less than four minutes from the time the mines exploded."

Neila stared at Cheral.

"Close your mouth, love," Cheral chuckled. "It isn't very becoming. She's the best of what family means. You can always count on her."

"I count on you and Kiile," Neila said softly.

"I'm glad, love. We're here for you, no matter what," Cheral smiled. "They're here."

"STSX1 AND APACHE PATROL FIVE ARE JOINING IN

LEFT ECHELON."

"Lead the way, Apache Four," Casi's calm voice said, filling the cockpit. "We'll fly formation left."

"Good to have you along," Keli said, and Cheral advanced the thrust levers.

Neila watched Cheral's movements and glanced at Cheral's face, seeing her features stiffen as she focused on the mission. Neila *felt* Cheral's concern and her sense of seriousness.

"Can you *feel* where Casi and Blaire are?" Cheral asked softly without looking at her, maintaining her focus on the distant sensation. Cheral took a strip of red material out of her utility pouch and fastened it tightly around her head, dropping the tails behind her right shoulder. "Keli, we're going to increase our speed."

"I don't *see* them, but I *know* they are beside us," Neila admitted in a whisper, studying the headband and looking back to see that Keli had put one on also. "Blaire is closest and Casi is next."

She watched Cheral push the levers on the left armrest forward more and felt the gentle change in ST12's push.

"It's on the far side," Neila said, and focused on the distant sensation.

"Major," Blaire's voice said, "the target seems to be a small transport, maybe a Class I or II with a crew of two. Kyddellan signature. Both crewmen are foreign."

"Thanks," Cheral said. "I heard you were getting very good at seeing the details."

"Thank you, Major," Blaire said. "And good afternoon, Neila."

Neila looked at Cheral in surprise and then smiled.

"You can answer her, Neila," Cheral said.

"Good afternoon, Cadet Lupis," Neila said to the cockpit. "I didn't know you knew I was here."

"Can't hide from us, young lady," Blaire teased. "Welcome to your first sortie."

"Thank you," Neila said. "I wasn't hiding." She looked at Cheral. *'Why does Captain Casi feel displeased?'*

'Because you are not in official training and I brought you on a potentially dangerous mission.' Cheral said, and smiled at Neila. *'Don't let it bother you, love. It is my decision who is on my ship and when. You have done nothing wrong. She just didn't know ahead of time and it surprised her.'*

"RENDEZVOUS IN FIVE POINT SEVEN MINUTES."

"Caldite combat language, Major," Keli said sharply. "ST record and translate, please."

"Apache One," Cheral said. "They're communicating with someone in the Caldite combat language."

"Confirmed," Casi said, her tone fully business. "Apache Patrol Five, *listen* for another ship. The commander was expecting them to try to sneak in and transfer a small collection."

'How would the commander know they would do that?' Neila asked Cheral.

'That's why he's the commander, love,' Cheral answered, and smiled at her. *'He figures out the possibilities and then listens to see which ones are most likely to happen.'*

'He's very smart then,' Neila said.

'Very intelligent. Both the commander and his mate are. When they tell us to do something, they have thought it out and have a reason. If there is time, they will let us ask questions, but if not, we ask later.'

'I understand,' Neila said. *'I think I like the commander and his mate very much.'*

Cheral nodded and pulled the thrust levers back. "ST, decelerate and drop into a formation with the freighter. I want to get a good look at it." Then Cheral called Casi and told her what she was planning.

"Apache One," Blaire said. "A Kyddellan fighter has left from a secluded place in western Australia. Nav computations indicate arrival in twenty-six minutes."

"Apache Patrol Five, do you have the coordinates the fighter came from?" Casi asked, and then continued when Blaire said she did. "Please pass them to Shadow Base and have Kiile send a squad to investigate what's there."

"Sent," Blaire said.

'Are you listening to all of this, Neila?' Cheral asked, and glanced at her.

'Yes. It's interesting. I mean I'm interested in hearing it,' Neila said.

"RENDEZVOUS IN TWO POINT FOUR MINUTES. WILL SETTLE IN RIGHT TRAILING ECHELON."

"Thank you, ST," Cheral said, and passed the ETA to Casi and Blaire. "Apache Five, I have a favor to ask."

"Go," Blaire said.

"I'd like to see if Neila can link with you," Cheral explained, "and then if she's successful, link again when you analyze the freighter and the fighter."

"We can try," Blaire said. "Neila, are you ready to try?"

Cheral nodded to Neila. *'Go ahead, love.'*

"Okay. What do you want me to link to?" Neila asked.

"Think of Apache Patrol Five and then of me and *listen* to what I'm thinking," Blaire explained. "If you can link with Cheral, you can link with anyone when they let you."

"Okay," Neila said, and thought about Apache Patrol Five, his size, his shape, and then focused on Blaire. *'Hey, you're wearing a headband too.'*

'Yes, I am. So is Cheral and so is Casi,' Blaire said in return. *'Now for something specific.'*

Neila turned quickly and looked at the surface of the moon, very close on her side of ST12. *'Oh my. What's that flat space?'*

'That is called Mare Nubium, and in a minute you will see a very large crater named Crater Copernicus. We will pass directly over it,' Blaire explained. *'Behind you, you can see Crater Tycho disappearing over the edge of the moon. I think we are linking just fine. Don't you think so?'*

'Yes, I do. Thank you, Cadet Lupis,' Neila said politely.

'You listen as we get closer to forming up with the freighter,' Blaire said. 'I'll let you know when I'm ready to analyze them.'

"Did you *hear* that, Cheral?" Neila asked, and Cheral smiled and nodded.

"You did very well, love," she said, and returned her focus to the mission.

"FREIGHTER ONE MILE."

"Thank you, ST," Cheral said. "We have him also. Please run the cloaking transmitter maintenance codes."

Suddenly an orange dot appeared on the scanner displays in each of the fighters.

"Sounds like the fighter coming to rendezvous saw him light up," Keli said. "He's started another conversation."

"Good," Cheral said. "ST, please scramble his communications and drop his veil and keep it down."

They were a thousand feet off the freighter's aft, right quarter, giving each fighter a clear view of the freighter's location when the veils "failed." They could *feel* the sudden confusion in the freighter.

'Follow my thoughts, Neila,' Blaire said, and started a detailed scan of the ship and the crew. 'STSX, please record what I see.'

"Apache One," Cheral said. "The fighter coming to rendezvous has had second thoughts. It is altering course, breaking off. You might want to follow him down or have someone meet him and give the marines some air support."

"TTYF8 and KCMM9 are escorting Forty-Two's squad," Casi replied. "They have the fighter lit up and will be waiting for him when he lands."

"Okay," Cheral said. "Time to give them the opportunity to surrender. Apache Patrol Five, give yourself some distance." 'Hold on real tight, Neila. They're going to shoot at us, but we'll be okay.' "ST, shields full, double forward and left side, all other shields on redundant core power. Set firing solution top and forward cannons, multiple volleys from each if they fire at us, number and duration are your choice."

"ALL FREIGHTER DEFENSES ARE ARMED."

"Give them the ultimatum and then drop our veil. Mark," Cheral said as ST12 repositioned another thousand feet away.

STSX12 hailed the freighter, demanding immediate surrender. When ST dropped his veil, the freighter gave its answer. Three of its cannon turrets fired, and ST instantly responded in kind. The freighter disappeared in a blinding flash and a boiling cloud of smoke and fire.

"Is everyone okay?" Cheral asked as the smoke dissipated and the few remaining shards of the freighter drifted away.

"Apache Patrol Five is okay," Blaire said.

"We're okay," Casi answered in a firm, though less formal tone.

"Very good," Cheral said. "Apache Four is returning to base. Thanks for the support."

'*Thank you, Blaire,*' Neila said in a tightly guarded thought.

⋏

When Cheral landed ST12 in the clearing outside the launch bay portal, she watched Apache One settle quickly through the veil canopy as she swiveled the pilot's chair to aft facing.

"Keli, please secure ST. Neila and I have a point to make," Cheral said, and quickly stood. "Neila, come with me, please."

Cheral was down through the floor portal before Neila was out of her jump seat. She hurried, threw her coat on, and caught Cheral as ST opened the aft portal. Cheral slipped her arm around Neila's shoulders and said softly, "I am extremely proud of you and what you have learned to do. But Shara is upset, a little angry, and I have to remind her of her own examples. What I say will be true, but how I act may seem strange to you. Okay?"

"Okay," Neila said, and Cheral led her down the ramp as Shara emerged from STSX1 and marched across the space between the two ships.

At the bottom of the ramp, Cheral slipped her arms under Neila's and scooped her up and swung her around, telling her how wonderfully she had done and how well she had handled the crisis. Cheral told her she'd make a top-rated fighter pilot out of her yet.

Casi stopped beside them and shouted, "Major Beeli!"

"Oh, Casi! Wasn't Neila just great?" Cheral said, ignoring Shara's shout. "Almost like Sedona and Sierra when you picked up the grandfolks for Thanksgiving. She can *hear* and link and *saw* everything Blaire showed her. I think she's absolutely amazing!"

Casi stared at Cheral and then at Neila. "I...I guess she was. But...she doesn't have Blues! Cheral, the girl needs Blues if she's going to fly! Especially if it's dangerous!" Casi looked away and back again, her anger suddenly out of place. "Get Neila some Blues!" Casi turned and marched back to STSX1.

Cheral stood holding Neila until STSX1 had lifted and disappeared through the veil. Then she turned, set Neila down, and hugged her again.

"I knew it would work! I just knew it!" Cheral said, still hugging Neila.

"Was she mad because of me?" Neila asked.

"Not you, love. She was being Shara, a wonderful mother hen that cares about all of her cadets and crews," Cheral tried to explain. "When our routine mission changed with the arrival of the visitor and she realized you were aboard, she thought about your safety. She forgot that your safety is your father's and my job and we were in the safest place we could be. We were aboard the best heavy fighter ever made. But the key is, she 'told' me to get you Blues."

"But she was angry when we landed," Neila said.

"Yes, she was. That's why I had to remind her. When I give you the 'history,' maybe tomorrow, of how we came to be here, you will see that Shara is just like everyone else, except she is extremely passionate about our safety. She has trouble understanding that we are also."

"So she's okay?"

"Very, love. We won't need to mention this tonight or ever again. Casi sees you belong here and will be well cared for,"

Cheral said. "So, let's go and get cleaned up and get ready to attend an important dinner meeting at Headquarters. And I think we have a very suitable outfit for the commandant's daughter."

"The one Kiile almost didn't let us get?"

"Yes, love. That's the one."

▲ ▲ ▲ ▲ ▲

Blaire had landed and was down Apache Patrol Five's ladder when STSX1 landed, and she stood in surprise, watching Casi as she marched toward Cheral and Neila. She knew Casi was angry, but did not hear her yell at Cheral, who was swinging Neila around in a proud and happy manner.

When Casi turned and hurried back to STSX1 and Cheral hugged Neila again, Blaire turned and went to her quarters. Inside, she flopped onto her cot and thought about the day and the mission and how well Neila had done and how calm she was in the face of the engagement. She attributed some of it to Cheral's calm explanations of what was going to happen next, but a lot of it was simply Neila. She had a strength about her.

Blaire pushed herself up, thinking about a shower, when she saw Sam's three presents she had stacked by her nightstand. After looking at them for a long moment, she admitted that she did miss talking with him, she missed their random, unscheduled lunches, and she missed how he was before she had made him so angry. Slowly she realized that even though she grew up thinking of him as a big brother, he had obviously stopped thinking of her as a little sister.

She shook her head, knowing that she was not ready for any kind of a serious man-and-woman relationship, and she admitted that if she had stayed in Riggin and reconciled, that was where Sam would have wanted to go.

She bent down and picked up the first present and slowly unwrapped it. She sighed when she saw the book of poems she "just had to have" when Sam had gone with her into the book section of Dawson's Drug Store. That was three birthdays ago.

She picked up the second present and again sighed when she held the colorful, handmade winter scarf. She wondered if Betti might have knitted it for him as she folded it and laid it on the cot beside her.

She had unwrapped the third present and was about to open the small square box when she felt Luc's urgent touch and the image of running through a hewn-rock doorway flashed in her mind. She saw weapons fire from all sides and men fall before her vision. Then suddenly it was still, and troopers came through a doorway across the room. Luc looked at a communications console and she saw his hand reach toward it, and slowly the room turned and went dark.

She clutched her chest and dropped the box when Luc's touch vanished.

▲ ▲ ▲ ▲ ▲

Forty-two stood in the transport's cockpit between the pilot and the nav-com officer. He leaned forward to look through the narrow windscreen in front of them, crouching down to see beneath the upper sill and the equipment panels mounted above it.

"TTYF8 is hovering over the open pit, sir," the nav-com said. "Major Franni says this is not an abandoned mine, but a specifically dug pit and shaft to emulate the abandoned gold mine pits in the neighborhood."

"Can she describe the layout?" Forty-two asked.

"Yes, sir," the nav-com said. "A printout is coming off the printer now. She says it is a single level, Y-shaped tunnel with large rooms between the arms of the Y. There is a small group of fourteen in one room at the back of the tunnel system and only six in the room near the intersection of the arms. She says the sense of the six is the same as the pilot of the returning ship. They are of the slavers, and the fourteen seem to be retained."

"Is there more than one way in?" Forty-two asked as he

retrieved the layout sketch.

"Yes," the nav-com said. "A cylindrical shaft rising from the room near the intersection of the arms. The main passage is through the wide opening at the pit—a hangar bay large enough for two Class Two Fighters."

Forty-two turned to the pilot. "Hover above the escape shaft and we'll drop a small squad to catch anyone that tries to leave by the back door. Tell TTYF8 what we're doing."

The nav-com passed the word to TTYF8 and the pilot maneuvered to the opposite side of the pit.

"Twenty-two," Forty-two said through the open cockpit hatch. "Here's a layout map. Position five at the escape shaft and collect anyone that tries to leave. Stay cloaked."

The transport settled to within a few feet of the ground and Twenty-two dispatched five troopers through the pilot-side hatch. The hatch closed and Forty-two turned back to the pit.

"Dispatch twenty around the lip," he said, and the pilot repositioned the transport and slowly drifted around the lip. Twenty-two timed the drops, and at equal intervals a trooper stepped out and dropped to the ground.

"What's the fighter's position?" Forty-two asked.

"If we don't spook him," the nav-com said, "he'll be over the pit in six minutes."

"Give everyone the status." Forty-two stepped into the hold and addressed the men. "Six minutes. When he's entering the tunnel, we'll drop into the pit and charge the tunnel. Twenty-two"—he handed Twenty-two a copy of the layout—"your squad will take the right arm and my squad will take the left. There are six holding fourteen captives, plus the pilot and those in the fighter. TTYF8 and KCMM9 will provide aerial cover. Pick someone to guard the ship and crew. Everyone else, stay cloaked until we enter the tunnels or engage."

Forty-two turned back to the cockpit. "Has there been any communications, in or out of the facility?"

"Only from the fighter after the commander stopped scrambling them," the nav-com said. "The fighter only said the rendezvous and transfer was not satisfactory. Nothing from the facility."

"As soon as the fighter is down, reinstate scrambling," Forty-two said. "I don't want them spreading the word, and I certainly don't want them telling anyone we're here, or have been here."

"Two minutes," the nav-com said. "Alert sent to all troopers and Q-Ships. Major Franni has him lit up."

Forty-two watched the scanner screen and the orange dot as it moved closer to their private position marker. *So far so good*, Forty-two said to himself as the dots merged, and the screen enlarged to show just their general area. With the topography of the pit superimposed on the screen, he watched the dot center over the pit, just offset from the mine entrance.

"He's descending," Forty-two whispered, and glanced at the seemingly empty pit through the cockpit glass. "Move in."

The transport moved over the pit and lowered, blocking the fighter's escape route.

"He's onto us!" the nav-com shouted. "He's hovering and starting to rise!"

"Drop our veil! Keep him under us!" Forty-two shouted in return. "TTYF, can you drop his veil?"

Suddenly, the fighter coalesced in the space under the larger mass of the transport. The pilot turned the fighter, but the transport blocked his move to the side of the pit. He moved quickly to the other side and the transport again blocked his route.

A bright flash erupted beneath the transport and the fighter began to spin slowly and lose altitude, finally bouncing to a sweeping stop on the pit floor.

"Ropes!" Forty-two yelled and hurried into the hold. "Open the side and aft hatches! Everyone down the ropes! Now!"

Forty-Two jumped and caught a rope and started down as members of his squad jumped for ropes and followed his lead. On the ground, he realized there were other ropes and marines descending on them all. A squad arrayed themselves around the fighter, and Forty-two glanced at the smoking right-hand engine as he led his men into the mouth of the tunnel. Twenty-two was right beside him.

Forty-two motioned to move ahead and Twenty-two slowly crept ahead on the right side, as briefed.

"The six are waiting at the arms," Franni's voice said in Forty-two's earpiece. He tapped twice to let her know he had heard her, and moved to his left. He passed a hand signal to Twenty-two to advise him they were waiting for them. Then he signaled a charge.

Together, Forty-two and Twenty-two rushed the right and left entry portals. Weapons firing, the squads flooded in behind them and suddenly it was over. The six lay sprawled on the floor and on top of desks in the center of the room. Forty-two turned and saw the communications console along the front wall, but when he reached to switch it off, the room spun and went black.

One Thirty-Two

Kiile landed the commandant's new personal shuttle in the yard between the main house and the barns at Headquarters. He opened the personnel hatch, extended the steps, and Neila and Cheral preceded him out into the yard. Neila stopped abruptly and smiled at the bright, colorful lights that stretched around the eaves of the main house. She turned to look at Kiile and then at Cheral.

"They're Christmas decorations," Kiile said, and took Neila's hand. "A very big holiday for many people in many countries, and they decorate inside and outside to express the joy of the season."

Cheral took her other hand and led them up onto the back porch.

Matti opened the heavy door and greeted them before they could knock. She took their long coats as they entered.

"My, my. But don't you two look absolutely splendid," she said as she appraised Cheral and Neila's fitted, knee-length dresses. "Please come in. The McIntires just got here and everyone's in the living room by the fire."

"Thank you, Matti," Cheral said, and led the way through the dining room.

Neila smiled as she took in the sight of the large table with its decorations and place settings already arranged. She was still surprised at the rich and comfortable feel of the great room, changed from her last visit with ribbons and wreaths hung all about. Then, sniffing the pleasant aromas in the air, she spotted the large decorated tree in the corner of the room, opposite the fireplace.

"A tree?" Neila asked, hardly believing her eyes. "Inside?"

"Yes, love," Cheral said softly. "More of our traditions."

"I think I like your traditions."

"Come over by the fire," Greg said as they reached the casual side of the living room. "You certainly look gorgeous, Neila." Greg was all smiles as he gestured to the loveseat and a nearby chair. "The girls will be out in a minute or two, but there is someone I want you to meet."

Greg turned to the couple sitting on the long couch opposite the loveseat.

"Neila, this is Doug McIntire and his wife, mate, Rose," Greg said. "You already know Colonel Kooich, his wife Leeana, and son Tayn."

Neila nodded hello to the Kooiches seated on the second loveseat, closer to the foyer. She turned and took Doug's extended hand. "Very pleased to meet you both."

"Their twins," Greg continued, "Kail and Kayli, are with the girls and Shara. They'll be out in a bit."

"Good to see you two again," Cheral said as Kiile led her to the fireside end of the loveseat and she sat down.

"Neila? Would you like to sit next to Cheral?" Kiile asked, and Neila followed his gesture and sat down in the middle.

She scooted close to Cheral and patted the space remaining beside her.

"Thanks," Kiile said, "but I'll take the chair so you won't wrinkle your pretty dress." He sat down just as Matti led Paul in and asked if everyone would like some cider.

When everyone nodded or said yes, she hurried back to the kitchen.

Paul turned to Cheral and took her hand. "Good to see you again, Granddaughter." And then he took Neila's hand. "And you too, Great-granddaughter."

She smiled and returned the greeting as Greg placed a straight-backed chair beside the fireside end of the loveseat.

"Thank you, Greg," Paul said, and turned to the chair. "These old bones like being close to the fire on chilly nights like tonight."

As he sat down, Shara led the girls and Kail and Kayli out of the hallway and into the living room. The children took chairs near the foyer. Shara stopped and smiled at Neila.

"You certainly look beautiful," she said, and took Neila's hand and gently pulled her up. "Let me take a look at you. My, my, you are beautiful."

"Mom," Sedona said, not so softly. "You're embarrassing her."

"Okay, okay," Shara said, and let Neila sit back down. "I don't mean to make you uncomfortable, Neila. I really want you to feel at home here in the valley. Cheral and Kiile know that if you need anything from us or for us to do, just ask." Shara turned to the overstuffed chair beside the fireplace and sat down.

Cara and Kym stopped at the edge of the living room, each holding a tray.

"For heaven's sake, Cara, come in and set those trays down," Shara said when she saw them.

They quickly served the cups of hot cider. "Annie says dinner will be ready in about fifteen minutes, Mrs. Shara," Cara said.

"Thank you, Cara," Shara said, and the house girls hurried back to the kitchen.

"Neila," Greg said, standing beside Shara in the overstuffed chair. "I heard that Doug's parents came from Somstri. Isn't that right, Doug?"

"Yes, it is," Doug said, and smiled at Neila. "And Greg tells me that you just came from there."

"Yes...we did just come from my grandfather's place in Belimoor," Neila said, surprise coloring her statement. "Do you know where that is?"

Doug smiled. "No, Neila. I've never had the opportunity to visit Somstri. My folks mated in Zeupa and immigrated to Earth before my sister and I were born."

"Did they immigrate to someplace called Colorado?" Neila asked in a whisper.

"Yes, they did," Doug said in surprise. "Why do you ask?"

Neila looked at Cheral and questioned.

'Neither Kiile nor I have told anyone what you told us, love. Not a word,' Cheral said. *'This is a surprise to us as well.'*

"What did your father and mother do?" Neila asked.

"They were heavy into farming and established a business to provide improved seeds for various crops. You know, blight resistance, better high-altitude and cold-weather yields, and things like that. They worked some farms in north central Colorado when they first arrived, but when Mom got pregnant, they moved to a city called Greeley and started their business. That's where my sister and I were born."

"What was your father's name?" Neila asked.

"Tom McIntire," Doug said, "and Mom is Karyn McIntire."

"Did he have a sister?"

"Yes, he said he did," Doug said, "but she didn't immigrate with them."

"Doug," Greg said when Neila shook her head. "You told me you talked to your dad about immigrating here and his past when you told him you were going to join the Force. What did he say about their lives before they came? I think you and Neila might have some things in common."

Doug looked at Greg and cocked his head. "Like everyone that immigrated and had to find a way to blend into the normal society, they changed their names to Terran names. Dad chose McIntire."

"My mother was Milna of Anthor," Neila said, taking a deep breath. "Her brother was Tor of Anthor."

Doug's mouth dropped open. "My dad changed his name from Tor to Tom, and because they didn't have last names on Somstri, he picked McIntire because it somehow reminded him of Anthor. I never knew what Anthor meant."

"Anthor was my grandfather and the father of Tor and Milna," Neila said, her expression slowly changing to a smile. "You are the son of my mother's brother. Have I come across the galaxy to find a true, blood cousin? Do we come from the same grandfather and grandmother?"

Doug smiled. "It seems you have, Cousin." Doug stood up and stepped in front of Neila. He extended his arms and hugged her when she stood up. He glanced at Rose. "Can you believe it? I've found a cousin?"

When they sat back down, Doug leaned forward and continued. "Dad told me that he was Tor of Anthor, but I didn't understand. And I didn't understand when he said Mother was Canri of Lomsi. But he always wondered if Milna was okay and happy."

"Tor was born first and Mother second by many years," Neila explained. "They were both born in Turell on Nevar, and Tor went to Belimoor on Somstri with Anthor when he and Gpama moved there. Mother stayed and grew up with Anthor's brother's family on the farm outside of Wiibsa." Neila's voice got heavy as she spoke. "That is where I was born...That's where Mother was..."

"You don't have to talk about this, Neila," Kiile said, and knelt in front of her. "If you don't want to. Doug heard about Nevar. He just didn't realize the importance of hearing. Let's talk about something else for now."

"Okay, Kiile," she said softly, and leaned forward until her forehead touched his. "I'm really happy to find a father and a cousin."

"Thank you, Neila," Kiile said, and moved back to his chair. "Doug, would you introduce Neila to your son and daughter. They have been fidgeting over here, eagerly waiting to meet her."

"My apologies, Neila," Doug said. "First, you were introduced to Rose. She's a local and I met her while going to school here. I was a little slow in asking her to marry me, but when I got around to it, she accepted and these two came soon after. Kail, Kayli, please come and meet your cousin."

Kail caught Kayli's hand and led her in front of the loveseat.

"It's our pleasure to meet you, Cousin Neila," Kail said, and extended his hand.

Neila smiled, leaned forward, and grabbed him in her arms. "From what I've seen since I've been here, family does not just shake hands. It's wonderful to meet you too."

She released Kail, saw his wide smile, and turned to Kayli. She grabbed Kayli and hugged her tightly. "It's wonderful to meet you as well."

"Thank you, Neila," Kayli said. "This is such a surprise. We had no idea."

"And I did not either," Neila said. "And I'm glad to meet you too, Rose."

"When Kiile and Cheral teach you how to navigate and travel on a remote—" Rose said.

"Travel on a remote?" Neila questioned, and saw Cheral's nod.

"When you do," Rose continued, "you'll have to come over and visit. If Doug's at work, you can visit with me and I can tell you all of the family secrets."

"Now, now, Rose," Doug said, and smiled and then looked at Neila. "She will, you know." Then Doug glanced at Kiile and Cheral. "Have you thought about giving Neila the history lessons you gave the kids?"

Cheral nodded. "I haven't told Kiile yet, but she will get the three lesson modules tomorrow."

Neila looked at Cheral, a wide smile filling her face.

"Tomorrow, after breakfast," Cheral said with a firm nod. "And then you can go with Kiile for the rest of the day."

Kiile was about to add his two cents' worth when Kym stopped at the edge of the living room and announced dinner.

▲

Dinner progressed in high spirits and the conversation gave Neila more insight into the nature of life outside, in the normal environment of the valley and town. Greg and Shara listed the key people in town that knew about the existence of the Force, explaining that Cheral and Kiile could give her a memory list of those in the outside world that she could get help from if she ever needed it. He mentioned that Jim Woods bought the ten-thousand-acre ranch just across the road from the Lazy D, Shelly's dad's place. He confirmed Shelly and Carrie would be moving into Marty's and Rusty's guesthouse at the end of

January and staying there until they could decide on what sort of a house to build and where to build it.

"Cousin Shara?" Neila asked during a lull in the conversation. "The framed images in the front room? Are they of you and your horses?"

"Yes, Neila," Shara said. "Many are of when I was young and rode in competitions. For trophies. And others are of the girls and a couple of students I have had. We even got Tayn to ride some, but I don't think his heart is in horses."

"You said I could learn to ride. When can that be?"

Shara glanced at Cheral. "If you can come out on Saturday, you can get familiar with the horses. Cheyenne's Bucky is here, and she will be here with the girls doing their exercises."

Neila turned and looked at Kiile and then at Cheral.

"I think that can be arranged," Kiile said. "We'll put horses down on your calendar for Saturday, Neila."

After dinner, Neila visited with Doug and Rose a bit before Rose said they needed to get Kail and Kayli home and in bed before it got much later. It was, after all, a school night. They escorted the McIntires to the front portico and watched their lights as they headed through the tree stand and the arch to the country road.

"Before we call it a night," Greg said as he closed the front doors and slipped the bolt, "Paul has a few things he wants to say. Would anyone like a cordial while we talk?"

Kiile and Cheral and Hench and Leeana accepted, and as Shara started to the kitchen, Neila asked, "Cousin Shara? May I have a little more of Matti's cider? It was wonderful."

"Certainly, Neila. Girls? Tayn? Anything?" she asked, and when they shook their heads, she went to the kitchen. Sedona and Sierra settled on the long couch to be closer to the conversation.

Shara returned and sat down on the hassock beside Greg in the overstuffed chair, and saw the girls smile at their usual routine.

"Greg, Hench, Kiile," Paul said in his smooth, soft voice.

"I have decided that since the original crisis has diminished greatly, and the school has rewritten all of my teaching syllabus"—he turned to Shara—"due to the efforts of a favorite great-niece of mine, and the instructors have embraced those changes enthusiastically, I am going to return to being a gentleman rancher and answer tactical questions only when necessary."

"What does he mean?' Neila whispered to Cheral.

"Excuse me, Paul," Cheral interrupted. "Neila, Grandpa Paul was a teacher at the Peace Force Academy in the Rings for many years and then went into the field. That brought him here, where he established the ranches. Remember my comments earlier about a history in the valley? Well, when Greg started the school at Shadow Base, he asked Paul to teach again."

"Oh. I understand. I think," Neila said.

"In about three days, you will understand more," Cheral said, and smiled. "Please continue."

"Thank you, Cheral. Anyway, I think the school is ready to continue without me in a classroom everyday. Therefore, since I did not 'officially' accept the position as instructor, though I greatly appreciated the pay, I'm not 'officially' resigning from the position. But I am going to stay on the ranch and help my foreman get things back in order."

Cara entered and passed the cordials to the adults and then a cup of cider to Neila. "Will there be anything more, Mr. Greg?"

"Not at the moment, Cara. Thank you," Greg said, and she hurried back to the kitchen.

Greg raised his glass to Paul. "I thank you for your unwavering support, Paul. Many students have benefitted from your years of guidance. Thank you."

Everyone sipped and Paul chuckled. "But you must admit, Greg. Your bride, my wonderful great-niece, made remarkable changes to the syllabus. My teachings were but a foothold upon which today's teachings grew."

"Many thanks, Uncle," Shara said. "Without that wise foothold, we wouldn't have what we have today. I'm glad you feel you can return to the ranch, even after so much has changed. I'm also glad you gave us those unexpected years of guidance."

"Now," Paul said, and turned to Cheral, "I want to talk to you about living in this valley. There are two people in my family that I think are interested in a life in the valley. Obviously, the first person is your cousin Shara. She fought and nearly lost her life to keep her ranch and to keep the freedom of this valley. And since Andrew and Nancy have passed many years ago, the other comes from my son's side of the family. You, Granddaughter, are the only one that has expressed any desire to be here in the valley. None of the others in your family have even expressed an interest in visiting our wonderful planet, much less this beautiful valley.

"I have talked to Shara about what I plan, and she is in agreement with my desires." Paul took another sip of his cordial. "I have two ways I can go, so what I want to know, Cheral, is whether you are going to stay here in the valley when you decide to retire. You have a family now, and a young daughter that needs a life in the real world, needs to attend regular school and grow in the community to have a local history and not arouse questions. Do you plan to give her that, or keep her sequestered at Obscure?"

"Grandpa, we've been talking about getting a place outside of Shadow Base," Cheral said. "I told Neila that how we do it was something we three would work on, to figure out a way. I know Kiile is in love with this valley as much as I am. I guess my answer is we want to be here. We want Neila to blend in and become part of the fabric of the valley as much as we want to become part of it. When I came back to school here, when Shara saved my life and showed me how much family is really here, and then Kiile became part of my life here, I felt I was home."

"Then," Paul said, and nodded to Shara's smile, "I guess my intention is this: I will divide the Rockin' H into two parcels. One parcel will add to Shara's Flying M's and the other will remain the Rockin' H. When looked at as a whole, together, the resulting two ranches will be the exact same size in area and acreage. Shara will keep the Flying M's and you, Cheral, will have the Rockin' H.

"The first stipulation is that I will remain on the Rockin' H, living there until I die and am buried there after. I will teach you and your family how to work it, run it, and keep it prosperous. This is the only home the Haaks have ever had on earth, and I want it to continue to be their home.

"The second stipulation is that the land can only go to heirs of the Haaks or Hawkins. That means Greg and Shara's heirs and Kiile and your heirs. If either family dies off, for any reason, the other gets the land. The best way to keep it is to not make the mistake I made. Have many children and teach them the beauty of ranching and the valley and the rewards of the Force."

Cheral looked at Shara then back to Paul. "I...I don't know what to say, Grandpa."

"Say 'thank you,' Cheral," Paul chuckled. "I want to live in the main house and continue to run the ranch as long as I can, and in the spring after the thaw, if you agree, I will build a 'guesthouse' suitable for you and your family and you will 'work' with me on the ranch. Neila can start school next year, so you will need to get her up to speed by then. How does this suit you, young Neila?"

"I...I too, don't know what to say, Great-grandpa," Neila said, and looked at Cheral and a smiling Shara. "I like the valley already and I want to live outside whenever we can. But this is too much for me to understand. Too much."

"Well, Neila," Paul said softly. "You have been subjected to a lot of changes in the past week, but I hope you see that we only want the best for you. Just like we do for Sedona, Sierra, Cheyenne, Tayn, and all of the others, we want you to have the best and I also want to protect what I have built. I only have Shara and her Greg, Cheral and her Kiile, and you children to help me do that."

Neila glanced at Cheral and then got up and bent to hug Paul firmly.

"Thank you," she said, and straightened. She looked around at Greg, Shara, the girls, the Kooiches, and Kiile and Cheral. "Thank you all. I am overwhelmed." She stepped over to stand in front of Kiile. "And thank you, Kiile, for coming for me and not ignoring me when I needed you. Thank you for bringing me to such a wonderful place."

Kiile reached out and pulled Neila onto his lap, the same way he had seen Greg and Shara do with their girls. He pulled her close, held her tight, and looked at Cheral. "You are very welcome, Neila. I thank Anthor every day for letting me know you exist and that you needed me."

"Grandpa," Cheral said softly, hesitant to intrude on the moment. "What do you need from Shara and me?"

"Nothing now. I will have the survey done and the papers drawn up. It'll take a few months, but in the meantime we need to talk about what your home will look like. If the spring weather cooperates, we can have a place ready by mid-summer."

"We will help with anything you need us to do," Shara said.

⋏ ⋏ ⋏ ⋏ ⋏

Blaire was standing just inside the launch bay beside the north wall when the controller opened the launch portal. She stood silent and unmoving as the transport drifted down through the opening and settled in the south half of the bay. When the aft portal opened and the ramp extended, she hurried forward and joined the small crowd that had formed beside the transport.

Four troopers carrying two litters quickly emerged and hurried into the complex. Twenty-two and two other marines followed them closely and disappeared through the hatch before Blaire could ask anyone for a status.

Then she let her shoulders sag, knowing a lowly cadet had no privileges in a circumstance like this; no one was going to stop what they needed to be doing to answer her unnecessary questions.

She turned and had started to walk back to the hatch she had used when she saw Colonel and Major Mooren hurrying her way.

"Blaire," Franni said as they reached her. "I thought we'd find you here."

"Hey, Franni," Blaire said softly. "Do you know how they are?"

Franni caught Blaire's shoulders and walked her inside. "Crem, you go on. I'll visit with Blaire a few minutes and then I'll be along."

"Okay, Fran," he said, and squeezed Blaire's arm as he turned and headed toward Billeting.

"The corporal from Twenty-two's squad took two projectile hits in the chest. He doesn't look too good, but at the moment he's still alive." Franni turned them down the short corridor to the Medical Wing. "Sergeant Stial was point for his squad, and got a hit in his upper chest and in his hip. The troopers got both of them on board and into Medical quickly, but they need the medics here to remove the bullets." Franni sighed as they stopped and sat in a couple of chairs in the small waiting area just outside the surgical rooms. "I wish our suits worked as well for projectile weapons as they do for laser weapons."

Blaire looked at Franni. "What do you mean?"

"Hasn't anyone explained our flight suits, or the marines' camouflaged uniforms?" She continued when Blaire waited. "They will stop a laser hand weapon and the energy damage a hit can cause. For projectiles, they just flatten the slug before they break through—making it worse, in a way, for the occupant of the suit or uniform. Larger, low-energy stuff is deflected, but a bullet can make it through the shielding."

"I didn't know," Blaire said, and glanced at the double doors closing off the corridor into surgery.

"Do you want me to stick around, Blaire?" Franni asked. "I can if you want me to."

Blaire shook her head. "No, Franni. Thanks, but I'll just wait a bit. I wasn't doing anything anyway. You go and unwind with

Crem. Get cleaned up and have a nice dinner or something. I'll be fine."

"You're sure?" Franni asked.

Blaire nodded and smiled as Franni got up.

"Call me," Franni said, and touched her forehead, "if you need anything."

"I will."

Blaire watched Franni turn and disappear into the corridor to Billeting. She settled back against the hard back of the chair to wait.

▲

Time slipped by like molasses pouring out of a jar in a cold January snowstorm, and Blaire was not sure what time it was when the orderly stepped through the surgery doors, crossed the room, and gave a clipboard to the male nurse manning the data and information desk. Blaire watched them talk, and finally the nurse behind the desk gestured toward her with a flick of his pen. The orderly turned his head and glanced in her direction. With a nod, he straightened up and walked over to her.

"Cadet Lupis?" he asked when he stopped and she stood up. "Who are you waiting word on?"

"Sergeant Stial, sir," she replied formally. "I am wondering how he is doing, sir."

"Relax, Cadet," the orderly said, and sat down in the chair beside the one she had been using. Blaire sat down and he continued. "Sergeant Stial is resting comfortably now. The surgeon was able to remove both bullets and had to do a lot of bone reconstruction in his right hip. Sergeant Stial's in bone rejuvenation now and will be moved to a medical couch in about another"—he looked at his timepiece—"fifteen minutes. Once he's been moved, he can have visitors, but I suspect he will be out for another hour or more."

"Could you let me know when he's been moved?"

"Certainly," the orderly said, and stood up.

"By the way. How's Twenty-two's man?"

The orderly stopped and looked at Blaire a long moment before he shook his head.

"Oh. Sorry," Blaire said softly. "Thank you, sir."

▲

Blaire sat and watched Luc through the protective shield of the medical couch. Time was still just as sluggish, but she felt better from the information the orderly had given her, and the fact that the staff had settled into a routine for checking on him and the information on the monitor had steadied into a normal rhythm.

With the waiting, she had started thinking about Sam and his presents, his continued effort to be sure he remembered her on her special occasions. He had never asked anything from her, always giving of himself, his time. And then she had messed it up.

She was wondering why she was sitting up, watching a man in Medical, a man she barely knew, when the chamber door slowly opened and Kiile stepped in. In reflex, Blaire stood up sharply, but realized Kiile was wearing civvies—nice civvies, but still civilian wear.

"At ease, Blaire," he said, and stepped to her and took her hand. "The orderly says he's doing very well."

"Yes, sir," she said, and gestured to her chair. "He's starting to come around. Sit down and talk to him when he sees you."

"But that's your chair," Kiile argued.

"I need to take a break, sir," Blaire said, gently pushing him toward the chair.

Kiile sighed and sat down and Blaire glanced at the couch as Luc rolled his head from side to side. She patted Kiile's shoulder and slipped out through the door.

Blaire, feeling Luc would be all right now, followed the corridor to the waiting area, then she turned toward Billeting and envisioned an overdue shower and sleep.

▲ ▲ ▲ ▲ ▲

Don Nikle hobbled back and forth in front of the kitchen counter, angrily waiting for the teapot to boil. He had forced himself to wait when the rendezvous time had come and gone. And when the time the fighter was supposed to land had come and gone without word, he had begun to get anxious. That was the first time he had tried to make contact with the fighter's base.

Now, hours later, he knew something was wrong. They should have been answering, just like they had earlier in the afternoon. Just like they should have when he tried to reach the ranch.

He set his mug on the kitchen table as he pondered the many *whys* running around in his head, and tried to carry the teapot and manage the crutch with his one good hand. He dropped the teapot onto the trivet and then dropped himself heavily onto the chair.

He poured the tea into his mug and admitted that his present condition would not send the strong, positive image he needed to invoke. He was barely more than a useless cripple. It had taken him most of a week to drive back to his sister's place after he was shot, his mind replaying the confused, frightening moments over and over. He did not know who had responded to his attack, but deep inside, he knew he did. They were the same ones that were one step ahead of him each time he tried something. And now, it appeared to him they may have figured out how to interfere with his communications abilities.

He finished his tea and worked his way upright, nearly falling when he leaned on the chair back, and the chair slipped. He caught himself with his club of a right hand, cursing loudly through clenched teeth at the sharp pain. He forced himself to straighten and stand.

In the living room, he eased himself onto the edge of the overstuffed chair and looked at the fresh blood that seeped through the gauze wrapping around his useless hand. He knew it wasn't getting any better, but the red streaks up his right arm concerned him. His leg was the same. The medicines he bought and had delivered to the house had helped at first, but now he knew they were not enough.

Unable to think clearly, he wiped the perspiration from his forehead and leaned back into the cushions. Maybe, he thought, he could make more sense of it after he slept. A short nap sounded good, and he wiped his forehead again and closed his eyes.

▲ ▲ ▲ ▲ ▲

Kiile was holding Cheral with one arm around her waist and Neila by the hand, still warm inside from the wonders of the evening as they descended the corridor of stairs. They crossed the launch bay and were almost to the main hatch in the north wall when it swung in and Seventeen stood aside, holding it open for them.

"Thank you, Seventeen," Kiile said, and gently pushed Cheral ahead of him and Neila behind her into the warmer confines of the facility.

"Yes, sir," Seventeen said. "May I have a quick word, sir?"

Kiile looked at Cheral and Neila as they stood together, Cheral with her arm around Neila's shoulders.

"We'll wait," Cheral said, and Kiile turned to Seventeen.

Kiile listened as Seventeen relayed his short message. Then Kiile nodded and Seventeen turned, nodded to Cheral and Neila, and then hurried down the corridor into the facility. Kiile turned and took Cheral's hand and walked them to their quarters in silence.

"Anything wrong?" Cheral asked as they entered and the ambient lighting brightened at their presence.

"A quick update on the other half of your mission today," Kiile said as he took Cheral and Neila's coats and hung them in the entry closet. "It seems that most of the investigation at the small base in Australia went well. They captured the fighter, its pilot, and released twelve captives that were on board. Forty-two and Twenty-two led their squads inside and neutralized six guards and released fourteen captives they were holding there. All in all, a very good recovery effort."

"You said 'most of' the investigation went well," Neila said, and caught Kiile's hand.

"Yes, love. I did," Kiile said. "I understand Forty-two was hit twice and is recovering in the medical wing, and Twenty-two lost one of his men." He looked down at Neila and then glanced at Cheral. "I need to go to Medical and make an appearance and see Twenty-two for a minute or two. You and Cheral should go ahead and get ready for bed, and I'll see you as soon as I can get back."

Kiile hugged Neila and kissed her forehead and then turned and kissed Cheral fully. "I'll be back as soon as I can."

⚓

"So, I am trying to understand," Neila said as she stopped in Cheral's bedroom doorway. She had bathed and dressed for bed and was brushing her hair when she restarted the conversation they were having. "Your grandfather is going to let you inherit his ranch while he is still alive?"

Cheral turned and threw her robe over her nightgown as she answered.

"In a way, I guess," Cheral said. "At least I will be the named heir even if he keeps the land until he dies. We'll just have to wait until he figures out all of the paperwork."

"Does this really mean we can live outside?" Neila asked.

Cheral nodded. "Yes, Neila. It looks like we can. And summer isn't all that far off."

"When does the 'thaw' happen?"

"Warmer weather usually comes in the month of May, sometimes earlier, in April," Cheral said. "Get the calendar from the kitchen and you can see."

Neila returned quickly. "It's now the middle of the month December. Right?"

"Right. Count the pages."

"I remember," Neila smiled. "Each one is a month, roughly four seven-turns, ah, weeks long."

"That also means we will need to get you caught up on the teachings you would have had," Cheral said, half out loud, "if you grew up here on Earth. You'll start in the fall with three years left, if I'm remembering right."

"Do you know what I have to learn?"

"No." Cheral smiled. "But I will find out what you should already know. Then we can start teaching you to be a normal Terran teenager."

"Will that be one of my duties?"

"I think it will, love," Cheral said and hugged Neila warmly. "And I think you will do just fine."

"Thanks," Neila said happily, then she remembered a question that had crossed her mind. "Cheral, I was wondering. If we hadn't, I mean, if 'you' hadn't wanted to live here in the valley, what was your grand... grandpa going to do with his land?"

Cheral stopped and looked at Neila and cocked her head. "I suppose he would have given it to Shara and the girls."

"Wow. He said she agreed with his idea to split the land," Neila said, half to herself. "Could she have disagreed and kept all of the land for herself?"

"I suppose she could have," Cheral said and hugged Neila's shoulders as they turned to the kitchen. "But, I think it's obvious she wants us here more than she wants grandpa's land."

"Cousin Shara has a good heart." Neila smiled and noticed where they were going. "Hot chocolate?"

"I suppose."

Friday, December 15

It was three in the morning. Seventeen stopped beside the back door of the two story house on Lone Pine. He glanced at the trooper that stopped at the other side of the door and tapped his earpiece. "Seventeen and Twenty-four are in position."

"Captain Glean says our target is in the living room at the back of the house," Thirty-two said in Seventeen's earpiece. "Short corridor from the door opens into the room. We'll enter through the front on your mark. Two sentries are watching the street. Everyone is cloaked."

"Good," Seventeen answered. "I have two watching the alleyway and two watching the outbuilding. We are ready. The lock has been tumbled and the door is unlatched. Mark."

Twenty-four pushed the door open and entered the corridor as Thirty-two announced they were in. At the mouth of the short corridor, Twenty-four stopped and Seventeen knelt beside him. He instantly saw the bandaged man in the reclining overstuffed chair, his head to one side, mouth open, eyes closed.

Seventeen crept closer and slowly stood up beside the chair. The man did not move and Seventeen tapped his earpiece again. "Captain Glean. The man in the chair is either asleep or unconscious. He is covered with sweat, right hand wrapped in gauze and bleeding. One leg wrapped and blood soaked."

"Seventeen," Debira said. "That is the man Nikle. From here, he seems to be unconscious."

Thirty-two stopped beside the chair and noticed the streaks on his arm and the swelling, then glanced at his wrapped leg. "Severe blood poisoning. We need to get him up to Medical."

Seventeen nodded, and within seconds a remote drifted in through the back door and stopped in front of the chair.

Twenty-four and the other marine poked Nikle, and when they did not get a response they leaned him forward and slipped a sling under his arms and around his chest.

"Secure his wrists and get him aboard," Seventeen said. "Once he's in Medical, be sure he's shackled, good wrist and good ankle to the restraint rings. If he gets away this time, I will have someone's head."

"Yes, sir," Twenty-four said, and the marine beside him nodded and helped as the remote lifted Nikle into an upright position. "Our remotes are waiting just outside."

Seventeen nodded and the marines followed the remote with Nikle out through the back door.

"Captain Glean," Seventeen said. "When the troopers have Nikle secured in Medical, please contact Shadow Base that we have him. We will check the house and outbuilding before we close up and rejoin the transport."

"Understood," Debira said.

⋏

Kiile's earpiece vibrated incessantly on the nightstand beside his bed, until he unwrapped his arm from around Cheral and reached for it. He slipped it on his ear and answered with a barely understandable "'lo."

Suddenly hearing the voice on the other end of the link, he sat up and blinked at the near darkness.

"You are sure?" he said as Cheral rolled over and sat up beside him. "Absolutely sure?"

Kiile nodded and smiled. "Well done. Thank you. We'll debrief at ten."

Kiile lay back against his pillow and pulled Cheral close.

"Seventeen and his squads picked up Nikle and are bringing him back," Kiile said softly.

"That's very good, Kiile," Cheral said, and cuddled into him.

"Apparently we wounded him pretty badly two weeks ago," Kiile said, still looking at the dim rock ceiling. "Seventeen said they have him in Medical for severe blood poisoning. He's not sure if Medical can pull him through it."

"It's good they have him in Medical," Cheral said, and fingered the hair on his chest and wrapped her leg around his. "But they have him taken care of, and since you woke me up so suddenly, you need to help me get back to sleep. Neila's sleeping and I need your undivided attention."

▲ ▲ ▲ ▲ ▲

"Your Highness," the voice from the communications console said when the prince told it to 'Receive.' "I'm Intelligence Officer Tmn. I have a message for you."

"Tell me the message," Prince Lukré said as he looked with displeasure at the garish decorations left in the late prince's—now his—office.

"Yes, Your Highness," Officer Tmn's voice said. "Our agents inside the Rings have confirmed the successful 'tampering' of several key servant-level aides within the governing families. Additionally, I am told the first phase of your plan is underway. The director himself accepted a hint that it would be good for him to personally meet with those in his staff that he regards the most highly and ensure their loyalty, all in the name of continued security and maintaining the Force's unwavering 'greatness.'"

When Officer Tmn paused, the prince asked if there was more.

"Yes. When the first meeting is set, I will inform you and you can alert your agents when to make their collection."

Prince Lukré smiled; the first since he gave the order to attack Nevar.

One Thirty-Three

Thursday, January 19

"How did you get everything into one truck?" Greg asked as he and Jim Woods carried the last of the boxes down the ramp and into the Lazy D's guesthouse.

"You don't acquire a lot of stuff when you live in a tiny two-bedroom apartment all of your married life," Jim said as he stacked his box with the others in the kitchen.

"Looks like you will have a little more space to spread out in," Shara said, gesturing to the large front room and the bedroom wing off to one side. "Have you two decided when or where you're going to build?"

"We have some ideas," Shelly said as she opened another box and stacked the dishes for rinsing. "We've been drooling over magazine pictures and home decorating videos, but Dad said he would like us to settle in and not jump into building right away. He says winter is not the best time to start construction."

"He's right about that," Greg said, and turned back to the moving van. "I'll fold the packing rugs and mats and close up the truck."

He stopped on the front porch and scanned the view. The meadows were open to the north, glistening with the remaining snow cover. The main house and guesthouse, sheltered in the southern stand of pines, had a restricted view to the east and west, but shared the beautiful view to the south, down the center of the valley.

He noticed Carrie Anne as she went into the stable, and then he entered the van and started folding the disorganized pile of rugs and mats. He was laying the last one on the stack in the front corner of the van's box when he heard a couple of cars stop beside the truck. He smiled as he looked around the opening and saw Wally, Carole with Ridan and Alyssa, and Deputy Lupis and Mandy get out of the two jeeps. Both women were wearing cooking gloves and carrying obviously hot casseroles wrapped in thermal towels.

"Afternoon," Greg called from the truck. "Everyone's inside."

"Thanks, Greg," Wally said. "I think Thom and Eddie will be out as soon as school lets out."

"Yeah," Greg said, and jumped down beside the ramp. "That's what I heard. They're bringing Sedona, Sierra, Cheyenne, and Tayn out with them."

He followed them inside and hunted up his cup and the water jug. As he finished his drink, Dan stepped up and asked softly, "Have you talked to Blaire recently?"

"Most every day," Greg said, and looked at Dan in question. "Something up?"

"No. No," Dan said. "She usually talks to us every few days and it's been close to a week since she did last. I was just wondering."

"I'll only say that she has been very studious." Greg smiled. "She's definitely one of our star students. Seldom takes time to do anything other than study and fly missions with the seasoned crews."

"I'm glad she's doing well and is busy," Dan said. "Keeps her mind focused on the right things."

"She's coming out with Kiile, Cheral, and their daughter Neila," Greg said with a smile. "I convinced her to take a break and they are somewhere between our ranch and here."

"Wonderful. Mandy will like that a lot," Dan said, and smiled. "Blaire says you've been taking care of her. Thank you for that."

"You're welcome, Dan," Greg said, "but Blaire doesn't generally need taking care of. She's very talented and has been helping the other cadets where she can."

Greg patted Dan on the back and turned him toward the kitchen.

"Are you still on duty?" Greg asked, and continued when

Dan shook his head. "Jim put a few brews in the cooler by the kitchen door, if you're of a mind. Jim thinks 'comin' home' is some kind of a cause for celebration."

Shelly stopped rinsing dishware long enough to give the new arrivals a tour and to answer the many questions asked as she led them through the house. Greg turned, *feeling* the Baines arrive. He stepped out onto the front porch as they stopped and the kids piled out. He saw his ranch's truck turn off the country road and waved as Kiile pulled around the main house and stopped beside the other vehicles.

The four girls and Tayn ran to the truck to happily greet Neila as she got out. Then they each said a polite greeting to Kiile and to Cheral before they turned and Sedona, Sierra, and Cheyenne ran to say hello to Greg.

"Where's Carrie, Dad?" Sedona asked, and Greg saw Sierra turn toward the stables.

"Follow Sierra," he said, and hugged Sedona. "Good to see you again, Neila."

"Thank you. It's good to see you away from the other places," Neila said, and smiled.

"Come on, Neila," Cheyenne said as she started toward the stables. "You need to meet Carrie Anne."

Greg chuckled at the excitement and eagerness of the children, looking so much like normal country kids that no one would ever suspect they were about to graduate as fighter pilots and Shadows.

"And how is Blaire?" Greg asked as the rest of the flock ran across the open yard.

"Very well, I think, sir," Blaire said, and smiled. "Sorry. It's habit I guess. I haven't been out of Shadow Base since Christmas. It's good to be outside wearing normal clothes for a change."

"Yes it is." Greg smiled. "Your dad was saying you've been too busy to talk to them. He was worried I might be working you too hard."

"Oh, no! I don't want him to—"

"I'm kidding, Blaire," Greg said, and held his hand up with a chuckle. "But you have been very focused."

"Yes, I guess I have," Blaire said, and let her gaze drop. "It keeps me from thinking about other things."

"Is there a problem? Do you need to talk to me or Shara about something?" Greg asked.

"Yes, there is a small one, but not something you can help with," Blaire said. "It's a personal thing and I have to figure out what I'm going to do about it."

"Sorry to ask," Greg continued. "If there is something about the training or the missions or your quarters...anything you need fixed—"

"No." Blaire smiled and blushed. "It's not that. I know what I want to do when it comes to the training and the work. I want to graduate and continue with what I've started. I want to be like Captain Tigs, like Franni and like Shar. I want to be able to help, to use my talents and gifts like they do to find and ferret out the slavers and maybe get some of the stolen people back. Those desires are not a problem."

"Okay, Blaire. But if you need help with anything—school, the job, or even with the people," Greg said. "You let either of us know." He tapped his forehead. "You know you can ask us anything, anytime."

"Thank you, Greg," Blaire said, and straightened. "That means a lot to me."

He smiled and noticed the flock of kids bunched around Neila and Carrie as they walked back toward the guesthouse.

"I guess I should go and say hey," Blaire said, and turned. She stepped off the end of the porch and walked toward the gaggle of happy kids and two fourteen-year-olds.

⚔

"Hey, Carrie," Blaire said as she joined the group. "How was your trip?"

"Hey, Blaire," Carrie said, and smiled. "Trip was good. Long, but good."

"Don't let these guys overwhelm you," Blaire said, and

smiled at the girls and Tayn and Ridan.

"I won't," Carrie said, and leaned close to Blaire. "Bet you can guess who I just saw in the stables."

Blaire looked at her and then glanced at the stables.

"I bet I can," Blaire said softly, and smiled.

"Well, I sure didn't expect a welcoming committee," Carrie said brightly, and smiled at each of them. "But this is great! I'm so glad to be out of that small apartment and the city."

"I thought you liked Lynchburg," Sierra said.

"I did," Carrie said. "Don't tell anyone, but the closer we got to moving, the more excited I got. I can see Gramms and Gramps every day and I can be outside and..." Carrie stopped when she saw Neila's sober expression. "Did I say something wrong, Neila?"

"No. Not wrong," Neila said, and forced a smile. "You just reminded me of sad times."

"I'm sorry, Neila," Carrie said. "I just get too excited and I didn't think."

"It's okay," Neila said, and let herself smile. "I have Kiile and Cheral and many cousins that I didn't know I have. Things have been good since I came here."

"Why do you call your dad 'Kiile'?" Carrie asked. "Don't you like him?"

Neila stopped her thought and stared at Carrie. "Yes, I like him very much. And Kiile is his name."

"Okay," Carrie said, and squeezed Neila's arm. "But think of it this way: everyone calls my dad by his name, Jim, but I'm the *only* one that can call him 'Dad.' Until I get a brother or sister, and I don't think that's going to happen, I like being the only one that can."

"I see," Neila said as they started walking back to the guesthouse. "I only have my father, since my mother and her family are dead."

"Well, that's true," Sedona said. "But I know kids at school that were adopted. They don't have a blood mother or father, but they call their adoptive parents 'Mom' and 'Dad.'"

"Why?" Neila asked.

"Because they take care of them—you know, food, clothes, home," Sierra added. "They are the kid's 'now' family, and they protect them, teach them, and do all the things that moms and dads do for their kids."

"Also out of respect, I guess," Tayn said, "because they chose to do all of those things for the kids. And you do have a family here, and it's the best you could wish for, Neila. Not that your mother and the family you lost weren't great and wonderful, but Kiile, Cheral, and all of your cousins are the very best."

"I know they are very wonderful," Neila said.

"Come on," Carrie said, changing the subject, "enough of all of that. Let's go see the house." She looked at Neila. "And Dad says Kiile and Paul are planning to build a house for your family this summer. That will be so wonderful, Neila. Come on."

"I'll catch up in a few minutes," Blaire said, and watched them head for the guesthouse before she turned to the stables.

▲

"Well, well," Sam said as the barn door slid open and Blaire stepped inside. "I was beginning to think you'd stepped off the face of the earth."

Blaire stared at his casual phrase and then, remembering that he could not know that she really had, smiled. "Just been busy. How have you been?"

"Busy too," Sam said. "I decided to stay on with Marty and learn the finer points of ranching."

"I see." Blaire smiled. "You look like it agrees with you."

"Same for you, I think," Sam said, and hung the leathers he was holding on a peg. "If your face is any measure, I'd say you've been getting a lot of exercise. Can't tell about the rest of you, though, with that heavy coat on."

"Yes," she said, and felt her cheeks flush. "I've been getting a lot of exercise. A lot of the training is very physical."

Sam watched her for a long moment and then picked up a feed bucket and walked over to the grain bin. "I guess you've found what you were looking for?"

"I guess I have, Sam," Blaire said. "I'm sorry I was so upset the last time we spoke, but I—"

"It's okay, Blaire. It was really my fault for not listening and helping when you asked for it."

"I've worried about the things I did and how much I've hurt you," Blaire said, holding his eyes as she spoke. "I want to apologize and say I'm sorry. I was much too naïve and immature."

"I know why you didn't come to my graduation," Sam said, "and I shouldn't have let it bother me so much. I'm sorry too." He watched her for another moment. "Will you be back in the valley anytime soon? I'd like to take you out once in a while if you'd let me."

"Thanks, Sam," Blaire said, and pondered how to explain. "I graduate in a couple of weeks and then I have to be away for rankings and equipment assignments." She held his eyes again. "I don't know where I'll be assigned. If I'm assigned close by, sure. I'd like that a lot. But I might not get to be close to home."

"What sort of work are you going to be doing?" Sam asked. "Your dad hasn't said."

"I haven't told them yet," Blaire admitted. "All I can say is it's undercover work. Investigations, data gathering, and anything else that is needed or can happen when one is in that environment."

"So it can be dangerous work?"

"Not usually, but sometimes," Blaire said with a slight shrug. "But only if you consider being shot at dangerous."

Sam stopped filling the bucket and just stared at her. "You're kidding, right?"

"Sam," Blaire sighed. "I can't give you any details. I know my choice affects the relationship you were hoping for us. But right now, I can't think about any kind of relationship beyond being friends, with you or with anyone. I have to be focused to do my job, and I don't know how long I will have to be this way."

"You know I've been in love with you ever since I met you, don't you?"

"Yes," Blaire said. "I finally figured that out after I made you so angry and started my new job. Like I said, I was very immature and vain and couldn't see past the end of my nose."

"And you still want to do this, whatever you are doing, anyway?"

"You know it isn't that simple," Blaire said. "I lucked into the career that I want—to help protect people and to fight for their freedoms. But it does come with a price. I don't expect you to understand and I won't ask you to. I won't ask you to wait for me or anything like that. I have nothing I can give to a relationship, and it would be unfair of me to lead you on, thinking I can. I don't want to lose your friendship again, but that is all I can give you now."

Sam straightened up and hung the bucket in the stall he had been tending. "Okay, Blaire. I want to be your friend too." He reached out and pulled her to him and hugged her tight. "I won't pressure you and I will pray for your safe return, to your folks and to the valley and your home. Tell me when you're in town and available and I'll see if I can work you into my hectic schedule."

"Thanks, Sam," Blaire said as he released her. She looked sideways and gave him a coy smile. "I am in town tonight."

⁂ ⁂ ⁂ ⁂ ⁂

Greg stood on the back porch of their main house and watched Kiile, Cheral, and Neila hurry across the short space in the backyard and climb into the commandant's six-man personal shuttle. They waved and Kiile swung the hatch down and secured it.

Greg waved when he saw Kiile through the cockpit window as he settled into the pilot's seat. When they lifted and cloaked, Greg went back inside.

Cara and Kym had cleared the dinner table and he saw Sedona and Sierra, their backs to him on the loveseat, talking with Shara, standing in front of the fire in the fireplace. He quickly crossed the room, stopped beside Shara, and slipped his arms around her shoulders.

"That was nice," he said, and kissed her gently.

He turned and pulled her with him as he sat down in the overstuffed chair to face their smiling girls. Shara curled up on his lap, her back to the fire and one arm around Greg's neck and shoulders.

"Well?" Greg asked. "How do you girls feel about having Carrie around full-time now?"

"We think it will be great, Dad," Sedona said. "And she's happy to be here."

"Dad?" Sierra asked. "Does Carrie have any talents or gifts?"

"I'm not sure," Greg said softly, "but I don't think so. Jim's blood is a Terran mix without any talented blood that we know of, and Shelly, like Carole, is a little more than a half Ferannian with some Somstri added in. So Carrie will be a little more than a quarter, and we haven't seen any predictable traits with less than a half-blood."

"But she could, couldn't she?" Sedona asked.

"It's possible, love," Shara said. "We just don't have any way of knowing if she will."

"But Ridan and Alyssa are strong candidates," Sierra said, and smiled.

"Yes, they certainly are," Shara said. "Wally is a full-blood and Carole is more than half, but neither of them have shown any emerging talents."

"Not completely so," Sedona and Sierra said together.

"They can both *read* our tags," Sedona said.

"And others," Sierra finished.

Shara looked at Greg and smiled. "That is true. Maybe they ought to be evaluated and see if STSX can do anything to enhance what they already have."

"It sure would be nice for Ridan and Alyssa," Sierra said.

"How so?" Greg asked, and looked at Shara as he gently helped her up.

"They need to be able to *hear* them like we *hear* you and Mom," Sedona said as Greg led Shara to the loveseat.

"We're joining you two," Shara said. "If you don't mind."

The girls quickly stood and let Greg and Shara sit down. Then they settled, one in each's lap, facing each other.

"This is better," they said together.

"We mean, we like watching you two together and all—" Sierra tried to explain.

"We know," Greg said, and squeezed Sierra as he reached for Sedona's hand.

"Now, as you were saying," Shara said, "it would be nice if Ridan and Alyssa could *hear* their folks, and it would be good for Wally and Carole to be able to *hear* them."

"It's more than comforting," Sedona admitted. "We like *hearing* each other, but we can't imagine what it would have been like if we couldn't *hear* you two while we grew up."

"It would certainly be different," Shara admitted. "And downright scary in times like these. We'll talk to Wally and Carole tomorrow."

Sedona tapped her forehead. "Ask them tonight, please. Billie turned nine in November and already has displayed the first of her gifts. Alyssa is older than Billie by seven months and may already have a gift or two, and Ridan is only six months younger. They need to be evaluated too."

"I see your point, girls," Shara said, and smiled. "And I agree with you."

Shara squeezed Sedona and held Sierra's hand as her eyes unfocused. They all knew she had contacted Five and had it relay her message and request.

"Wally said they would come by after lunch," Shara said, and squeezed Sedona again. "I knew there was a good reason we keep you two around."

They laughed and Greg's expression slowly turned somber.

'*INCOMING MESSAGE FROM DIRECTOR AGL36Q.*' STSX said in their minds.

Greg looked at each of them. "I guess we'll listen to what the director has to say." '*Please read us the message, STSX.*'

'*TO: HQZL09-ES.*

'*FROM: PEACE FORCE HQ DIRECTOR AGL36Q.*

'*HAVE REVIEWED YOUR LIST OF CADETS FOR GRADUATION AND THEIR ACCOMPLISHMENTS. FOUR OF THE CADETS LISTED ARE RECOGNIZED BUT ARE NOT REGISTERED. EXPLANATION NEEDED. REQUEST FOR CADET BLAIRE LUPIS NEEDS FURTHER EXPLANATION. REQUEST FOR CAPTAIN ANI TIGS GRANTED. PLAN A MEETING IN MY CONFERENCE ROOM IN THE RINGS ONE WEEK AFTER GRADUATION. ALL GRADUATES ARE TO BE PRESENT.*

'*I ALSO WISH TO INTERVIEW AND REVIEW THE EVALUATIONS FOR EACH OF THE NON-REGISTERED TALENTS YOU HAVE IDENTIFIED. INCLUDE THEM AND THEIR GUARDIANS IN THIS MEETING. IN PERSON, PREFERRED. EOM.*'

"Oh my," Shara said softly. "All of the kids with talents?"

Greg smiled and shook his head slowly. "Just those in our happy little 'family,' Bren."

"We'll need one of Kiile's transports," Shara said, and slowly smiled. "So Kiile, Neila and Cheral, and Lieutenant Quil should also go."

"Is the director angry, Dad?" Sierra asked.

"You can't tell if he's angry or not," Shara said. "At least not from his messages, and sometimes, not even when you're talking to him." She looked at Greg. "I guess he finally figured it out."

"What?" Sedona and Sierra asked together.

"That your dad is training you children"—Shara smiled a guarded smile—"that are too young to be trained by the Peace Force. Your dad took on a lot of responsibility for all of you. If anything had happened to any one of you, the Force would not have stood behind him."

"But you said it was necessary," Sierra said, and looked at her dad with concern.

"It was absolutely necessary, love," he said, and smiled. "And I'd do it the same all over again if I had to."

Sierra hugged Greg as tight as she could. "If that old director gives you any trouble over your decision, I'll give him a piece of my mind."

"Me too," Sedona added, and Greg chuckled.

"Politely, I hope," Greg said softly. "You've proven my decision was the right one. Each one of you have. I'll not worry about the director too much. He really is an honest and good man."

"Well, if he isn't happy with your accomplishments," Sedona said, and planted her fists on her hips, "we can just retire and let him fight this battle by himself."

Greg laughed and had to wipe tears from his eyes before he could say anything in response. Instead, he just grabbed Sedona's hand again and squeezed Sierra.

"You just might have the right idea, Sedona," Greg said.

"What are you saying, Greg?" Shara asked, suddenly realizing the real possibility in Sedona's statement.

Greg smiled at her. "You know I've thought about it and you know I don't think it's the right time. But the time is coming, Bren. It'll be twenty-eight years in March for me and it was twelve for you last October."

"You're not retiring before I can," Shara said firmly. "I still have at least—"

"Mom. Stop," Sedona said, and smiled. "No one's retiring. And we're just getting started and you two are going to be here for us as long as we need you. So stop it. Okay?"

"Okay, loves," Shara said. "But I—"

"Mom!" Sedona and Sierra said together. Then softer, Sedona asked, "Instead of that, will one of you tell us what happened with Don Nikle? I don't *feel* him anymore. Neither of us do."

"Well, I guess we can explain it to our favorite cadets," Greg said, and settled into the telling of Seventeen's raid on Nikle's sister's place in the northern Chicago area.

"Evanston, actually," he said. "He was badly wounded from the near capture down by Community, east of Grants. He would've died of severe blood poisoning if Seventeen and his squads hadn't gone after him when they did."

"I remember *feeling* him when they brought him to Shadow Base," Sierra said. "Neila said Kiile was greatly relieved when Seventeen succeeded."

"Yes, he was," Greg admitted.

"What about all of the equipment Blaire found at his place?" Sierra asked.

"Communications equipment," Shara said. "Just like Franni suspected after Blaire *searched* his place and discovered the equipment."

"Like the target generation the remotes do?" Sierra asked.

"Yup," Greg said. "And after he 'talked' to us, we knew where he placed receivers and Seventeen sent squads to remove them."

"So why don't we feel him anymore?" they asked together.

"Because we took his memories in a brain scan and took away his desire to continue collecting slaves," Greg said simply. "And then Seventeen took him to wherever they keep dangerous prisoners."

"Took away his desire? Can that be done to anyone bad?" Sierra asked, pondering a thought.

"I suppose," Greg said, and looked at Shara, "to some degree. We haven't tried to alter desires before Nikle."

"It's like hypnosis, isn't it," Sedona surmised.

"Yes, I guess it is," Shara said. "Why? What are you

thinking?"

"Nothing really," Sedona admitted. "I'll let you know when I get it put together. Too many questions right now."

"Okay. When you get it put together. We won't pry," Greg said. "But I think it's time for you two to get ready for bed. Then we can have some of Matti's hot chocolate before lights out."

"Okay, Dad," they said together, and jumped up. "You tell Matti and we'll get ourselves ready."

Chuckling, they watched the girls hurry around the furniture and down the hall. Shara got up and started for the kitchen. "Enough for four?"

"Certainly, love."

▲ ▲ ▲ ▲ ▲

"Would you look at all of those stars," Sam said, looking up into the clear night sky as they walked south on Cleary.

Blaire looked up and smiled, but caught herself before she mentioned how many more they could see if they were in the right place. "They are so beautiful," she said instead. "Won't see so many when the moon gets up, though."

"Yeah," Sam agreed. "I thought you were crazy for wanting to walk when I came to pick you up, but you were right, definitely. It's not any colder than normal and the view is beautiful."

She glanced at him and knew he wasn't talking about the stars. "You said you wouldn't push."

"I'm not pushing. Not really," he said, and smiled. "Just being truthful."

She smiled and decided to let it go. "I've been so cooped up, studying and doing my exercises and drills, that I wanted to spend as much time as I could outdoors."

"You picked a good night for it," Sam agreed.

"I didn't remember Jerry's having such great dinners," Blaire said. "Is it me or have they changed their menu?"

"A bit of both, I think," Sam said, and smiled. "You haven't gotten out recently, and they did hire a new cook and his ideas for the evening menu have been well received."

"Well, it was wonderful. Thank you, Sam," Blaire said, and smiled as she turned back to the street and the odd sensations she was beginning to *feel*.

They walked on, making small talk as Blaire studied her rising sense of foreboding. Something wasn't right, and she casually looked up each street and alley they passed. Just past the college, she saw a man standing under the street light at Maple, in front of Willy's Auto Shop.

"Is that Tim Hill?" she asked as they got closer. "There, across the street."

"I think you're right," Sam said when he studied the man that started across the street toward them. "Wonder what he wants."

"'Lo, Sam. Blaire. I though that was you," Tim said as he stopped a few feet in front of them, blocking the sidewalk.

Blaire's senses went to full alert. Her hair tingled. Tim's stance, nervousness, and manners were unsettling, and she glanced at Sam, wondering if he was missing the signs or just exceptionally calm under pressure.

"Sam," Tim started. "I've got a problem and I need some help."

"What kind of problem, Tim?" Sam asked.

"I got a guy after me for some money I owe him," Tim explained, but Blaire was not buying it yet. "Can you loan me some?"

"Probably not, Tim," Sam said. "How much are you looking for?"

"Five hundred," Tim said. "I need it quick. Tonight."

"Don't have that kind of cash on me, Tim," Sam said.

"The ATM. Can you get it out?" Tim was starting to sound panicky. "I can pay you back next week."

"Sorry, Tim," Sam said. "I don't have it to give you."

"I need it. I need it now!" Tim shouted, and Blaire saw the change in his eyes.

"Tim! No!" She stepped in front of Sam just as Tim pulled the semiautomatic pistol from his waistband.

She swung his gun arm up over his head and brought her knee up sharply into his crotch. The gun went off and she hit him squarely in the face with a right jab. Tim fell backwards and Blaire kicked the gun away as she knelt and rolled him facedown.

"Get something to tie his hands," she said without emotion. "Shoelaces, strips of cloth, anything. He won't be out very long and we only need hold to him until Deputy Saulter gets here."

Sam unlaced one of Tim's boots and looked at her. "Deputy Saulter knows? How?"

Blaire looked at him and knew she could not tell him she had called WL-One. "The gunshot. I'm sure he heard it. He... should be walking the Main Street beat about now."

She tied Tim's wrists and was standing with Sam beside him when Deputy Saulter pulled up in his star-emblazoned, hard-topped jeep.

'WL-One. *Tell him what I told Sam,*' Blaire said, and smiled as the deputy got out. She saw him hesitate and glance at her, then he turned and greeted Sam.

"Hello, Blaire," he said as he stepped up on the sidewalk and looked at the body on the sidewalk. "I was just up a few blocks on Main when I heard the gunshot. What happened?"

Blaire smiled at the deputy and then resumed her somber expression as Sam explained what transpired.

"Blaire was amazing," Sam said in conclusion. "She saw everything coming and was ready for it."

Deputy Saulter smiled at Blaire.

"Do you have an evidence bag?" Blaire asked. "You'll want it for his pistol, nine millimeter like your standard issue."

"I'll get it," Deputy Saulter said as he finished his notes at the end of Sam's explanation. He put his digital pad in his jacket pocket and retrieved the pistol.

He placed the bag with the pistol in a pouch and put it in the metal lockbox in the back of the jeep. He opened the rear passenger door, went and folded Tim over his shoulder, and dumped him unceremoniously into the back seat. He strapped him in using the cinch straps instead of the normal seat and shoulder harness.

"That ought to hold him until I get to the office," the deputy said as he shook Sam's hand. "Glad to see you're all right, Miss Blaire."

"Thanks. I'll let Dad know what happened," she said, not saying that he probably already knew.

The deputy waved and got into his jeep, and they watched as he turned back to Main on Juniper. Sam turned and studied Blaire with a keener eye as they walked east on Maple.

At the end of the first block, he asked how she did that.

"Just my training, I guess," Blaire said, and looked at him, her expression still somber. "I learned what they taught me very well, Sam. I'm not the same Blaire Lupis you knew three months ago or before. I don't worry about being taken care of anymore, but more about taking care of others now."

"I certainly see that you're different," Sam said with a smile. "You're confident, able, and seem to know what you're doing. I'm happy for you. Happy that you have changed into a strong woman." He saw her expression take a serious turn. "I mean that in the best possible way, Blaire. I really do."

At Hunt, they turned south and walked the last block to Blaire's parents' place in silence. When they reached their front door, Sam turned her to face him.

"You call me the next time you're in town and are available," he said. "Tonight was wonderful, barring the Tim Hill incident—which, by the way, you handled better than I could have ever thought to do."

"Okay, Sam," Blaire said softly, looking up, realizing how close they were.

Sam caught her face gently between his open hands and kissed her softly. He held her lips to his as long as he dared, and then slowly relaxed. Her face still close, he watched her and her eyes as she slowly opened them.

"Goodnight, Blaire," he said softly as he pulled his hands away from her face. "Please take care of yourself. For everyone else that needs you, if you won't do it for me. Goodnight."

She caught the doorjamb to steady herself and watched Sam as he walked down the drive to his jeep, parked in front of the house on Oak. He waved as he got in and she waited until he was gone before she forced her legs to move.

Knowing her mom and dad were asleep, she called Two for a ride out to the ranch and her fighter. She touched her lips and smiled. It was her first kiss and the first time Sam had ever tried to kiss her. Thinking of his tender touch and the sensations that had tingled all the way to her toes, she was glad Sam was the one that had kissed her.

⋀ ⋀ ⋀ ⋀ ⋀

"Can you fix one of your cups of hot chocolate," Neila asked Cheral as they returned to their quarters, "before we go to bed."

"I suppose," Cheral said, and went to change into her sleepwear. "Just one cup, though."

"You didn't like the drink at the Mess?" Kiile asked as he unbuttoned his shirt and followed Cheral into their bedroom.

"No. Not really," Neila said as she went into the kitchen area and started getting the ingredients out. "It didn't taste like Cheral's. Not rich and creamy, I guess. Too watery."

"Ah. You're turning into a connoisseur of hot chocolate," Kiile said as Cheral stepped back into the kitchen area, tying her robe about her.

"Now, young lady," Cheral said as she took the handled pan from the cabinet and the milk from the chiller. "Go wash up and get dressed while I heat the milk and get things started."

"Okay, but let me watch you put it together," Neila said, and hurried to her room.

Cheral smiled and watched her disappear through her door and heard the shower water start. She turned to the task and was pouring the milk when Kiile came out and sat on one of the stools at the counter.

"You know, Kiile," Cheral said softly. "She brings so much excitement and life to our family. I can't imagine what it would be like without her."

"So you like having a daughter and all of the extra caring and remembering and work," Kiile teased. "Instead of being young newlyweds, focused on just each other?"

"Actually, I do," Cheral said. "We've been together, in a manner of speaking, for so long, we might not have liked just being the two of us."

"Well, love." Kiile smiled. "We do get our times together, and we have our times together with Neila. I love both. The two of you help me see my world as it should be."

"Thanks," Cheral said as she set the pan on the stove unit and began stirring as it warmed.

It only seemed like a minute or two before Neila came back out wearing her robe and drying her hair with a towel.

"You weren't in there very long. Did you wash completely? No places missed?" Cheral said and smiled at Neila.

"Yes. Everywhere," Neila said, and sat down on the middle stool next to Kiile. "Will you brush my hair while the milk warms? Then I want to help make the magical potion."

"Magical potion?" Kiile asked as he took the brush and turned Neila. "Where did you get that from?"

"Carrie Anne," Neila said. "She calls it a magical potion because she says when it's done right, it tastes so very wonderful, and because of how grand it makes her feel, especially in the winter just before bedtime."

"I think I would have to agree with her," Cheral said, and glanced at the pan as she stirred.

"Will my hair be dry enough when it gets warm?" Neila asked, suddenly concerned.

"If not, your dad can finish brushing while you drink yours," Cheral said. "It'll be dry enough before you go to bed. Did you like meeting Carrie and visiting with everyone today?"

"Yes. Very much," Neila said happily. "Does Carrie know how and why I am here?"

"I don't think she knows the whole story, love," Kiile said. "Her folks, Jim and Shelly, both do, but I don't know if Jim has told Carrie everything about the Force and what we do. I know cousin Shara has been flying her and Shelly back and forth for years, so she knows more than most."

"I was wondering, because sometimes she said things like she might know," Neila said, "and other times like she didn't know anything. She's strange."

Cheral watched the steam rising from the milk and glanced at Neila. "I think we're about there. Would you want to get a spoon and taste it to see if it's warm enough?"

"Sure," Neila said, and got up. She turned to Kiile and hugged him, kissing his cheek. "Thanks, Pada." Then she hurried to the drawer and picked out a spoon.

Kiile watched in happy surprise as Neila tasted the milk and followed Cheral's instructions and comments, adding and stirring the ingredients in. Satisfied that Neila had it right, Cheral got the cups from the cabinet and set the sealed container of fluffed sugar cubes beside them. Neila slowly poured until all three cups were even.

"Can I put the cubes in?" Cheral asked, and opened the container.

"I'd like to, if that's all right," Neila said as she set the pan back on the stove and turned the setting to its lowest value.

"Okay. I don't mind," Cheral chuckled, and watched as Neila took the sugar tongs and gently placed an equal number of cubes into each cup.

Then Neila slid the cups across the counter to their three places. She took her previous place next to Kiile and Cheral took the one next to her.

"You did that very well, Neila," Cheral said, and took a sip from her cup.

"Cheral?" Neila asked without looking at her. "Are you going to adopt me and be my new pama?"

Cheral coughed and looked at Neila. "Would...would you like that?"

"Bdor only came around when he wanted to be with my mother," Neila said slowly, and concentrated on her cup, sipping as she thought about things. "He didn't want to be my father, maybe because I already had one. But he didn't seem to want to be his sons' father either. He just wanted to be alone with my mother. We were not a family." She sighed and sipped again. "You act like Pada does, like you want me to be here. You tell me what is right, what is wrong, and what I should not do. You tell me when I do things wrong and show me how to do them right. You tell me that I did good when I do things right. You get things I need to be a part of this world, and show me how to use them. You treat me like I am part of a family, a real part of a real family. I like that."

"I do too, love," Cheral said softly, and glanced at Kiile's grin. "Very much. I want everyone to like you and to be proud of you and to be pleased they know you."

"Today, Sedona talked about people who have adopted children that are not theirs by birth and made them part of their families," Neila continued. "And I think they are good for doing that." Neila sighed and looked at Cheral with a tight smile. "I have Pada and am very thankful he came to get me when I had nowhere to go, but you came and had no reason to. I am not your daughter, but you care and treat me like I am. It has been confusing, knowing you want me here and yet I don't belong to you. I need to belong to you too, like I belong to Pada, so you can be my pama and I won't feel confused anymore."

"I would love to be your pama, love," Cheral said, and hugged her tight. "I don't know what I would do if you weren't here with us."

Neila smiled and straightened.

"Promise you won't be mad at me," Neila said, and turned to look at Kiile. "I asked cousin Greg about adoptions and he said that in a situation like ours, he has the forms that need to be filled out and sent to the director."

"You did? Today?" Cheral asked, holding her expression neutral.

"Yes," Neila said. "I asked him after Sedona, Sierra, Cheyenne, and Carrie and I talked about people that adopt kids. I hope that was all right. Carrie said I should just do it and apologize later if I shouldn't have. I just didn't want to wait and keep being confused."

Cheral chuckled, leaned to her, and hugged her tight again. "You did just fine, Neila. Just fine."

Kiile began brushing her hair again. "I think we will visit the commander—sorry, Cousin Greg and Shara in the morning and get these forms filled out. Maybe we should go right after morning Mess."

One Thirty-Four
Saturday, January 20

Greg, Shara, Hench, Leeana, Tayn, and Meara were already sitting at the dining room table when Sedona and Sierra came out of the hallway for breakfast.

"I know it isn't a school day," Shara said, "but I didn't expect you to sleep in. Matti was going to hold breakfast, but I told her that if you two weren't hungry, the rest of us were."

"Sorry," Sedona said, and hurried to her chair beside Shara. Sierra sat down in her place between Sedona and Meara. "Morning, Meara," they said together, and then looked at the Kooiches and greeted them.

"We would have been out sooner, but we had to check something out first," Sierra said as Cara and Kym started bringing platters of eggs, bacon, ham, shredded and fried potatoes, a bowl of yogurt and fruit, and carafes of juice, water, tea, and coffee.

"What something did you have to check out?" Shara asked as the girls began filling their plates and passing the platters around.

"It seems we had the same dream last night," Sedona said as she poured herself a glass of orange juice and passed the carafe to Sierra.

"The same dream?" Greg asked, and stopped to look at the two girls. "How can that be?"

"We're not sure," Sedona said, "but we both seemed to have linked with someone. It was like we were watching someone very far away."

"Watching someone?" Shara asked. "Did you see what this person looked like?"

"No," Sierra said. "That's the strange part." She took a bite and smiled at Sedona. "Before we went to bed, something was nagging at us, like in our minds, but not where we could really tell what it was."

"So we held hands," Sedona said, "like we do when we need each other's help seeing something or...defending ourselves."

Shara glanced and Greg and Leeana and then back at the girls. "So you linked. What did you see?"

"We *heard* a man speaking in a strange, gruff voice. In a different language," Sierra said, "but it was like we were speaking. We understood him."

"What was he doing?" Shara asked softly, her interest piqued, her focus keen. "I've had that same kind of feeling before."

"He was talking to a group of people around a large table," Sedona said.

"Not like this," Sierra said, "but a conference table, like the one at Shadow Base that you use for formal occasions."

"He was talking about someplace called Calash," Sedona continued. "He said, wherever this place is, it has a population of one point two million."

"He said his present fleet was not large enough," Sierra said. "I'm not sure what his fleet is. But he said he needed three times the number of ships he has now if they are to be successful on Calash."

Shara turned to look at Greg, suddenly feeling concerned, and called STSX.

'STSX, *where or what is Calash?*'

'*THIRD PLANET IN THE GOBIAL SYSTEM. SMALL PLANET MASS WITH LIGHT GRAVITY; ZERO POINT SEVEN SIX THAT OF EARTH. INDUSTRIAL ECONOMY WITH HIGHLY SKILLED LABOR. LAST CENSUS SET POPULATION AT ONE POINT TWO MILLION INHABITANTS AND WORKERS.*'

Sedona and Sierra finished eating while they listened to STSX's reply.

"We want to link with you," Sedona said, "Dad, Leeana, Blaire, and Franni, and see if we can *hear* this Prince Wilmet again. We think he might be trying to help the slavers."

Shara was suddenly ashen; her mouth moved but words did not come out.

"What's wrong, Mom? You're scaring us," Sierra said.

"The only Prince Wilmet we know of, girls," Greg said softly, and glanced at Hench, Leeana, and Meara, "is Warlord Prince Wilmet Kiese Lukré, the replacement for the late Warlord Kiese of Knobaal."

"The one Mom killed?" Sedona whispered. "We're hearing the evil prince behind the slavers?"

"Oh god," Shara said, and covered her mouth. "You mustn't let him hear you. He can't know who you are. Greg, this can't be."

Greg hugged Shara tight and tried to calm the panic rising in her mind. Leeana moved to his side and held her arm around Shara as well. Meara quickly knelt beside her.

"He doesn't *hear* us, Mom," they said together.

"Our thoughts are blocked," Sierra said softly. "It's okay, Mom."

"Why were you thinking about him? Why did you *hear* him?" Shara asked.

"We think it was because," Sedona said, nodding her head slowly, "we were talking last night about changing a bad person's desires to do bad things."

"And somehow," Sierra added, "we found Prince Wilmet and *listened*, together."

Greg looked at Sedona and then at Sierra. "So you're saying you can enhance each other without physically touching?"

Sedona and Sierra looked at each other. "I...guess we can. Once we *found* him, I guess we *kept* listening, even after we fell asleep."

Shara took Sedona's hand in her left and then Greg's in her right.

"Sierra, please take Sedona's hand," Shara said, "and Leeana, please take Hench's and Greg's hand. Tayn, Meara, you might as well join in too." Then she looked at Sedona and Sierra, and took a deep breath. "Try to show us what you *heard*."

C.3486.787

"I must agree," Camerso said as he selected a robe from the royal clothespress, "that everyone feels your speech last night gave the council something to think about."

"You know what I said?" Prince Lukré asked as he settled the long under-tunic over his shoulders.

"No," Camerso said. "Only that those in attendance felt your message was strong and to the point. I will only know what you say behind closed doors if you tell me."

Prince Lukré smiled and studied his Gentleman's Gentleman. Camerso had been the personal assistant to the late Prince Kiese and had stayed in the palace while they searched for a replacement after the prince's untimely death. When they had selected him as the prince's replacement, they offered Camerso as his personal assistant and Man's Man to help him adjust to his new role. Prince Lukré knew he had a lot to learn and a lot to prove.

"Have you ever heard how Prince Kiese died?" Prince Lukré asked.

"No, sir," Camerso answered. "I only know that Prince Kiese had been fighting many ongoing battles with what was reported as a phantom fighter group from the Galactic Peace Force. For many decaturns, every shipment of slaves had been intercepted, the freighters boarded, and the captives taken away, presumed returned to their home worlds. He became enraged and single-mindedly focused on stopping the interceptions. He laid traps and ambushes, all to no avail. Finally, he arranged a large confrontation force and set out with many battlecruisers and battleships to face this phantom force. There were some reports from the battle scene, but most were chaos- and panic-filled as each battlecruiser was destroyed. One report said a cruiser exploded after only being hit three times. Then the reports ceased and reconnaissance teams found nothing but fragments and debris when they searched for survivors."

"Any clues to the identity of the phantom force?"

"Only that on a few occasions," Camerso said, "the prince told me Intelligence said that the freighters reported seeing a single heavy fighter with a red band around its forward body. Usually, that was just before the transmissions ceased."

"And no reports of this phantom force after the prince died?"

"No, sir," Camerso said. "Of course the collections and transporting of slaves by the Traders' Union ceased at the same time."

"You seem to know a lot of details, Camerso," Prince Lukré said. "Do I need to watch what I say in front of you?"

"No, sir," Camerso said. "I only know what Intelligence told me when they interrogated me after it was apparent the prince was lost, and those few things the prince told me himself. I had no knowledge of the prince's plans or intentions until Intelligence told me what they knew. I have spoken of this to no one until now."

"He was decisive," Prince Lukré said, and took a deep breath. "I understand he did not take council from others easily, doing only what he believed to be the right way to the ends he wanted."

"I understand you are decisive yourself. The attack on that agricultural planet in the Botuni System," Camerso said as he brought the robe to the prince, "caught a number of the council by surprise. I believe it was a well-placed blow at the appropriate moment."

"You think they liked that bold stroke?" Prince Lukré asked.

"I think, sir…" Camerso stopped and smiled, holding the robe for his inspection. "…that stroke separated you from the other considerations and possibly secured your appointment."

"I was pleased that it worked as well as it did," Prince Lukré said, "but the yield was far too small. The concentration of sleep gas was far too strong for the population of that planet. I told that stupid general to take care when he arranged for the attack, but did he listen? No! I wanted slaves, not corpses. He cost me nearly three quarters of the yield."

"Yes, sir," Camerso said as he stepped back from the prince without turning away.

"Told him to test his dosage, but do you think he listened?" Prince Lukré turned and held the robe in front of him as he gazed at the mirror. "Again, no! Well, he won't make that mistake again."

"I heard he will not," Camerso said. "Is this robe acceptable for your Throne Room meetings this morning?"

"Yes, Camerso," Prince Lukré said, and turned back to face him. "I think the council also understood when I made the general and his aides test the dosage on themselves." Lukré smiled. "As I told them, it was too strong. But when I launch my next attack, it will be correct."

"Will that be soon, sir?" Camerso asked as he unfastened the buttons and eyelets and opened the robe for the prince. "Another successful collection will cement your place among the council as our new warlord. They will stop asking their tiring questions."

"After I 'discuss' the failed Terran collection six turns ago with that over-assuming, self-empowering Aide Chimr, I will announce to the council two collections I have planned," Lukré said with a twisted smile. "One about the size of Nevar and another significantly larger in numbers. Soon, Camerso. I will not say when, but very soon."

Prince Lukré was still smiling with an evil twinkle in his eye as Camerso helped him into the heavy ceremonial robe. As he straightened and adjusted the weight of the garment, a sudden wave of nausea swept over him and the room threatened to spin. He caught the arm of the large chair beside his desk and swung himself into it before he fell inelegantly.

"Are you all right, sir?" Camerso asked, and stepped close but did not touch the prince. "Shall I get the Potions Master?"

"No! No, Camerso," the prince said. "It will pass."

Prince Lukré sat for a long moment and stared at the bright, chaotic, multicolored carpet. "I wonder if these dizzying colors in the rugs and hangings are upsetting me. I felt the same stab of unbalance and spinning when I returned to this room last night after the meeting with the council."

"I will have them changed immediately," Camerso said, and straightened. "Something more soothing? Calming?"

"Yes," the prince said with more emphasis than he felt. "Solid colors fading from vivid by the entry to softer colors in the study. That would help, I think."

ᗩ ᗩ ᗩ ᗩ ᗩ

"Okay, Neila," Greg said as Cheral got up from STSX's nav-com's chair. "It's your turn. Come and sit down and sign your name under Cheral's."

Cheral smiled and handed Neila the stylus as she stepped out of the way and let Neila pass. "You can still change your mind, love," Cheral added.

"*Gogalum.* Nope," Neila said confidently, and Kiile smiled when the word from her native language slipped out. She sat and followed Greg's gesture to where she should sign. "You belong to Kiile and I belong to Kiile, and this way, we belong to each other too."

Writing slowly and clearly, Neila added her mark to the document's image. Finished, she looked up at Greg and smiled.

"STSX," Greg said softly. "Please add my signature, name and rank and ID. Print a copy for Kiile and his family and send the document to the director for the Ring's official records."

"DONE. COPY BEING PRINTED."

Greg took the thin sheet as it emerged from the slot in the console to their left, and handed it to Kiile. He looked at Neila and smiled.

"May I be the first to congratulate you, Neila?" Greg said, and extended his arms to hug her. "And to officially say how happy you've made us all by being here."

Neila went to Greg and hugged him tight. "Do I really belong to Cheral now?" she whispered.

"Yes, Neila," Greg answered. "It is official and your dad will get a Records' time stamp report within an hour, our time. It's as official as it can get."

Neila turned and hugged Cheral, and after a long moment she hugged Kiile and expressed her thanks to both of them.

"Okay," Greg said as he stepped to the central chamber and gestured to the floor portal. "I think coffee, tea, juice, or maybe some of Annie's hot chocolate is in order. Anyone care to join me?"

⚔

Sitting between Sedona and Sierra, Neila sipped her chocolate and smiled. "Annie's chocolate is not the same as our recipe, Mom. What does she do that's different?"

"I don't know, Neila," Cheral said, smiling at Neila's use of the term. "Maybe she'll tell you if you asked her nicely."

"Can I?" Neila asked as she pushed her chair back.

"You may," Shara said, and nodded.

Neila got up and went into the kitchen. After a few minutes, Neila came back into the dining room smiling. "Thank you, Annie. It tastes really nice." Neila went to Cheral and handed her a folded piece of paper. "This is Annie's recipe. It has four things we don't use, and a fifth ingredient she says she adds for special occasions. Can you see if we have them?"

"I sure will," Cheral said as she glanced at the list before she tucked the paper into her shirt pocket.

Neila returned to her chair and Sedona asked if she had time to go riding with her, Sierra, and Cheyenne. Neila looked up at Kiile and smiled when he said she did.

"Dad has things to talk to Kiile about anyway," Sierra said softly. "And Cheyenne and Aunt Jill and Uncle Nick are almost here."

Neila closed her eyes and thought about Jill, then smiled. "I *feel* them. Are they on the road that comes from town? Not flying?"

"Yeah. On the road," Sierra said.

"They are going into town to the grocery store after they finish here," Sedona explained.

"Where's Tayn this morning?" Neila asked, deciding it was okay to be a little curious.

"He's helping Hench and Leeana at Shadow Base," Sierra said. "They knew we were riding today and Tayn decided he wanted to go with his dad instead."

"He doesn't like to ride?" Neila asked in surprise.

"He likes to ride," Sedona and Sierra said together. "Sometimes."

"He likes it better," Sierra said, "if he can go over to the CW and ride when Billie rides."

"Aah," Neila said softly, and smiled. "He prefers Billie's company to other girls."

"Right," Sedona and Sierra said together.

"He likes the rest of us and some at school," Sedona said, "but not the same way he likes Billie."

"The boys on Nevar had their 'special' girls, too," Neila said, and finished her chocolate. "They were very possessive, but didn't mind going after the others when they felt like it."

"I don't think Tayn's 'going after' anyone, Neila," Sedona said. "And we girls do have a say in who we want to like, or if we want to like anyone. We don't have to like any of the boys if we don't want to."

Neila smiled, remembering her conversation with Cheral when she had first arrived. "I know. Mom told me."

"Dad?" Sedona asked, turning and interrupting his casual conversation with Kiile. "How does the weather look for today? Is it good enough for us to go up on the ridge?"

"I think so," Greg said, and *felt* for STSX. "No farther, though. That's far enough for what's left of the day. Dark will come early."

"We know," Sedona and Sierra said in unison.

"And there are still a lot of deep pockets in the foothills,"

Sierra finished, "between the ridge and the foothills."

"Deep pockets?" Neila asked.

"Places where the snow hides drop-offs and chasms," Sierra said. "If your horse steps off into one of those, you both could be hurt, bad. Maybe worse."

"The snow is still four or five feet deep in the foothills," Sedona explained. "The wind moves it around, making some places less deep and others deeper. The snow can make a deep ravine look like a pasture."

"You two keep an eye out on the clouds," Shara said. "STSX will alert you if anything comes in early. We are supposed to get more snow before midnight."

"Yes, Mom," they said as one, and smiled.

"We won't go beyond the first ridge," Sierra said, and looked up at the back door. "Chy's here. Dad, can Neila ride Dílis? He's gentle and sure-footed. Better than the buckskin."

"Certainly," Greg said. "You girls ride safe. Be smart."

"We will, Dad," Sedona said as they got up from the table. "Don't worry."

He watched them as they eagerly grabbed their coats and hurried out through the back door.

▲

"That's what the Director said," Greg explained to Kiile, Cheral, Nick, and Jill as they settled in the living room with their coffee. "He wants to personally interview each of the children—the non-registered talents, as he put it."

"That's what? Four?" Nick asked, counting on his fingers.

"Six at the moment," Greg said. "And Wally is bringing Carole and their two for evaluation after lunch. We evaluated Kail and Kayli last week, and even though they have the signs, they haven't actually begun to *hear* yet. Doug, on the other hand, does have a couple of gifts he hasn't told anyone about. He also wants to interview you, Kiile, because your talent waited so long to reveal itself."

"Like Nick, I still count four," Kiile said. "Who're the other two?"

"Billie Baine and Neila," Greg said. "I'm hoping he'll register the younger ones early and simply log the older ones that are already registered. We're going to need one of your transports to carry the non-pilots and some of the parents."

"Yes, I remember you saying Billie was *hearing*, but why Neila?" Nick asked, surprised.

"Her talents are undocumented, and I think she has a few surprises," Greg said with a smile for Kiile and Cheral. "The Director agrees that we have an unusual number of talented offsprings and is very curious about this fertile incubator we have—especially for what that means to the Force."

"What about the cadets?" Kiile asked. "Are you going to have a normal graduation ceremony?"

"Yes," Greg said. "Promotions, as usual, for Blaire and the three older cadets, Huml, Milik, and Ilistr, but I can't promote the children yet, even though I have them listed as cadets. Ani will go with us, but she'll come home with a Q-Ship."

"Are you planning on taking three Q-Ships?" Cheral asked.

"Yours, KKLC14, and ours," Greg answered with a nod. "Each with a patrol fighter. With all of the children in one place, I want adequate security and am thinking maybe a fourth Q-Ship would be wise. I'd like TTYF8 along, but someone has to mind the store and watch the home front."

"LTVC21 was a big help on Nevar," Cheral said. "Debira has good senses about her."

"Which patrol fighter pilots are you thinking about taking?" Jill asked softly. "Nick and I will be going, so I'm wondering if you want us as part of the escort or just to travel as Chy's guardians."

"Under the circumstances," Greg said, and smiled at Jill, "I am leaning toward both of you and Blaire with your patrol fighters. I'll talk to Hench and see what he thinks when he comes back to the ranch for lunch."

"And the schedule?" Kiile asked. "I'll need to get things organized."

"Graduation is planned for the second of February," Greg said. "And the next class will arrive with their fighters on Wednesday the fourteenth. If the Director's available, I'm hoping to meet with him on Friday, the ninth, our time."

"With a transport, it'll take an extra day. We'll have to leave no later than Tuesday the sixth. Maybe Monday would be better," Kiile said as he studied the calendar on his digital pad. "I'll make the arrangements."

▲ ▲ ▲ ▲ ▲

Blaire walked down the corridor from the Mess, and with her mind full of answers to the questions on the digital pad she was carrying, she turned into the Billeting corridor and nearly ran into the marine hobbling with a cane, going in the same direction. She stopped, suddenly seeing him as he turned to see who was about to collide with him.

"Luc," Blaire said in surprise. "I'm so sorry. I was going over the questions for Monday's exam and didn't see you." She took a deep breath and exhaled slowly. "How are you doing? I haven't seen you in almost a week."

"Hey, Blaire," he said softly, and leaned back against the wall. "Okay for a very lucky idiot."

"How's that?" Blaire asked. "I heard your raid on the Australian facility went very well. Twenty-six captives rescued and returned."

"The facts of the engagement are nice," Luc said, and waved his cane in front of him. "But we lost one and I'm hobbling around, dependent on this stupid cane to keep me upright."

"Aah, yes," Blaire said, and looked him in the eye. "I won't diminish how bad it is to get wounded, but there are twenty-six captives and many in your squads that are very grateful for the mission and its success. Everyone's sorry you got wounded, but they are very appreciative of your courage and determination to save the captives and effectively execute your operation."

"Sorry," Luc said, and glanced down at the floor. "I don't

mean to be feeling sorry for myself. I'm just not used to being forced to take time off, especially for recuperation."

"Well, you do it very well," Blaire said, and smiled at him. "I know it isn't easy, so do something to fill your time and mind while your body mends. Pretty soon, you won't have time to."

"Thanks," he chuckled. "I heard you were here when they brought me in."

Blaire stared at him. "I...saw them bring you and the other one in and I did check on you after surgery." Blaire swallowed and took a deep breath. "Commandant Kiile sat with you and I heard he was there when you woke up."

Luc smiled. "I heard you were there a lot longer than that."

Blaire shook her head slightly. "Don't read anything into my checking on you. I knew who they brought in and I wanted to get facts on your condition. I checked on the other marine also, but he wasn't as fortunate as you were."

Luc studied her face and smiled. "Okay. Thank you for your concern for a fellow soldier." Then he changed the subject. "I hear your class is graduating in a couple of weeks."

"On the second," Blaire said. "And I've got so much to do to get ready for the final exams. Galactic astronavigation, and a recitation on the political makeup of the Kyddellan systems, and the governmental characteristics of the Knobaal Warlord and his new empire."

"And I bet there is a general retesting of everything you learned from the time you got here and started studying."

"Yeah. Something like that."

"Makes me tired thinking about it. Good luck. And I promise there will not be any unfavorable outbursts from the marine contingency during your celebration. Now, I need to get back to my quarters and get some rest. Maybe I'll see you at Mess or sometime around the facility."

"Most likely. Glad you're up and around, Luc," Blaire said, and started down the corridor to her quarters.

▲ ▲ ▲ ▲ ▲

"Well, Wally, Carole," Greg said as they settled in the living room of the main house and Matti brought a tray of cups and a carafe of coffee. "I have reviewed STSX's evaluations and have some surprises for you to think about."

Wally looked at Carole, sitting beside him on the loveseat, and then at Alyssa and Ridan on the long couch beside Greg in his overstuffed chair. Shara was watching with a warm smile from her place on the footstool beside Greg, and Nick and Jill listened from the second loveseat.

"What kind of surprises?" Carole asked, a hopeful smile filling her expression.

'Alyssa? Do you hear me?' Shara asked as she turned to look at Alyssa.

Her sudden stiffening and surprised expression were all Shara needed.

'Can you answer me?' Shara continued as Alyssa looked around to see who was *talking.*

'Y...yeess,' she said uncertainly in her mind.

'Ridan?'

Ridan looked around and smiled when he saw Shara's gaze on him.

"It seems your youngsters have not told you that they are among our gifted children," Greg said, and smiled at both of the children. "How long?" he asked them.

"S...since school started," Ridan said softly. "Aly and I *talk* to each other a lot, but not to anyone else."

"Who do you *hear* and not *talk* to?" Shara asked, glancing at a startled Carole.

"We're not sure," Alyssa said softly. "Mostly just voices and murmurs."

"I...hear murmurs all the time," Carole said. "Is this normal?" She looked at Wally. "Do you?"

Wally nodded and looked at Alyssa and Ridan. "Do you *hear* words and sentences?"

"Yeah," they said, almost in unison.

"It seems," Shara said softly, smiling hugely, "we have a bumper crop of empathic children. Our two, Cheyenne, Tayn, Billie, and Neila, and we expect Kail and Kayli to start very soon. We also have a rather large count of adults." She nodded to Jill. "Jill, Cheral, Kiile, Leeana and Hench, many marines, and all of our flight crews."

"But we don't," Carole said. "Not really. Just murmurs."

"I would like to have you both spend four sessions with STSX," Greg said. "He has a series of implants that he's given others to help jump-start or enhance a budding capability. It's a session, two days off, then another session, and so on. He helped me, Cheral, Kiile, Jill, Ani Tigs, and other pilots in our squadron to develop and increase our capabilities and to fine-tune them."

"The sessions are harmless in all other aspects," Shara said. "If your mind is ready, you will respond to the sessions. If not, then everything will remain the same and develop at its own rate."

"Since they can *hear*, I'd sure like to share that with them," Carole said, and smiled at Wally, Alyssa, and Ridan.

"We can do the first session today," Shara said. "If you'll stay for dinner, we can start, eat, and relax a bit before you head back into town."

Carole looked at Wally's smile and said, "I think that's a great idea."

Shara got up and went to the kitchen to let Annie and the house girls know they would have ten extra for dinner. She stepped back into the dining room as Sedona led the other three girls in. Neila quickly hung her coat on a peg in the coatroom and hurried through the rooms to the fireplace.

"I didn't know it could be sooo cold," Neila said as she held her arms open and tried to hug the heat.

Sedona, Sierra, and Cheyenne quickly joined her and

hoarded all of the heat they could.

"Sorry, Neila," Sedona said. "I didn't think it would be this cold."

"Temperature has been dropping all day," Shara said as she returned and sat down on the footstool. "You guys settle on the hearth. Hot chocolate is on the way. Is it snowing yet?"

"Flurries. Nothing heavy," Cheyenne said.

"Where's my mom and dad?" Neila asked, looking around the room.

"They went back to Shadow Base for a little bit," Greg said. "The Kooiches and the Beelis will be back before dinner." Greg looked at Alyssa and Ridan. "May I tell them?"

"Tell us what?" Sedona asked, and looked at Alyssa.

"We can *talk* and *hear* like you all can," Alyssa said with a smile.

'*Wow! That's great!*' Sierra said. "I was thinking maybe you could. Something you said in school last week. This is great!"

⚔

"STSX1, KKLC14, and STSX12 will be the core three Q-Ships," Greg said as he leaned back and let Cara collect his and Shara's dinner plates. "And you said you thought LTVC21 would be good for our fourth."

"Yes," Hench said, and sipped his coffee. "With all of us gone, I just can't bring myself to take TTYF8 with us. That would leave the base without leadership, and in dire straits if a serious attack or something of any magnitude arose."

"I agree," Greg said. "It will leave eight Q-Ships, most of the Class Twos, and the newly graduated cadets for local defenses. Hopefully, we have Nikle's followers disorganized enough they won't be an immediate threat."

The children sat quietly, finishing their desserts and listening eagerly to the adults making plans, certain that if they interrupted or made a sound, they would be sent away.

"I agree," Hench said, and studied his cup, "that Nick, Jill, and Ani are the right choices for our escorts, and I also agree

Blaire should be included as the fourth."

"Kiile," Greg said, and looked at him and Cheral. "I will plan on you transporting Wally, Carole, and Alyssa and Ridan, and Thom or Eddie and Billie, Doug McIntire, and any marines you feel we should have to provide security when we land in the Rings."

Kiile nodded. "I can do that. What about Rose and their children?"

"I'll have to ask," Greg said. "Kail and Kayli have not started yet, but Rose may want to go with Doug. He's the one the Director is interested in, and we won't have enough Q-ships to carry another patrol fighter."

"I will have the transport reconfigured," Kiile said, "to have adequate sleeping provisions and a secondary galley. Should I consider extra bunks in case the other children want to travel aboard? Let me know about Rose, Kail, and Kayli."

"Let's see," Shara said softly, and looked at the children. "Cheyenne can travel in either of the host ships for Nick or Jill."

Cheyenne nodded. "I'll go with one going and the other coming back. We can all communicate without having to be in the same ship."

"Very true," Shara agreed, "and I assume Tayn will either travel with his folks or on the transport."

"He's welcome to do either," Leeana said, and smiled a knowing smile at Tayn.

"I'm planning on Sedona and Sierra traveling with us," Shara said, and looked at Neila.

"I'm like Cheyenne," Neila said. "I will probably travel one way with one and the other way with the other."

"Okay," Kiile said, and smiled. "I can arrange for these possibilities plus a squad."

"One more thing I will ask," Greg said, and slowly looked at each of them and each of the children. "This trip will not be discussed with anyone that is not specifically traveling on it. If it must be discussed, those discussions will only be in private where no one else can witness you."

"You expect trouble?" Kiile asked, and looked at Hench.

"Maybe. It's an uneasiness I have," Greg admitted. "The Director has never called a group together specifically for being 'talented.' He has never liked having a large number of his operative Shadows collected in one place. He has the evaluations on each of those he has asked to come and has reviewed them. He really doesn't need to interview them, but he says he wants to, and there is something bothersome about that.

"Therefore, I want everyone involved to be watchful for casual inquiries or open questions. I want all such inquiries reported to me, Hench, or Kiile, either directly or through our mates, immediately." He looked at the children again. "This includes you. Understand?"

"Yes, sir," they all said, and nodded. Sedona tapped her forehead and looked at the others.

He took a deep breath and exhaled slowly.

"I sure hope I'm wrong and just being a paranoid parent," Greg said, and smiled. "Anyone want anything else to eat or drink?"

᛭ ᛭ ᛭ ᛭ ᛭

"I haven't felt you this worried in a long time," Shara said as she slid between the fleece sheets.

Greg tossed his soiled clothes into the hamper and stepped into the bathroom to get ready for bed.

"Like I said, I hope it isn't really anything," he said as he dried his hands, switched the bathroom light off, and crossed the room to their bed. "But this is one time I feel we should really be prepared rather than just looking prepared."

He slid in and stretched out beside Shara as she snuggled as close as she could.

"After Kiile, Cheral, and Neila left," Shara said softly, "I tried to *touch* the Director. But even with STSX's help, I could only tell he was in the Rings. Not where exactly, or if he was alone or working or anything definitive like that."

"Part of that is the way the Rings are constructed," Greg said, and curled his arm tighter around Shara. He *felt* the girls and knew they were asleep. "When we are inside the complex, we should be able to tell, just like when he used to test us for access."

"I hope so," Shara said. "Your feelings are making me nervous too, and I'd like something to show us we're being overly concerned."

"Me too, Bren," Greg said. "But after eavesdropping on the new Warlord Prince Lukré this morning and *hearing* what he told his valet, I don't think I am. I want to talk with the Director and see if we have enough evidence to go after him."

"Sometimes," Shara admitted, "I wish we could just swoop in and take him out and level his empire in the name of all that's decent and good."

"Me too, Bren. Me too." He held her for several long moments and then chuckled. "Did you ever think Kiile could switch to being a father so quickly?"

"No, actually," Shara said, and joined his warm thoughts. "And Neila asking for Cheral to adopt her. It's only been thirty-some days, and I must admit, I haven't seen Cheral as happy as she was today when Neila called her 'Mom.'"

"STSX says," Greg said, "Kiile has settled nicely with his being able to *hear,* and that has to help make Neila feel secure."

"You mentioned this morning that Neila had a few surprises up her sleeve," Shara said. "What did STSX tell you?"

Greg chuckled and tickled Shara lightly. "She's *telekinetic,* love. Like Doug only a lot stronger."

"Really," Shara asked, but it wasn't a question.

"Cheral said Neila can easily lift large objects and move them," Greg said, "but I don't think she realizes how."

"And that was in the evaluation you sent to the Director?"

"I'm sure he will test her somehow," Greg said, and rolled onto his back, pulling Shara with him. "But we will see what he does when we get there. Right now, I have something to talk to you about." He gently caught the sides of her head and pulled her to him, kissing her until there was only one thought between them.

One Thirty-Five
Friday, February 2
Graduation Day: Class ASCT-48

Blaire followed the other cadets into the Flight Ops briefing room and stood in front of the chairs beside Coli. Glancing around, she noted that Cheral and Lieutenant Quil were standing at the far end of the curved row. *Feeling* Neila, she looked more closely at Cheral and saw a blond head moving on her other side. Blaire smiled, knowing Neila knew her way around the facility better than anyone and could go anywhere inside without fear, yet she never missed an opportunity to be included when something important was happening.

Blaire glanced around at the sound of the door reopening, and watched as all of the other pilots entered and arrayed themselves in front of the seats arranged in the rows behind the graduating class. When the pilots had all found places, they turned forward and fell silent.

"Please, be seated," Colonel Kooich said, standing at the podium at the end of the table with Leeana, Colonel and Major Mooren, both Captain Jordans, both Captain McIntires, Captain Casi, and the commander seated behind it.

Blaire sat down.

"My congratulations to you eight cadets and to you, Lieutenant Quil," Colonel Kooich continued. "Today marks the successful conclusion to the forty-eighth class in the Apache Squadron Combat Training School. You are a small class, but no less deserving and no less trained.

"As a point of history, when the first class was formed, many of you probably had no idea that you would be here, starting a career such as this. Four of you, for certain, had no ideas at all."

Caiti, Coli, Keely, and Tayn smiled and laughed.

"The first class, by the time of graduation, was attended by four cadets, one captain and nine nav-com lieutenants. The commander, a colonel at the time, had previously, and quite successfully, trained his mate in the art of being a Shadow, a nav-com officer as well as being a QShip Pilot, and seeing that success and the short time he had accomplished the training in, the Director challenged him to repeat it by starting an official training class. By the time the first class had progressed to near graduation, the Director named us the Apache Squadron Combat Training School—ASCT in short.

"The first class graduated fourteen Combat Pilots with Distinction. The following four classes per Terran year averaged eleven graduates per class. Today we see nine more join the esteemed ranks of the five hundred and twenty ASCT graduates that have gone before you. Class ASCT Forty-Eight raises the total graduates to five hundred twenty-nine. Congratulations.

"As you know, we have a unique circumstance in Class Forty-Eight. Four of you are not yet registered in the Rings, being underage, but rest assured, your progress, every step of your training and your performances, have been keenly watched by the Director himself. You four have satisfactorily completed and demonstrated your ability, and in most cases far exceeded the requirements of this school. You have mastered the skills necessary for self-defense, defense of others, hand-to-hand combat, data gathering and analysis—in other words, the abilities necessary to become a Shadow. You have further chosen and mastered the skills necessary to become not just fighter pilots, but QShip-qualified fighter pilots."

Someone started clapping and Hench waited until everyone had joined in. When the praise diminished, he continued.

"Surprisingly, the youngest cadets showed this class, this school, how narrow-minded we were in our thinking and in our judgment. Cadet Caiti and Coli Geaardt are the only students that have ever completed their entire flight combat exercises, from the first to the last, while *Dancing in the Dark.* Cadet Blaire Lupis, Cadet Keely Dnar, and Cadet Tayn Kooich completed all except their first engagements *Dancing in the Dark.*"

Again someone clapped, and with a few whistles for emphasis, Hench was forced to pause a moment. Blaire saw each of the parents behind the long table openly smiling at their children and their accomplishments.

"It is not necessary for me to include the numbers from the official kill record, since each cadet and Lieutenant Quil scored the maximum attainable for the class. For the first time since the classes began target generation training, no one failed to make a kill or killed a 'friendly' by mistake. Again—"

The applause and whistles forced Hench to pause again. He smiled at the class and slowly held up his hand, calling for silence.

"Again, we, the proud administrators of this school, congratulate each and every one of you, Class ASCT-Forty-Eight."

Colonel Kooich turned to Colonel Mooren. "Colonel, will you assist me with the honors? Class ASCT-Forty-Eight, please rise."

The front row stood as requested, and Blaire kept her eyes forward even though she wanted to see if Neila was standing to see. She quickly hid her smile and resumed her poised stance as Colonel Kooich and Colonel Mooren marched the length of the row and stopped in front of Lieutenant Quil.

"Lieutenant Quil," Colonel Kooich began. "You are presented with a Certificate of Graduation for the nav-com Transition Training Program and are awarded a Space Pilot's Ribbon with a Q-Ship Qualification Pin, and a Fighter Pilot Ace's Cross with a Braid of Distinction. For your assistance at Nevar, you are awarded a Distinguished Service Star for Actions Beyond the Call of Duty and a grade promotion to captain. Congratulations, Captain." He took the awards, ribbons, and lapel bars from Colonel Mooren and handed them to Keli.

Amid an outburst of applause, Colonel Mooren repeated Hench's congratulations and they stepped aside and stopped in front of Cadet Huml.

"Cadet Huml," Colonel Kooich said in his "official" tone. "You are presented with a Certificate of Graduation, a

Full Shadow Ribbon, a Space Pilot's Ribbon with a Q-Ship Qualification Pin, a Fighter Pilot Ace's Cross with a Braid of Distinction, and a promotion to under-lieutenant." Colonel Kooich shook Lieutenant Huml's hand.

"Congratulations, Lieutenant," Colonel Mooren said, shaking Lieutenant Huml's hand.

The colonels moved to Cadet Milik and repeated the speech, passed Cadet Milik his Certificate, Ribbons, Pin, Ace's Cross, and under-lieutenant lapel bars.

They shook hands and moved to Cadet Ilistr. They repeated the procedure and moved to Cadet Tayn Kooich.

"Cadet Tayn Kooich," Colonel Kooich said. He repeated the speech, and the presentation of the Certificate of Graduation, the Full Shadow Ribbon, the Space Pilot's Ribbon with a Q-Ship Qualification Pin, and the Fighter Pilot Ace's Cross with a Braid of Distinction, but stopped before the awarding of rank. "Cadet Tayn Kooich, I have added a personal endorsement for promotion to the rank of under-lieutenant for the Director at the time of his interview. It is our sincere hope the Director will look past the short time remaining until you are officially of age to register and that he will bestow upon you the rank you so earnestly deserve. Congratulations, Cadet."

Colonel Mooren repeated his congratulations and they moved to Cadet Caiti Geaardt. After Colonel Kooich gave the same speech with the same comments regarding his endorsement for promotion, they moved to Cadet Coli Geaardt and then to Cadet Keely Dnar.

"Cadet Keely Dnar," Colonel Kooich said after giving the speech he had given to the other cadets. "I will forever be impressed with how well you studied, learned, applied, and demonstrated your skills and understanding of the subject matter and the goals you were working for. You are a bright example of one giving her all to reach her goals and to keep up with and stay equal to the others, incorrectly assumed your superiors. You, as much as anyone in this room, deserve the Director's understanding and honest appraisal, age aside, and the rank owed you. Again, congratulations, Cadet Keely Dnar."

The room was dead silent as Colonel Mooren gave Keely his Congratulations.

"Now, Cadet Blaire Lupis," Colonel Kooich said as he stopped in front of her. After he had awarded the Certificate, the Full Shadow Ribbon, the Space Pilot's Ribbon with Q-Ship Qualification Pin, the Fighter Pilot Ace's Cross with its Braid of Distinction, and her under-lieutenant's lapel bars, he smiled at her. "In addition, it is the decision of this body to award you with two Distinguished Service Stars for Actions Beyond the Call of Duty for your assistance in defending Shadow Base against the tunnel intruders and for your assistance in locating and the eventual capture of Don Nikle."

The applause and whistling forced Hench to wait again before he could finish.

"Commander?' Colonel Kooich said, and turned to face Greg. "Do you have anything to say to Class Forty-Eight?"

"Yes, Colonel. Thank you," Greg said as he rose up and stood behind the table. "It gives me great honor to celebrate the accomplishments of Class Forty-Eight. Each of you have exceeded what are considered the toughest and most demanding requirements in the Galactic Peace Force. To accomplish, in three months, all that the Academy requires in four years—or in ninety turns compared to fifteen hundred turns, as was pointed out to me—is a testament to your abilities and determination. I offer you my sincerest congratulations.

"After today, some of you may be relocated, by choice or by assignment, to other posts with similar, but different challenges. Those that do move on, I hope you will take with you fond memories of your time as Class Forty-Eight. Whether you move to a new assignment or not, I want you to know that it has been my great honor and privilege to serve you and to prepare you for the life ahead. Make the Force proud and always strive to help your fellow officers and those needing your assistance.

"In closing, I will announce that for the next forty-eight hours, each of you new graduates are officially 'off-duty.' Take the time to rest and relax, decompress. I will expect each of you back here Sunday, no later than noon, each one relaxed and recharged, ready to receive your next assignment. Thank you, and again, congratulations, Class Forty-Eight. Dismissed!"

⟡

Blaire was happily lost in thought as she walked down the corridor and turned at the intersection at the entrance to the Mess. Planning to get a snack and a drink, she did not hear Sergeant Stial call "Lieutenant" as she walked past him.

He called again, but included her name the second time. "Lieutenant Lupis," he said, and she finally heard him, stopped, and slowly turned around.

He saluted her and she quickly returned it and then saw his lips spread into the warm smile.

"I heard you were promoted to lieutenant," Luc said, and stepped closer. "Congratulations."

"Thank you," she said, and smiled back at him. "Sorry, I didn't hear you. I was focused on getting ready to head out and wasn't thinking about anything else."

"Head out?" he asked, and scrunched his brow.

"Yeah." She smiled again. "We've been ordered to take the next forty-eight hours off. Without delay, we're 'off-duty.'" She stopped and looked at him. "Oh, my. I'm just running off at the mouth, Luc. How are you getting along? It looks like you've outgrown the cane."

He nodded. "No more cane. Thanks for noticing."

He walked with her as she went down the serving line and selected her sweet roll and a cup of coffee. "I'll be back Sunday for an assignment briefing. Maybe I'll get lucky and get somewhere close by."

"I'd like that, Blaire," he said when she turned toward the corridor. "Maybe I'll see you Monday and you can let me know where they send you."

"Sure," Blaire said, and nodded. "Keep the Fort safe while I'm gone."

"I'll do my best, Blaire. You enjoy your time off, but don't party too hard, or fall off any bridges or anything like that. We need you back in one piece—your normal happy, confident, stiff-laced, purpose-filled self, all in one piece."

"Yes, sir," she said, and smiled. "I'll try, Luc."

Blaire turned and left the Mess. She walked slowly to Billeting and her quarters, thinking about Luc's words and his description of her.

▲ ▲ ▲ ▲ ▲

Sedona and Sierra were huddled together at the table near their favored, windowed corner of the school cafeteria's lunchroom, talking with Cheyenne. Tayn and Billie stopped and slid into chairs across from them.

"What's up?" Tayn asked softly. He and Billie already knew Sedona and Sierra had sensed something, but they were not certain of what.

"More of the prince stuff," Cheyenne whispered, and took another bite of her lunch.

Tayn looked at Billie, concerned. They knew about Sedona and Sierra's dreams and their sudden, unexplained link to the evil prince, and now their tone made him concerned.

"Is it bad?" Billie asked.

"Eat and act normal and listen in," Sedona said. "We need to pass this along to Mom and Dad."

"Okay," Tayn said, and led by example, taking a large bite of his sandwich.

'Mom, Dad?' Sedona asked, knowing they were back at Shadow Base having lunch with Kiile, Cheral, and Neila in the Mess after they had dropped her and Sierra off at school.

'We're here. What's wrong?' Shara answered.

'Prince Lukré,' Sierra said. *'He just had a conversation with someone and he was told his next collection had been set up. We didn't get the whole conversation, but it has something to do with someone that's in the Rings or that works in the Rings or...We don't know, but it has some connection with the Rings.'*

'Don't let it upset you,' Shara said. *'If you want, we can review*

what you heard *after you get home this afternoon. Maybe there is something there that wasn't obvious.'*

'*Maybe,*' Sedona said. '*We already asked STSX to check, before we called you, and he didn't find anything.*'

'*Okay,*' Greg said softly. '*Still, don't let it bother you. Keep* listening *and we'll try to* listen *too. Hearing* them, *maybe we can stay a step ahead of them and spook their horses when the time's right.*'

'*Thanks, Dad,*' Sierra said, and almost smiled. '*We'll let you know if we* hear *any more.*'

▲ ▲ ▲ ▲ ▲

It was full dark and snowing lightly when Sam stopped in front of Dan and Mandy Lupis' house. He hurried to the door, rang the chime, and smiled when Blaire, dressed in fitted slacks and a fitted, floral-print top, opened the door and let him in.

"Are you ready?" he asked, "or do I need to wait?"

"Hey, Sam," Dan said from where he and Mandy sat in the living room near the fireplace. "Good to see you."

"Hi, Dan, Mandy," Sam said, and turned to see them. "How was your day?"

"Good," Dan said. "Enjoying the early shift for the next few days. Everything okay with you?"

Sam nodded and Blaire smiled at her father's normal inquisitive routine. She took her coat from the closet and handed it to Sam.

"You two kids have fun," Mandy said as Sam helped Blaire slip into her coat.

"We will, Mom," Blaire said, and turned to the door Sam was holding open for her.

"Goodnight," Sam said, and waved as Blaire stepped out and he closed the door behind them. "You look very nice tonight." He took her arm as they stepped off the porch and walked to the driveway. He nodded to her jeep parked in front of the double garage. "That's a sight I was thinking I might not ever see again."

"What? My jeep?"

"Yes." He smiled and looked at her. "Your jeep in your parents' drive. There was a time, not too long ago, I might have said I wouldn't be lucky enough to see it happen again."

He opened his jeep's door and helped her in.

"You should know," Blaire said as he slid in and closed the driver side door, "I'll always come home and visit the folks."

"Yeah," Sam said a little cooler than he meant to as he started the engine. Then he turned and smiled at her. "Are you hungry? Really hungry?"

"Yes," she said, and smiled back at him. She started to mention that the Mess had great cooks, but she missed the meals she grew up with and the going out to eat. "I do believe I am."

Sam went around the corner at Kelly and back to Amos on Maple. He turned north on Amos. "Friday night in a school week," he said, and gestured to Main, just a block over. "The kids are cruisin' already. Main's tied up all the way to the bridge."

"I forgot about that," Blaire said, surprised that she had. "Guess I've been keeping my head down too much. Definitely not getting out enough."

Sam chuckled and Blaire saw he was feeling better; the dark caution in his mood had started to ebb.

At River Street, Sam turned to Main and then and crossed the north bridge. He took Mill Road east and turned at the first left.

"The Stone Fence?" Blaire asked in surprise when she saw the restaurant peek out from behind the thick stand of tall pines.

"I was sure you haven't had a good steak in a while," Sam said, and glanced at her as he swung the jeep into the parking lot. "I know it's a little early, but I could only get a reservation now or a lot later."

"The time is fine, Sam," Blaire said as he parked the jeep.

"Simply wonderful. I was too keyed up to eat much at lunch, so this is really great."

Sam helped her out and led her in through the double set of front doors. A pleasantly dressed woman greeted them, checked Sam's name off the reservations list, and led them to a table by the large fireplace.

"Thanks, Patty," Sam said as he helped Blaire with her chair.

"You're welcome, Sam. Excuse me—Mr. Reeds," she said, and smiled.

"Patty? Do you know Blaire Lupis?" Sam asked by way of introduction. "Patty was a year behind me in school."

"Nice to meet you, Blaire," Patty said. "Please don't be offended that I don't remember you, but I was so self-absorbed in school, I missed getting to know a lot of very nice people."

Blaire smiled. "I often feel the same way. It's nice to meet you, Patty."

"Thanks. Bobby will be your server tonight. Enjoy your meal," Patty said as she slipped the menus in front of them, nodded, and then turned back to her post.

"And how do you know Patty?" Blaire asked, trying to keep the question from sounding like she was prying or that she suspected some kind of a relationship.

"She was a friend of mine's girlfriend," Sam said, and smiled at Blaire's obvious question. "We saw each other when Mark and I went for coffee or a beer."

"Aah," Blaire said, but suddenly *felt* Sam's mood shift again. "What is it, Sam? Did I ask something I shouldn't have?"

"No. It's nothing you've said, Blaire." Sam leaned forward and looked at her. "Just remembering. Patty and Mark got married in her last year of school and they had a little girl. He went to work at the mill and she tried to be a stay-at-home mom. That lasted a year."

Blaire suddenly felt the reason wasn't the obvious one.

"He got caught between one of the big felling machines and a tree they were cutting down. It was over in an instant and Patty was left with just her and their little Nicole."

"How terrible," Blaire said before she could think of the right words to say.

"Yes, it was," Sam said, and took a deep breath. "They're managing the best they can. Actually, Patty's looking better tonight than I've seen her look in a long time. Her folks have helped a lot, and Mark's have as well. But it takes time to climb out of that kind of a hole."

Then, against her will, Blaire looked down at her menu, remembering her conversation with Sedona many months before. "Another girl," she muttered softly to herself.

"What? Another girl?" Sam waited, watching her, curious.

Blaire looked up and shook her head. "It just surprised me. A few months ago and then again a few weeks ago, I was in a conversation about the number of girls that are born here, compared to the relatively few boys. It's a consistent fact, but a curious one."

"Consistent? How so?"

"Records I've studied as part of my training show the trend is nearly a hundred years old," Blaire said, and sipped her water. "Four girls to every boy, give or take a few over the years. I said it must be something in the water."

Sam stared at her, but didn't say anything.

"I was kidding, Sam," Blaire said, and Sam slowly relaxed. "There is nothing wrong with the water." And she sipped hers again as if to prove her point.

Sam was still chuckling when a pretty brunette stepped up to the table.

"I'm Bobby and I'll be your server this evening. May I get you something besides water to drink?"

Sam forced his chuckles down to a smile and asked, "Blaire? What would you like?" Then he cocked his head and continued. "I know you're old enough for wine or beer."

She smiled at him, but suddenly felt like he thought of her as a child again.

"Bobby," Sam said without waiting. "We'll have a chilled bottle of your house Chardonnay."

"Very good," Bobby said. "And dressing on your salads?"

She took their requests and hurried off to get their order started. Sam looked at Blaire, and reached out and took her hand.

"I didn't mean it like that, Blaire," he said softly. "It was insensitive of me. I'm sorry. You are not a child and I certainly don't need to be reminding you of things, especially your age. Please don't be angry. You're a beautiful woman, and I still find myself surprised by how beautiful you are. Sometimes when I'm with you, I just can't get the right words to come out."

Blaire took a deep breath, knowing that he was sincere in his apology.

"Okay," she said, and smiled. "I won't be angry. I want to enjoy this evening with you and not be reminded of how juvenile I was growing up. This is now, and I'm not the same girl I was back then."

"You certainly are not," Sam said, and smiled. "But I loved that girl too. And I couldn't always get the right words out then either. Please remember that."

"Okay," Blaire said, and took her hand back as Bobby came up and set wine glasses and the customary cutting board with two loaves of bread in the center of the table.

"I'll be right back with your wine," Bobby said, and smiled at them.

Blaire watched her go and turned back to Sam, cocking her head. "And how do you know Bobby?"

"My, my, but you're inquisitive tonight," Sam chuckled. "Glory and I have known Bobby and her brother almost as long as we've known you, Blaire. She was in Glory's grade when we started school here, and her brother was in mine."

"Sorry," Blaire said, and smiled. "I missed that, knowing who you knew while we grew up. I think I can count all of my friends on one hand."

"Well, don't worry about that," Sam said, and opened his menu. "Just because I know who some people are doesn't mean they're friends. Some are and many are not. Now, what are you in the mood for? Do you have a choice in mind or do you want me to order for you?"

"Oh, I have a choice," Blaire said, and winked at him, "but it would be interesting to know what you would pick for me."

"Now why, if you already know what you want, would I risk your good opinion of me by choosing something different?" He smiled, but refused to rise to her bait.

Bobby brought the wine and poured for Sam to taste. He did and then nodded. Bobby filled Blaire's glass and then his and then set the bottle in the chiller beside the table.

"Have you decided on a main course?" she asked, and proceeded to take their orders. "I'll have your salads out in a minute."

As she walked away with their choices, Sam picked up his glass and raised it toward Blaire. She mimicked him as he said, "A toast to the most beautiful and mysterious friend I've ever been lucky enough to know. May all of your futures be good ones."

"Thanks, Sam," Blaire said, smiled, and sipped her wine. Her eyebrows slowly rose as she realized the house Chardonnay was not a typically cheap wine.

"They have their house wines specially pressed and carefully grown," Sam said knowingly. "It's a closely guarded secret, but because they do all of that, more people than not drink the house label over the more well-known labels."

"I can see why," Blaire said, and nodded. She set her glass down and looked at him. "I guess you probably figured out that I graduated today."

"I had it figured close," Sam said, "and yes, since it was a Friday and you said you had two days off, it's obvious something significant has happened. And graduation was my first guess. Congratulation, Blaire. I'm very proud of you and happy you have found what you were looking for." He raised his glass to her again. "Do you know what is going to happen next?"

"No," Blaire said, and took another sip of her wine. "I have to report back by noon Sunday, and then sometime in the afternoon we'll be told what comes next."

"So," Sam said, his tone guarded, "you don't have any ideas where or what? Possibly?"

She shook her head as Bobby stopped tableside and served their salads. Blaire straightened and unfolded her napkin, and when Bobby had gone, she looked up at Sam again.

"I can't talk about any of the details, Sam," she said, wishing she could. "I'm sworn to secrecy, and my successes or failures can be affected by who knows what about me. I hope you can forgive me. Even if I knew where I was going or what will happen, which I don't, I still couldn't tell you. I feel very bad that I can't share that part of me."

Sam smiled. "As I said, 'to my mysterious friend.' I'm not angry and I understand. At least I understand that it isn't that you don't want me to know where you are." He took a bite of his salad and cut a slice of bread for her and then for himself. "I want you to always remember that I'm thinking about you. Wherever you are and whatever you're doing." He straightened, realizing he was leaning over the table and whispering. "Now, let's enjoy a wonderful dinner and the time we have. I promise I won't ask you any more inappropriate questions. Well, not about your work."

She smiled and took a bite of her salad.

⅄

"I can hardly waddle," Blaire said as she hung on Sam's arm.

He led them across the parking lot and helped her into his jeep.

"Looking at you," he said, smiling warmly as he settled himself behind the steering yoke, "I'd say you exercise often enough to have a pretty high metabolic rate. I'm betting you'll be famished by breakfast."

"You may be right," Blaire laughed. "That was so very good. Thank you, Sam. But you shouldn't have spent so much on me. That was expensive, with the bottles of wine, the desserts, just everything."

"It was worth it," Sam said, and started the engine. "But

124

only if you really liked it."

"I did, Sam. I really did," Blaire said, and smiled, holding his eyes for a long moment.

Sam finally reached out and caught her hand and squeezed it, breaking the spell developing in the moment.

"It's too bad there isn't a good place to go dancing," he said as he pulled out onto the street and turned toward Main. "I'd really like to take you dancing."

"Why?" Blaire asked. "You know I haven't danced much. I can't be very good."

"I know," Sam said, and smiled. "It's just a legitimate way I can hold you and not have to explain why to anyone."

Blaire knew she was blushing, thankful it was night and only the passing streetlights flashing through the windows threatened to expose her condition.

"Frankly, Blaire," he said, and concentrated on the street as he crossed the north bridge. "I wish it was warmer and I could take you for a night ride out to one of the rock outcroppings to watch the town lights, or to sit out and enjoy the falls, or any of a million other things I'd like to do with you."

"Sam," Blaire said, forcing herself to not rise to his words. "You promised you wouldn't push."

"I know I did, Blaire," he said as he slowed and turned east on River and then south on Amos, again avoiding the Friday night traffic jam of high school kids. "But I can't change how I feel. I won't cause you any discomfort or put you in a compromising position by asking you to come to my place, but I really don't want to end our evening so early."

"Tell you what," Blaire said. "Let's pick up another bottle of wine and go to Mom and Dad's place. They are already in bed since Dad has the four a.m. shift. We can enjoy the fireplace, a little more wine, and each other's company without causing any raised eyebrows. You game?"

"Thanks, Blaire," Sam said. "That sounds great."

At Oak, Sam turned west and swung into the side parking for the convenience store across the street from Hap's. Blaire got out and went in with him and picked out a few snack items while he picked out a couple of bottles of Chardonnay.

"Look," he said, and showed her the bottles. "The Fence's house label. I didn't know they were selling it locally."

Five blocks east on Oak and Sam parked behind Blaire's jeep in the drive in front of her folks' house. He paused and looked at the falling snow before he followed Blaire up onto the porch and then inside. He set the sacks on the kitchen counter as Blaire slipped her coat off and went down the hall to let her folks know she was home and that Sam was with her.

When she came back to the kitchen, she had her coat in hand and took his to the closet by the front door.

"Didn't want Dad to hear a noise and come out armed and ready to fight off an intruder," Blaire said softly as she came back to the kitchen.

"Good idea," Sam said as he opened a cabinet, looking for glasses.

"Top shelf on the left," Blaire said. "There are some stemless, insulated wine glasses there."

"Ah, I see them," he said, and quietly retrieved a pair. He put one bottle in the refrigerator and opened the other. He watched Blaire stoke the fire in the fireplace at the back of the family room as he poured the wine.

He remembered the small family room and the deck behind the garage from his many visits while Blaire was in elementary and high school. He remembered when Dan had bought the house instead of having a place built out of town like the newer deputies had done. Sam smiled at the memory of the house-warming party Dan had thrown, inviting all of the deputies, including his dad and most of the close neighbors.

"Does your dad still have neighborhood barbeques?" Sam asked, carrying the wine glasses into the family room.

"In the warmer weather," Blaire said, and pulled an end table close to an overstuffed chair. "Put those here," she said, and went back into the kitchen for a bowl and a bag of mixed nuts. When she stopped beside the table and chair, she studied the fire a moment. "Good enough."

He looked around at the two separate overstuffed chairs near the fire, and the loveseat—set back a little farther and between the two chairs for a clear view of the fire. Before he could ask, she took his hand and pulled him to the chair beside the end table and sat him down. Then without comment or question, she settled in his lap with her legs over the arm of the chair nearest the end table.

"How's this?" she asked, seeing the surprise on his face. "It isn't dancing, but you won't have to explain anything to anyone."

He smiled and slipped his arm around her waist, and she let him gently pull her against him. "I think this may be better than dancing," he said softly.

"Now, if you could hand me the bowl and the bag of—"

He turned her head to him and kissed her gently but firmly. She knew she shouldn't, but she felt herself wilt against him. Her hand held his head and her lips to his. Finally, she had to take a breath and slowly let their lips part. She inhaled and he kissed her again.

After another long moment, he relaxed and let her breathe. Her heart racing, she laid her head on his shoulder and tried to think, certain that she should not be letting this happen. When he handed her a wine glass, she still had not thought of a good reason why she should stop. She took a larger-than-normal sip and slowly swallowed it, but her mind kept returning to his gentle yet passionate kisses, his genuine care for her—even during the years when he was angry with her, and even when she was young and clueless as to why he was always around.

He touched his glass to hers and smiled. "To you, dearest Blaire. May you always remember that you are loved."

She smiled at him and laid her head back on his shoulder.

"I told myself I can't have any kind of a relationship. I don't know how to be in one, much less a long-distance one," she softly admitted, and took another sip. "After you kissed me on the porch, all I could think about was seeing you again and kissing you again. I'm having so many unfamiliar feelings right now, and I don't know what I should do, or which way I should go.

"Some of my friends fell into relationships in training, and now they are faced with separations, unknown distances and durations. Some are heartbroken and others say it's okay—it was fun while it lasted and now they have to move on—but I'm not built that way. I can't just jump from one relationship to another. And now, I don't know what to do about you."

"About me?" Sam asked, surprised.

"Yes. I've always liked you, and I was angry at myself when I realized what I had done and how angry I had made you. But it wasn't until that day in the barn that I truly felt how angry you were and I suddenly felt lost. My world, the one I thought I knew, was gone. So I made a new world, filled with new faces, new purposes, and new friends. I fit where I had never been before and I found a new home. I was satisfied, happy, pleased with my new abilities.

"And then..." She sipped her wine again. "...I saw you when Jim moved Shelly and Carrie Anne into Marty's guesthouse. That day, a lot of things changed. I think I finally saw you, and how you felt about things—about me. In the weeks that followed, I looked forward to today, but not just graduation. The time off and the possibility of seeing you again, to see if you really felt the way I thought you felt.

"And now, I have a dilemma. I want to be in both of my worlds—two worlds that don't meet, don't comingle, overlap but don't touch. It's unfair to you, and to me, to try to spend my time in both worlds, yet I can't choose between them. I am both.

"I am needed in my new world, Sam," she whispered, and emptied her glass. "And you and my folks are the only reasons I want to be in my old world."

Sam set his glass down and pulled her to him. She let him hold her tight against him.

"It's okay for you to be in your new world, Blaire," he said softly. "I know you belong there. And it's okay that I'm here in your old world. I'll be here for you to visit. In time, maybe we can work out a better solution." He squeezed her. "I waited twelve years to get the chance to kiss you. I can wait a few more to see if we get to have a future together."

She pushed herself back and looked at him. "Why, Sam? Why would you do that?"

"You know, Blaire, I don't think you're half as smart as everyone thinks you are," he said, and slipped his arms under her, stood up, and set her back onto the chair. "Now, I'm going to get the bottle of wine that we so foolishly left on the counter."

After a moment, Sam returned, and she watched him refill her glass and then top his off and set the bottle on the end table. When he bent down to scoop her up again, she curled her arms around his neck and kissed him firmly. She did not interrupt the kiss even as he lifted her up, turned around, and slowly sat down on the overstuffed chair. Slowly, she finally relaxed and let her lips release his. She opened her eyes and looked at him.

"I guess I'm just realizing that I don't know what I'd do if you weren't here for me," she said, hoping she was not sounding too much like a mushy teenager.

"Let's not test the 'not being here' part," Sam said, and smiled. He handed her the wine glass and took his. "I'll tell you what. Maybe this will make it easier for you. You do what you have to do and see me when you can, and I'll be here until you tell me you don't love me or that you love someone else."

She looked at him and studied his calm, confident expression for many minutes. "Can I see you tomorrow?"

He smiled at her and kissed her quick. "Of course. I work tomorrow, but you can come out for lunch and maybe we can do dinner again after I get off. Maybe somewhere a little less expensive. I don't want to give you the wrong impression and have you think I'm made of money or anything like that."

"Jerry's is fine with me," Blaire said. She pulled his head to her and kissed him again.

One Thirty-Six
Saturday, February 3

"I understand your point, Thom," Wally said as he leaned forward on the round table in the small marshals' office conference room.

"Greg says Billie has to go," Thom said softly, "just like he says Alyssa and Ridan have to go. Eddie won't let Billie go unless she's with her, and you know how nervous Eddie can get. She's never traveled much, let alone going off planet. She'll fall apart if I don't go with her."

"I understand, Thom. Really. I do," Wally said, stressing his words. "But Carole and I have to go too."

"You'll just have to let Ted or Dan handle the office," Thom said, "and there will still be five deputies and Sam here in town, and Clay, Hawthorne and Grants, the Niles Ranch and Community are covered by the deputies down there. So we should be good with us both away. After all of these years, are you still having doubts that they can do their jobs?"

Wally rubbed his chin, shook his head, and looked at Thom. "No, Thom. They'll do fine, and they have Kenny to watch the dispatcher's desk." Wally shook his head again and smiled. "Maybe I'm the one that's being overly nervous about going off planet."

"It isn't like they can't talk to us if they need help with something." Thom smiled.

"Yeah," Wally agreed.

"Okay, Wally," Thom said, then sat back in his chair and took a sip of his warm coffee. "I'll tell Greg all three of us are going."

Wally nodded, stood up, and opened the conference room

door. He glanced around the empty office and smiled, looking back at Thom. "I wonder how many are going. Has Greg said anything to you?"

"No," Thom said. "I think he told me you were going only because we needed to agree on being gone at the same time."

Wally nodded. "I wonder how many others."

▲ ▲ ▲ ▲ ▲

"I've got most of your things cleaned and folded," Rose said as she poured herself a cup of tea. "I'll get you packed tomorrow."

"I can still ask Greg if you and the kids can go," Doug said, feeling Rose's resignation.

"No," she said. "Greg asked me to help out with the daily patrols. He didn't say why, but I think with the school's graduation, he's redistributing the patrol fighters and maybe reassigning some to other places."

"Yeah, maybe," Doug said. "We haven't had the same level of threat for a long time. Just the Nikle issues since Labor Day."

"I was sooo relieved when they finally captured him," Rose admitted with a sigh. "I told Pat Brownly he'd been caught."

"I bet that made her feel better."

"Some, of course," Rose said. "I just can't imagine what she went through." Rose shook her head and looked at Doug over the rim of her cup. "She's going to help me with the kids, after school on the days I have to work."

"You told her you're working?"

"Yeah." Rose smiled. "I told her I had a part-time job making deliveries and running errands for different businesses. It's a bit of a lie, but the essence is true. And I've clued the kids in so they will go along with the story."

Doug smiled. "I heard Pat is teaching again."

"Yeah. She's more comfortable now since Wally put her through that self-defense training class. I think she's going to be all right."

"I also heard she's seeing Abe some," Doug said, and smiled. He winked.

"Yes, but I don't think it's gone that far yet. She has finally realized Abe was never angry that she couldn't have kids of her own."

"We'll just have to keep our fingers crossed for them," Doug said as he got up and refilled his cup. "More tea?"

▲ ▲ ▲ ▲ ▲

For the first time in a long time, Blaire admitted she felt happy. Actually happy. She thought about the obstacles that were still between her and Sam, but his acceptance of her, his *wanting* her, and his willingness to wait and let her make up her mind about how she felt about him—or whatever else she needed time for—surprised her.

She tried to pay attention to the county road as she turned off the main highway north of town and headed west. She was pleased last night's snow was light and the plows had made quick work of pushing it aside. At the drive to the Lazy D, she swung in and drove slowly back to the stables where Sam was working.

She parked her red jeep beside the sliding door and picked up the thermal cooler with their lunch in it. It had also been many months, she remembered, since she had had lunch with Sam on the ranch. It was just before she blew up at him, ran to Shar for help, and changed her life forever. The memory sobered her for a moment, forcing her back to the obstacles she didn't want to think about—at least not today. She promised herself she would think about them later; maybe tomorrow. Maybe after she knew what was going to happen next.

She smiled, closed the jeep's door, and turned to the stable.

With cooler in hand, she heard Sam talking to someone as she put her shoulder to the door panel and pushed. He was standing near the center of the main aisle when she stepped in and he waved to her.

"...nothing new in the last two weeks," he said to someone unseen, and motioned for her to the office where the first two stalls on the right should have been. "That's right, Wally. I'll let you know if I hear anything. Okay, I'll swing by the office after I get off work. I have a *date* tonight, so I can't stay long." He smiled at Blaire when she stopped in the office doorway and looked at him. "Yes, Wally. You know her. See you later. Bye, Wally."

Blaire saw him tap his ear and realized he was wearing an earpiece.

"I didn't know you had one of Wally's earpieces," she said as she went in and set the cooler on the desk.

"Yeah. Couple of years now," Sam said, and followed her into the office. He stopped behind her and slipped his arms around her waist and gently hugged her. "I hope this is all right. I've been waiting for you to get here all morning."

She slowly turned in his arms and wrapped her arms around his neck.

"Me too, Sam," she said softly, then pushed herself up on her toes and kissed him. "I've spent all morning trying to think of all the reasons I shouldn't be letting this happen, and I just can't seem to focus on any one of them for very long. I'm scared I'll be leaving and you will turn into someone I used to know."

She buried her face between her arm and his neck and held him.

"We can keep in touch through your folks, Blaire," he said softly, resting his cheek against her head. "However it works out, like I told you last night, I'll be here until you tell me to go away. I know things can change. Maybe things will work out better than you think they might. We just have to wait and see."

"I know," she said, and slowly lifted her head and smiled at him. "I know, Sam."

He smiled and slowly turned her to the desk. "Let's see what you brought for lunch," he said, and reached for the cooler.

"Connie's chicken wraps," she said, and began taking the

paper-wrapped sandwiches out. "Good, they're still warm. And her sweet pasta salad and her homemade chips."

"And I see water, two cans of cola, and are these hot teas or coffees?" Sam set the beverage containers on the desk as Blaire pulled the straight-backed chair up beside the desk chair and sat down.

"One of each," she said, and reached for the tea. "I figure something warm to start with and then maybe water or soda after."

"That'll work," Sam said, and sat down in the desk chair beside her.

He handed her a wrap and one of each of the sides.

"If you don't mind my asking," Blaire said as she started eating, "what do you do for Wally? I figured he had all of the bases covered with his tribe of deputies."

"Just odds and ends," Sam said, and sipped his coffee. "Errands. You know, running documents over to City Hall or the bank."

"You can't do that after you get off work," Blaire said, and stared at him.

Sam smiled. "Nope. That's the early morning stuff." He ate a little and then continued. "I do a few other things for him. You see, there was a time when a girl I knew grew up and became the most beautiful woman I've ever known, and suddenly I couldn't sleep at night. She was still too young for me to be openly serious about her. So I was talking to Wally one day and he said he was short-handed and needed someone to watch someone for a couple of nights and see where he went, what he did between work and going to bed. So I volunteered. That was a couple of years ago, before things started getting tense again."

"Hmm," she uttered through a mouthful of pasta salad. "Are you still watching people for him?"

"Sometimes," Sam said nonchalantly. "Mostly I just listen to what folks say around town, like Dad does down south. Feeling the temperature of the water every now and then."

"The temperature of the water? Does Wally think

something's going on?"

"He doesn't say," Sam said, and took a longer sip of his coffee. "Got to remember to tell Connie how good these wraps are."

"I think she knows, Sam," Blaire said, and chuckled. "It's the only thing you order when you go there."

"Yeah. I guess you're right." He smiled and then looked at her. "But they are very good. You have to admit."

Blaire shook her head and ate a few chips and absently focused on the wall, looking toward the main house. She was not really looking at the wall, but was suddenly thinking of tomorrow again, focusing much farther to the south. She ate another chip before she heard Sam.

"Blaire. It'll be all right. It will. I promise you, it will."

She turned, hearing his words, and he reached out and pulled her to him.

She straightened and forced a smile. "Yeah. I know." Then she finished her wrap and tossed the empty side containers and the wadded wrappers back into the cooler. "When should I expect you?"

"Is six okay?" he asked. "If you don't want to, I understand."

"You better not try to weasel out of our date," Blaire said emphatically, holding his eyes sternly. "I want at least one more night like last night to remember."

"I wouldn't think of missing an opportunity to be with you," Sam said as he stood up. "Especially if there's a chance of repeating last night."

She stood up and looked up at him, smiled, and then pushed herself up on her toes and kissed him. "All right then," she said. "I have some shopping to do for a friend of mine and then some things to do at Mom and Dad's place. I'll see you at six."

"At six," Sam said.

▲ ▲ ▲ ▲ ▲

Sam parked his jeep in the lot behind the marshals' office and entered through the back door. He noticed Thom was at his desk and Kenny had gone for the day.

"Hello, Sam," Wally said from the file cabinets.

"Afternoon, Wally, Thom," Sam greeted. "Any coffee left? Or should I ask how old the coffee is that's left?"

"Getting pretty thick," Thom said, and started putting papers into his desk drawers.

"I think I'll pass then," Sam said, and grimaced at Thom. Then he turned to Wally. "You wanted me to stop by?"

"Yup," Wally said as he slipped a file folder into the open drawer and then pushed it closed. He glanced at Thom. "Tell Eddie and Billie hi for me, Thom. You going to that cookout thing they're having at the school tonight?"

"I don't think so," Thom said as he locked his desk, switched his monitor off, and slipped the small monitor beside it into his jacket pocket. "Eddie was going to fix something special at home tonight, so I'm looking forward to a quiet evening with my two girls."

"Sounds like a winner. `Night," Wally said as Thom stepped out through the back door and closed it behind him.

Wally placed another file in another drawer before he turned to Sam and gestured to the conference room.

"Greg contacted me today," Wally said as he closed the door behind him. He switched on the air conditioner wall unit and selected fan only. Then he sat down. "There are a number of things happening and there are a few people from Obscure that are going to be gone for a few weeks."

"I know you and Thom are going to be gone," Sam said. "Related?"

"Greg has a feeling there may be a mole, either in the ranks or trying to get into the ranks," Wally said as if he had not heard

Sam. "The remnants of the Family have tried to get a look inside Obscure for over twelve years now—ever since it was captured and Greg took it over.

"He has Major Franni Mooren *listening* for anything unusual, especially anything that mentions a departure or that a number of people are missing. He asked for you to coordinate with Franni and help *listen* for the next three or four days."

Sam nodded. "May I use one of your remotes?"

"Greg said to take Five," Wally said. "Once you're there, you can release it until you've done all Crem and Franni need. You can call for it when you need it again. You still have quarters there?"

Sam nodded again. "When?"

"Tomorrow night about midnight," Wally said, and rubbed his chin. "He asked that you *contact* Franni on your way in and she'll tell you where to meet her. Wear khakis. He doesn't want anyone but Crem and Franni to know you're there."

"I see," Sam said softly. "Sounds like something serious is riding on this one."

Wally nodded and glanced at his watch. "What time are you meeting Blaire?"

"Six," Sam said, and smiled. "A nice quiet dinner at Jerry's, so don't come bothering us."

"Have a good evening, Sam," Wally said, then got up and went into the main office area.

"I'm hoping to, Wally," Sam said as he followed him out. "Don't forget to turn off your 'white noise.'" He gestured to the conference room as he opened the back door.

Sunday, February 4

Blaire settled Apache Patrol Five into its assigned spot and started the power-down sequences. When she opened her canopy, she realized her ground crewman had positioned the ladder and was quietly waiting at the bottom for her to deplane.

"Sorry to take so long," she said as she hurried down the ladder. "I shouldn't make you wait in the cold so long."

"No problem, Lieutenant. Congratulations on your graduation and promotion," he said as she returned his salute. "Is there anything more you need?"

"I don't think so, Corporal," Blaire said, then smiled and turned toward the portal hatchway and the corridor of steps.

Inside, she stopped at the bottom of the stairs and watched, absently captivated as five mechanics worked on a new Class 2 patrol fighter, placing repulsion pads with STSX1 hovering above it. The bright red stripe was vibrant against the matte gray finish, and she noted the numeral 17 painted just below and behind the canopy. She wondered whose fighter it was and why they were aligning it with STSX1.

She pulled herself away from the sight and hurried across the launch bay and through the hatch on the north wall. At the first corridor, she turned left and hurried to Billeting and her quarters.

She palmed her door open, tapped the door lock to 'Secure' when it closed, and dropped her duffle beside the door to the necessary. Checking her timepiece, she knew she had more than half an hour before their briefing.

She turned to her communications terminal and toggled the blinking message annunciator.

"Seven messages?" she asked herself out loud, seeing the queue. She tapped the replay and listened.

The first was Emli on Friday, looking for someone to party with, and the next three were from Ilistr, trying to borrow civvies. The fifth one caught her attention. It was from the commander.

"Lieutenant Lupis, please access your computer terminal for a private message. Read and ask any questions, in private, before you attend the briefing at twelve hundred hours on Sunday, small Flight Briefing Room."

Blaire stared at the terminal for a moment, then quickly checked the remaining three messages. She was surprised the last one was from Luc.

"Lieutenant. It's Luc. I'd like to ask you to have dinner in the Mess Sunday evening after you get back. Just personal. I won't ask about your assignment or anything. You know how to reach me if you're interested. Thanks."

Blaire shook her head, erased the messages, and went to her computer terminal. As she sat down, the terminal booted, and in a moment settled with the home screen waiting. She logged in and went to her messages. There was only one. It was also from the commander.

"Blaire. Commander Geaardt. I must ask that you do not speak to anyone after you get this message and before you come to the briefing. You are not yet on duty, so no one within the facility should try to discuss anything official. Do not engage in any personal conversations. I will answer any questions you have before the briefing or during the briefing. A situation has arisen that demands the utmost secrecy. Twelve hundred hours in the small Flight Briefing Room. This message will automatically erase when it is closed."

Blaire reread the message and stared at it a long moment before she closed it and toggled the terminal off. She looked at her timepiece and hurried to change.

▲

Blaire stepped into the small briefing room and was surprised to see only the commander, Casi, Colonel Kooich, and Leeana seated in four of the five chairs arranged in a circle in the center of the room.

"Ah, Blaire. Please close the door and come in," Stran said, and gestured to the one empty chair.

She did as he instructed and sat down before the four of them.

"Did anyone try to engage you?" Colonel Kooich asked.

Blaire smiled. "Sir, you know no one did. And I have not replied to a request to have dinner with Sergeant Stial."

"Yes, you're right," Hench said, and smiled. "We do know."

"Blaire," Stran began. "You know the plan was to take you

and Captain Ani Tigs to the Rings for a ranking ceremony, as I called it."

She nodded.

"Well, that was only a partial truth. First, I have asked the Director to assign you with a Q-Ship and he rightly has reservations. No one has ever asked for a Q-Ship for a new graduate. Second, Captain Ani Tigs will be assigned a Q-Ship and she will be promoted accordingly."

"Thank you, sir," Blaire said. "I am very surprised and I am grateful that you feel that way about me."

"The Director may not agree to assign you a Q-Ship," Stran admitted, and smiled, "so I am assigning you a new patrol fighter and you are being attached to my personal squadron."

"Is that the one in the launch bay?"

"Yes. You are officially Apache Seventeen attached to Shadow Base and the commander's wing," Stran said. "And your new ship has a few 'special' upgrades."

"Sir?" Blaire asked in surprise.

"Your ship," Stran said, "has both turrets upgraded to quad cannons with a second core power unit buried within it. Like Apache Squadron Q-Ships, both core power modules have shields, weapons, cloaking, and can provide full ship's power. I've also installed two engine upgrades. It isn't as fast as our Q-Ships, but it is significantly faster than any Class Two fighter. I do plan on exchanging the engines soon with higher-thrust units. I've also added a long-range scanner capability to the existing scanner." Stran rubbed his chin. "There was something else. Oh, yes. It wouldn't work. I wanted to install an empathic module to the central computer, but STSX could not figure out a way to make one work on a patrol fighter."

Blaire stared at the four of them. "I don't know what to say."

"Don't say anything," Stran said softly. "Don't say anything to anyone. We are the only ones, outside of the maintenance crews, that know of the changes. You and your ship are unique. You have a specially trained and assigned maintenance crew, specifically for your ship. Get to know the five of them, personally, as close as friends. They are the only ones that may touch your ship. If anyone else tries to work on it or gain access to it, you must report them immediately."

"Yes, sir. I understand," Blaire said, and then asked, "Can Seventeen speak directly with STSX1 or the other Q-Ships?"

"No, Blaire," Casi said. "Not empathically. Only QShips and pilots can do that, and as you've done before, you still can, personally."

Blaire nodded and waited.

"You were chosen for the mission to the Rings for a second reason," Stran said, and expanded on his concerns and fears for the mission. He explained his concerns for the safety of the children and the adults, being brought together in a manner that would make them vulnerable. Stran reflected on how he felt this was an uncharacteristic move on the Director's part, and how that made him feel the need for utmost secrecy. He explained that he felt there might be a problem developing inside Headquarters, and the Rings might not be as safe as they had been led to believe it was.

"Blaire," Casi said, "you are not to tell anyone you are on this mission. The others on this mission will not tell anyone else either. No one except us and Kiile know who is going. I will announce the full roster after we launch, have grouped, and are in flight. If anyone asks about this mission, or any expected mission, *tell* us immediately." Casi touched her forehead.

"Yes, ma'am."

"This afternoon," Stran said, "I want you to take Seventeen on a shakedown. Wear your helmet so no one can easily recognize you. Take an unused route to and from Billeting. Test everything, record everything, and then review the results after you get back in your quarters."

"I think," Casi said, "you ought to tell Sergeant Stial that you can't have dinner with him. Another time, but you shouldn't tonight. Stay in your quarters. Eat in. I know you will know what is going on with the preparations, but stay out of sight and keep things to yourself."

"We will gather for an oh four hundred launch tomorrow

morning," Hench said. "Wear your helmet, go to your ship half an hour before launch, and the initial mission information will be on board, waiting for you. Everyone will board their ships so it is not obvious we're planning a mass launch until we are gone. We'll update everyone once we're up."

"You think we have a spy in the ranks," Blaire said, suddenly realizing the *why* behind the cautions.

"Yes. It's possible, Blaire," Stran said. "We're actually going to launch veiled over a half-an-hour time span to make it less obvious, but you're right. Somehow, information about Apache Squadron is getting out. Franni and the others are *listening* to see if anything is said about our departure."

"Blaire," Casi said, and caught her hand, "I hope you realize you are a very significant and trusted part of our command. You are special to us and to our operation here. Now, go and get a bite to eat and Apache Seventeen should be set out side and ignored by the time you're finished. Take it for a flight. Your new ground support crewman can be trusted. He is one of your five and will handle the ladder without any questions."

"Thank you, Commander, Captain," Blaire said, and stood up. She nodded to Hench and Leeana. "I think I'll get a snack and take a walk."

She smiled and turned to the door, closing it softly behind her as she headed back to the Mess.

Monday, February 5

C.3486.803

"We're in the practice area, Casi," Stran said from the nav-com compartment. "You can drop your veils and start grouping everyone."

"Thanks," Casi said, and smiled at Caiti in the right jump seat and then turned to Coli in the left. "STSX, hail the squadron. Drop veils and form up on Apache One."

Caiti and Coli turned and looked around as the QShips, patrol fighters, and the two transports coalesced out of the vast

143

darkness.

"For everyone's information, Apache Flight is a flight of ten," Casi announced to the ships. "Four QShips and four patrol fighters, as you can see, and two transports. Apache Seventeen will join up with Apache One, STSX1, Apache Ten will join up with Apache Four, STSX12, Apache Fifteen will join up with Apache Two, KKLC14, and Apache Sixteen will join up with Apache Five, LTVC21. Our transports will have call signs Apache T-One and T-Two. The patrol fighters will please commence join-up."

Casi swiveled the pilot's chair to aft facing and watched as Apache Ten, Fifteen, and Sixteen maneuvered to align with their hosts. Apache Seventeen slipped behind and below STSX1, out of Casi's direct vision.

"You'd think Blaire has done this a hundred times," Caiti said, watching Apache Seventeen with her eyes closed.

"I know," Coli said. "She's so smooth and precise."

"Caiti, watch the helm while I get Blaire aboard," Casi said as she slipped out of the pilot's chair and drifted quickly down through the floor portal.

Within the normal time window, each Q-Ship announced their patrol pilot was aboard and secure. Casi returned to the cockpit and took the open jump seat. "Blaire, you're welcome to sit up here or down below. Your choice."

"Thanks," Blaire said, and joined them on the instructor's seat.

"All ships. As I said I would," Casi began, "I will give you a quick briefing. To begin with, the Director requested the physical presence of each of our new talents for interviews in the Rings. We feel this is a strange request and is a bit out of character for the Director, but he is the director, so we are taking our lot to see him. Interestingly enough, he did not request the new talents by name—again unusual for the director. That said, we are very concerned and we have put a number of steps in place to possibly help keep us anonymous and unnoticed. Thus the odd departure. Because of the strangeness of the request, we fear the request may not actually be from the Director's hand, and we also feel there is the possibility of a mole either inside Shadow Base or watching Shadow Base.

"We will discuss our plans for while we are in the Rings later in the flight. Now for who is with us and where they are.

"Caiti, Coli, and Blaire are with us on STSX1. Neila is with Cheral and Keli on STSX12. Ani, in Apache Ten, is with them as their cover. Keely and Tayn are with Colonel Kooich and Leeana on KKLC14. Cera, in Apache Fifteen, is their cover. Jesi, in Apache Sixteen, is LTVC21's cover. Wally, Carole, Alyssa, and Ridan Lima, Thom, Eddie, and Billie Baine, and Doug McIntire are on Apache T-One with Kiile and marine Twenty-two's squad of twenty. Apache T-Two has a second detail, marine Forty-two's squad of twenty for security. Are there any questions?"

Each Q-Ship and both transports replied they did not have any questions.

"Very well then," Casi said, and nodded to Caiti.

Caiti swiveled the pilot's chair to forward facing. "STSX, does everyone have the coordinates for the first leg?"

"AFFIRMATIVE."

"On my mark," Caiti said, "Apache T-One will accelerate and lead the flight to the first coordinates, Bravo-Charlie-Oboe. Apache T-One will go to full thrust, maximum cruising speed. Apache Flight will match speed and follow. Cloaking on. Sensor blocking on. Shields full. Is Apache Flight ready?"

Each ship reported ready.

"Apache T-One, mark!"

The cluster of ships began to accelerate with Apache T-One, and quickly vanished into the darkness.

⚠

After a couple of hours had passed, Coli switched with Caiti as the flight commander, and Blaire asked Casi if they could talk in private. Casi nodded and gestured to the floor portal.

"What's up, Blaire?" Casi asked as they settled into the double-wide seats on the sleeping deck and strapped themselves in.

"A bit of a personal dilemma," Blaire said as she tightened the strap across her lap. "You know Sam Reeds, Deputy Thad's son."

Casi nodded.

"Two weeks ago he decided I was finally old enough to let me know how he felt about me. You know we had a bit of a problem for a few years, and I really never expected anything to develop between the two of us."

"I remember you mentioning something about that when you came to us," Casi said. "Is this part of your dilemma?"

Blaire nodded. "He kissed me for the first time two weeks ago after a very pleasant dinner out, and we had two dinner dates this past weekend. Both ended up very nice, very close, if you know what I mean."

Casi smiled. "He's helped you for many years. I'm glad you worked things out."

"But that's the problem. We've worked out the 'between us' things, and now with graduation into my new world, I don't know how to work out the 'his world' versus the 'my world' issues. I know Sam has been working with Wally some and he knows I was interested in the police work Dad and Wally did, but I don't know how to be with him and not let something slip out. I'm hoping you can help me. I really don't want to lose Sam, but if I have to go somewhere for any length of time, I don't know what I'll do."

Casi smiled. "First off, you should tell him what you're doing."

"What?" Blaire stared at Casi. "I can't do that. I swore to never—"

Casi held up her hand and Blaire stopped.

"I can see that Sam is much more capable than I realized," Casi said. "You didn't notice and that is something. That he hid it from you is incredible. And he didn't notice either."

"What are you talking about?" Blaire asked, separating her words.

"Sam and you! You hid your tag from him, didn't you?"

"Sure. I had to," Blaire said softly. "I couldn't let him sense something was different."

Casi smiled. "And he hid his because he had to. He's one of our agents, Blaire. He's been a Shadow since you were nine, I think. Yes, ten years now. He's a captain."

Blaire knew her mouth was hanging open. "He's...an agent? A Shadow? A captain?"

Casi nodded. "He's one of our best at *listening*. Almost as good as you are."

"He can *hear*?"

Again, Casi nodded. "He doesn't have your gift for perception, but he has very keen *hearing*."

"You said ten years. Two years after we met?"

"He knew about our secret life from his and Glory's rescue," Casi said, "and then his dad trained to become a deputy and learned Wally's secrets, the remotes and our connections. Sam saw it all and made a decision."

Blaire slowly smiled. "Does he have a 'registered' name?"

"Donl Just. Spelled *J-S-T*."

"And will I get a 'registered' name?" Blaire asked.

"You might. Your Dad's registered name is Lomr," Casi said, and smiled. "But you might want to wait and see how things work out with you and Sam. You might not want to register a name more than once." Casi winked.

Blaire felt her cheeks warm and knew she was tuning red. "What does Sam do? I know he helps Wally and listens to the talk around town and helps Marty at the Lazy D."

"The Lazy D is his obvious job, and helping Wally is another obvious job," Casi said. "You know, so people can see how he supports himself. In his second life, just like you, he is an undercover agent. He goes where we need him to see what he can find out for different things we face. He did the groundwork the day before Seventeen and Thirty-two collected Nikle."

"Does he fly, too?"

"No," Casi said, and smiled. "He didn't go for that option,

but he may want to reconsider once you tell him you're a pilot and are ST-Class Q-Ship qualified. I think he'll be surprised." Casi turned more serious. "Blaire, don't let this—this new job and the differences in our worlds—come between you and Sam. On purpose, he hasn't let you 'see' him, just like you haven't let him 'see' you."

Blaire smiled and blushed again.

Casi chuckled and rolled her eyes. "You know I don't mean physically. But if you two decide to get past this concern of yours and get together, it can work and you can live without any of the 'public' knowing you have second lives. You're doing it now and Sam's been doing it for a number of years. You'll find it's easier when you both know and work together. Look at Doug and Rose and their children. Look at Nick and Jill and Cheyenne. Look at us or my uncle Paul. Even Cheral and Kiile are going to move outside and start a 'public' life in the valley. Neila will start in the public school in the fall. It takes some work, but it really isn't that hard."

"Thanks, Casi," Blaire said, and smiled again. "And if I'm in yours and the commander's wing, does that mean I'm assigned to Shadow Base, Obscure?"

"Yes, Blaire," Casi said. "You're officially part of the 'Ladies' Brigade' and will live and operate out of the valley. You're actually on Stran's staff, the same as Hench and Leeana, Crem and Franni, Nick and Jill, and Doug and Rose."

"What do Nick, Jill, Doug, and Rose do?"

"They are our personal protection and you have just joined them. They are the ones closest to us in a conflict. The marines come next," Casi explained. "In addition, each of your tags carries a special endorsement. When one of you speaks for the team, your word carries the same importance as if Stran said it himself. If one of you gives an order to another Peace Force agent or Shadow, it is the same as if Stran or I gave it."

"Wow!" Blaire said, and just stared at Casi.

"Use the new power and authority with care," Casi said, "but if you need to use it, use it with confidence. If the orders are not obeyed, disciplinary actions will be taken."

"I'm surprised that the commander has this much faith in me," Blaire said softly.

"Don't be," Casi said. "You're an officer in the Galactic Peace Force now. The uncertain girl that came to us three months ago doesn't exist anymore. Never forget that." Casi stretched and glanced at the time over the medical couch. "Let's go up so I can relieve Coli."

"Yes, ma'am," Blaire said, and followed Casi up to the cockpit.

One Thirty-Seven

'One of the squad leaders mentioned in Mess that he hadn't seen Twenty-two or his squad this morning,' Sam said. *'That isn't a surprise, since his squad is around twenty men and they usually Mess about oh-six-hundred.'*

'I expected someone would notice at mealtimes,' Franni answered. *'I'm watching two people on the north side of the ridge between Saddle Horn and Cantle Ridge. They seem to be hikers and are only speaking in voice. I've asked Seventeen to see if they can be relocated without causing too much of a problem.'*

'Seventeen talked with a different squad leader and apparently Seventeen is in charge,' Sam said. *'Kiile, Cheral, and Neila are not here and two transports are gone.'*

'So are a number of other ships,' Franni said, *'but that's not what we're listening for.'*

'I know, but so far no one has mentioned anything about them being gone. Maybe because they are in and out so much anyway.'

'That's what the commander is hoping,' Franni said, and Sam could *feel* her smiling. *'Keep listening inside and we'll keep looking around out here.'*

'Will do,' Sam said, and settled back into cushions of the overstuffed chair in his unmarked quarters.

▲ ▲ ▲ ▲ ▲

"Director Stansh," Prince Lukré said without looking up from his desk or the data console beneath its clear desktop. "What does Intelligence have for me this morning?"

The director closed the door behind him and stopped in front of the desk, straightening into a waiting, rigid posture after taking a quick glance around at the softer colors and textures of the redecorated office.

"Our agents confirm they have the Peace Force director's undivided attention," Director Stansh said with a slowly growing smile.

"Very good," Prince Lukré said, and looked up. "And the meeting?"

Director Stansh's smile faded. "The Director called for the meeting as you planned, but his offices have not confirmed a response."

Prince Lukré rubbed his chin. "When?"

"Three turns," Director Stansh said. "If we believe what little we know about this elusive squadron of heavy fighters with red stripes, their commander will comply with the Director's bidding."

"Have our agents tried to force any information from the Director?" Prince Lukré asked, and toyed with a stylus on his desktop.

"No," Director Stansh said. "We fear a loss of consciousness would be detected by his offices."

"A connection?" Prince Lukré said, not quite a question.

"Yes, sir," the director said. "There are long-standing stories of the communication capabilities of certain individuals within the Peace Force."

"Yes, yes," Prince Lukré said, and picked up the stylus. "I've heard that. Has he told anyone he is being entertained by our agents?"

"We do not think so," Director Stansh said uncertainly. "We cannot be certain, but there were no inquiries or questions when he announced he would not attend a number of his normal meetings."

"But you are not certain," Prince Lukré said, and stared at the director.

"No, sir. We are not certain."

"Three turns, you said," Prince Lukré said, and turned his

chair to face a wall mural. "That should mean the commander and his staff are en route to the scheduled meeting."

"Yes, sir," the director said, relieved the prince had changed the point of his questions. "But we also cannot confirm that. In the four thousand, three hundred plus turns since the squadron first appeared, we have not been able to locate their base. We have searched a number of possible systems, but no evidence of their existence has surfaced."

"Then we wait," Prince Lukré said, and turned back to the director. "I presume all other arrangements have been made."

"Yes, sir," Director Stansh said. "We have agents embedded to assist with the meeting. Once we have the commander and his staff, we will have their key group of talents, as the Director called them."

"Do not be too confident," Prince Lukré said sharply. "There is a reason they are called Shadows." He held the director with his stare, and then quickly waved him away. "And that they have remained elusive and undetected. I will await your update in three turns."

C.3486.806

"I can't believe they let the whole flight in cloaked," Caiti said from the nav-com compartment.

"Is Approach and Departure Control working properly?" Coli asked.

"Yes," Stran said as the inner iris opened and they led Apache Flight into the main bay in front of the headquarters complex. "STSX, contact Headquarters and find out what time the Director's meeting is. Then have all Apache Flight go to optical and empathic communications only."

"HEADQUARTERS DOES NOT HAVE A MEETING TIME SCHEDULED," STSX said.

Stran looked at Casi. "We are a day early, but he should have set a time."

"HEADQUARTERS SAYS THERE IS A WELCOMING

153

RECEPTION AT SIXTEEN HUNDRED HOURS TONIGHT FOR YOU, CAPTAIN CASI, COLONEL KOOICH, CAPTAIN LEEANA, CAPTAIN KIILE, AND MAJOR CHERAL."

"In two hours," Stran said. "I don't like it. Sure feels like something's up, inviting only the six of us, the top people in Apache Squadron? Makes me nervous."

"All Apache Flight, IFF off. Apache T-One and Two," Stran said, "Do not dock. Apache One, Apache Two, and Apache Four, we will release our fighters, then drop our veils and dock as expected. Apache Five, you can release Apache Sixteen at your discretion. All fighters remain cloaked and 'at ready.' Do not dock. Approach let six in—they do not realize we are ten."

"Affirmative," Apache T-One said.

The others quickly replied in kind.

After the pilots transferred and the patrol fighters separated, Apache Seventeen took her position above and behind STSX1 and Stran dropped their veil. He saw KKLC14 and STSX12 materialize, and *felt* Apache Ten and Fifteen take positions similar to Apache Seventeen. He swiveled his pilot's chair to aft facing and monitored STSX as he slowly spun in place and backed into the berth reserved for them. He watched Hench settle in the next berth, and Cheral in the berth just beyond him.

"STSX, you look like you've done this before," Stran said, like he always did.

"OF COURSE I DO."

"You just can't take a joke, can you?" Stran chuckled.

"THERE IS NOTHING FUNNY TO LAUGH ABOUT."

"You're right," Caiti said softly, and looked at Stran.

"Are you sure this amount of secrecy is necessary?" Coli asked as Casi came forward.

"Yes, love," Stran said. "Until we are sure of what the state of affairs is here. Never let your—"

"—guard down," Casi said, finishing his sentence. "Remember that, girls. It has saved our lives more than once."

"We know," Caiti and Coli said together.

"Well, we have two hours," Casi said. "Let's do a little snooping before we accept. But we'll probably have to accept."

"Yeah, we will," Stran said. "Okay, let's do a little sniffing around. Girls, you too, and get Cheral, Keely, and anyone that can search to snoop. STSX, where is the reception to be held?"

"HEADQUARTERS, MAIN CONFERENCE ROOM ON THE SECOND FLOOR OF THE ADMINISTRATION BUILDING."

"That's also unusual," Stran said. "Receptions are usually in the reception hall. You remember it, Bren." Stran smiled at her, remembering the details of her first visit to the Rings and the award ceremony.

"Yes, I remember," Casi said, and smiled. *'Okay, Cheral, Ani, Blaire, Keely, Caiti, Coli, link with me and let's check out the buildings around the bay. Something feels fishy, not yet normal.'*

'We're here,' multiple voices said in Casi's head at the same time. *'Show us.'*

▲ ▲ ▲ ▲ ▲

"Thanks for letting Neila stay with Caiti and Coli," Cheral said as they entered the administration hall and followed the information monitors.

"No thanks necessary," Casi said. "There's no way we would make her stay alone on ST12. Tayn and Keely are on KKLC14. They can go over to LTVC21 if they decide to later." Casi turned to Stran. "I hope this wasn't a formal affair."

"No request for dress Blues," Stran said, and glanced around, "so clean Blues ought to be satisfactory."

They stopped at the entrance to the large conference room and a man in a white uniform greeted their seven and noted their names on the guest log.

"Commander," the man said when he finished making his entries. "Our sensors tell me you are wearing active weapons on your persons."

"We are," Stran said, and held the man's eyes without apology.

"That is highly unusual, sir," the man insisted.

"No, it isn't."

"But, sir. This is a quiet, social event to greet you, your staff, and a few of our other esteemed officers."

"Then, it won't be necessary to use them," Stran said firmly, still holding the man's eyes.

"Yes. Yes, sir," the man finally stammered. "I suppose that is correct." He nodded and stepped aside. Keli chuckled softly under her breath.

"There are three inside entrances, not counting the two kitchen accesses," Casi said, slowly glancing around the room.

"And three outside passageways to the balcony outside," Cheral added, "and one staircase from it to the walks around the front of the building."

"I don't think the Director is here," Leeana said softly. "And a couple of waiters do not have tags."

"Strange," Casi said. "I noticed that also."

'There are fifteen among the kitchen and wait staff,' Caiti said softly to Casi, *'without tags. And there are two near the far balcony doorway with tags that are acting strangely—like their implants didn't take correctly or they're having trouble remembering what the tag is.'*

'Thanks, love,' Casi said. *'I see what you're talking about.'*

'Leeana is right,' Caiti continued. *'The Director isn't there. Show us what he feels like and his ID and we'll try to see what's keeping him.'*

'Okay,' Casi said, and thought about the Director and the mixture of his sense.

'Got it,' Caiti and Coli said together. *'We'll let you know when we find out. Watch those guys without tags and the other two with the funny ones.'*

'Thanks,' Casi said, and smiled.

156

"What's the smile about?" Stran asked when he saw her smile.

Casi relayed the conversation she had had with Caiti and Stran nodded. "Yeah, I was starting to count the no-tags. A couple of them are carrying hand weapons, including some in the kitchen."

They went to a portable bar set near the windowed wall on the balcony and ordered drinks. Walking among the crowd, Stran commented that the gathering was not as large as he had first thought it was—maybe only a hundred strong. He looked for other Blues and noted only four other couples. The rest were in assorted business attire and all had appropriate tags.

Cheral told Kiile she needed to find a necessary, and Keli admitted to the same need. Kiile said he would go with them, and they worked their way across the room and slipped out through an inside entrance near the kitchen side of the conference room. Stran watched them leave and then turned back to his conversation with Hench and Leeana.

▲ ▲ ▲ ▲ ▲

Caiti, Coli, and Neila were sitting in the double-wide cushioned chairs when Caiti heard Casi's description of the conference room and Leeana's comment on the Director's absence. After discussing her sensations with Casi, Caiti reached out and *felt* for the Director's sense. When she got a faint touch, she knew his general whereabouts but couldn't pinpoint him.

'Blaire,' Caiti said, *'we need your help to find the Director for Mom. I have a faint touch, but you are better at looking inside buildings and things than we are.'*

'Sure,' Blaire said. *'Show me what you have and I'll try.'*

Caiti and Coli let Blaire link with them and felt Blaire set to the task, slowly scanning the administration hall, one floor at a time.

'The upper floors are arranged like fingers off a central tube, facing the central bay,' Blaire said, describing what she was

seeing. *'There are twelve floors above the six administration levels, and he seems to be in the very center finger of the next-to-the-top floor. His apartment is the entire finger and he is in a large entertainment room, sitting in a chair with his back to the expansive wraparound windows. Strange—there are four men with him and they have very jittery tags.'*

'Jittery, like they are unsteady?' Coli asked.

'Yes,' Blaire said. *'Like the ones in the conference room you told Casi about. Like they can't remember them.'* Blaire hesitated a long moment, searching the sensations she was feeling. *'I don't think the men are friendlies. I'm going to move closer and see if I can feel anything more.'*

Caiti and Coli looked at each other and then at Neila.

"Are you listening to all of this?"

Neila nodded. "I doesn't sound very good."

'Tayn, Keely,' Coli said. *'Listen in and be ready to move if something happens. I'm starting to feel like Dad did.'*

'We're listening,' Tayn said. *'KKLC is standing by. We're ready if you need us.'*

'Thanks. Alyssa, Ridan, Billie,' Coli continued. *'Listen in and keep your folks and Squad Leader Twenty-two up on what's happening.'*

'Got it,' Alyssa said.

⚔

Blaire hovered Apache Seventeen in front of the central finger and settled in front of the second level from the top. She could see the men much clearer with only the copper colored one-way windows between her and them.

She *listened* and *felt* the men. All were armed, and the fifth, the Director, seemed restrained in a chair. Softly she *touched* his mind, not wanting to startle him if the men were watching closely.

'Director AGL36Q,' she whispered. *'I'm Lieutenant Lupis of Apache Squadron. Touch my tag. Are you being restrained against your will?'*

A long moment passed and she began to wonder if he heard had her.

'Yes,' the male voice said softly. *'These men are agents of Prince Lukré.'*

'We thought they might be,' Blaire said. *'Can they tell you're talking to someone?'*

'So far, no,' he said. *'There are fifteen or more agents at the party they set up for the commander.'*

'He knows. He's playing their game while we look for you.'

'You've been looking for me?'

'Of course, sir. Let me arrange a surprise for your captors.' Blaire shifted focus. *'Caiti, Coli, he is being restrained by four agents of Prince Lukré. We need some of the marines—'*

'Four have formed up on your location, cloaked, on remotes. Four more are almost in place inside, just outside the Director's door. Give us a minute while we try to slip the lock. Oh, and I sent ten to the conference room—five in and five out, just in case.'

'Thanks. I see them.'

⋏

Coli turned to Neila and smiled. "Time to use some of your secret talents. Let's look at the Director's door locks."

Neila stared at Coli a moment before Caiti smiled at her. "We know. You and Doug both have the same 'secret.' Link with us, please, and see what you can figure out."

⋏

'Blaire,' Coli said, *'it's your show. The main entry is unlocked and the marines outside will come in when you tell them.'*

'Thanks,' Blaire said, and *touched* the Director again. *'Director. I am sorry, but we have to come in through your beautiful windows. Can you turn your chair over when I break them?'*

'I can. What are you going to do?'

'I have reinforcements. You just get as low as you can so they don't shoot you when they try to shoot us. I'll give a countdown in a second. Coli, tell the marines I'm counting down. On my mark,

I'll blow the windows and the marines can go in from both sides.'

'Okay,' Coli said, and Blaire *heard* her contact Twenty-two in the hallway outside the Director's door.

Blaire entered two firing solutions into the top cannon for a widespread double shot, one to each side of the grouped men. "Systems armed, short-range set," she said out loud to herself.

'Okay, Coli. Three, Two, One.' She saw the Director throw himself sideways and the chair roll over. 'Mark!'

The fighter-length span of copper-colored window panels burst outward, pushed by the building's pressurized conditioning system, and the four marines beside her dropped their veils and charged through the flying shards into the room. Blaire saw the marines rush through the main entry door, and in a furious burst of laser fire, the four startled captors fell into lifeless lumps on the Director's floor.

Sensing Twenty-two, Blaire reached out to him to ask about the Director, but Coli and Caiti's screams suddenly interrupted her.

▲ ▲ ▲ ▲ ▲

"Coli says Blaire found the Director," Casi said softly. "She says he's in his quarters and is being detained by four men."

Stran nodded. "I think we should work our way around the room and slip back out."

Leeana nodded and then looked at Casi. "Tayn says he's powering up KKLC in case Blaire needs help."

Stran touched STSX1. "Coli has STSX up and ready also. We need to hurry."

They were halfway around the room when two couples in dignified dress engaged them in conversation. Stran and Casi tried to be courteous and pleasant and finally moved on, explaining they needed to circulate.

Casi looked up. "Coli called Twenty-two for assistance and Blaire has been talking with the Director. They're going to storm his apartment."

"I *heard*," Stran said, and looked at Hench. "We need to get up there to help."

A loud hiss, a sudden drop in air pressure, and the sounds of glass falling outside startled everyone. Casi looked up again as Stran pushed on the door to the inner corridor, but it did not open. He shoved again and still it resisted.

"Locked!" he shouted, and turned as the room suddenly filled with a dense fog. They *felt* the five men closing in as dizziness swept over them. Casi fired her Brekshiir and two fell. Stran moved in front of Casi and fired; two more fell. He saw Hench's Brekshiir fire, but didn't see who he hit.

He turned and caught Casi's arm, but the dizziness and darkness consumed his mind and he fell unconscious beside her, among the others stricken in the room.

⋏ ⋏ ⋏ ⋏ ⋏

Kiile, Cheral, and Keli were walking back toward the reception room when they felt the floor shake, the drop in pressure, and heard the faint waterfall sounds of glass. They hurried and reached the double door they had used when they left, but it would not open at Kiile's push. He started to put his shoulder to it when a marine materialized beside him.

"Wait, Commandant! There's been an attack," the marine said. "The doors are locked and the room is filled with a sleep gas. Please step aside so we can blow the doors." He gestured for Kiile to take Cheral and Keli to the building's main entrance.

Kiile grabbed Cheral's hand and led her and Keli away as the other marines materialized in the corridor and pulled breathing masks over their heads. He heard one of them call for Series Two canisters and he hurried.

'Neila?' he and Cheral called together. 'Are you okay?'

'Yes!' Neila answered quickly. 'The commander and the Kooiches have been attacked.'

'Yes, we know,' Kiile said. 'The marines are trying to get in.'

161

'They have been taken,' Neila said. 'They are not there anymore. Coli is flying and we are following them.'

'Where? Following where?' Cheral asked, deep concern coloring her thoughts.

'They are being taken to the civilian port on the other side of Headquarters,' Neila said. 'Blaire and Twenty-two's marines rescued the Director and now she's going with us. Tayn, Apache Fifteen, and Apache Ten are also following.'

'Where is everyone else?' Cheral asked.

'The transports are okay,' Neila said, 'and Apache Five and Apache Sixteen are standing guard in the bay.'

'Okay. You're in good hands with Caiti and Coli' Cheral said. 'We're heading for ST12.'

⚔ ⚔ ⚔ ⚔ ⚔

'Twenty-two!' Blaire shouted. 'The commander's been attacked! I've got to go. Do you have everything under control?'

'Yes, Lieutenant,' he answered. 'Go!'

Blaire backed Apache Seventeen away from the gaping hole where the Director's beautiful windows had been and turned to face the docking bay.

"Apache One," she said in her helmet mike, "where are they?"

She had *reached* out to find the commander when Coli answered.

"They're being taken to the civilian port behind Headquarters," Coli answered. "They are unconscious and were taken from the reception room almost immediately. Follow us."

~

"STSX, KKLC, cloaking on, shields full, sensor blocking on. Keep IFF off," Coli said. "Caiti, get Bay Control to open the shortcut to the civilian port."

Caiti contacted Bay Control as Coli swung STSX toward the passage she *felt* between the two ports.

"Apache One," Bay Control responded. "We do not have a clearance for you to pass through."

"Bay Control," Caiti said in a soft, steeled voice. "This is not a request. Either you open the portal or Apache One will make one!"

"Bay Control," Blaire said immediately following. "I am Apache One's personal escort and Commander Geaardt orders the portal be opened!"

"But, I don't have you painted—"

"OPEN the portal! Now!"

Coli added thrust, sensing the separation of Stran and Hench from Casi and Leeana.

"They're putting them on two different transports," Caiti said. "Apache T-One, contact Forty-two. We need marines in the civilian port. The commander and Colonel Kooich are being taken aboard a transport there. Captain Geaardt and Captain Kooich are being taken aboard a second transport."

"How far to the portal, STSX?" Coli asked.

"ONE THOUSAND TERRAN YARDS," STSX said. "PORTAL IS OPENING."

Coli dove through the opening, followed quickly by Tayn in Apache Two and by Apache Ten, Fifteen, and Seventeen.

One of the two civilian transports had moved out of its berth and the second was in the process of releasing its moorings when Coli entered the shipping bay.

"STSX, take out the engines on the one still in its berth," Coli said as Apache Ten and Seventeen descended upon it. "Keep it from leaving."

Two cannon bursts and two bright explosions at the stern of the freighter silenced its engines. It slowly drifted against the docking pier and stopped. Coli maneuvered STSX around the freighter to ensure it wasn't going anywhere.

"The marines are here," Caiti said, sensing the stream of remotes carrying the marines, two at a time, onto the dock. "They have the hatches open and have gained access."

A very long moment passed before STSX announced, "FORTY-TWO REPORTS THEY HAVE FOUND THE COMMANDER AND COLONEL KOOICH. THEY ARE ALIVE AND WILL BE TAKEN TO MEDICAL ON APACHE T-TWO."

"Okay Coli," Caiti said softly. "Let's go get Mom and Leeana."

Coli nodded.

"Apache Two, Apache Fifteen, Apache Seventeen," Coli said in a calm, stern tone. "We will join up after we leave the shipping bay. Apache Ten, please return and assist Apache Four when you are able. Thanks for the help, Ani. Apache One and Two are going after the second transport."

▲ ▲ ▲ ▲ ▲

Blaire was sitting on the instructor's seat, with Caiti and Neila in the right and left jump seats as Coli focused on Casi and Leeana's location. Tayn, Keely, and Cera, in Apache Two, followed in close formation as Coli single-mindedly pursued the fleeing Kyddellan freighter.

"THIRTY MINUTES TO INTERCEPTION."

"Do you want us back in our fighters?" Blaire asked.

"Sorry, Blaire," Coli said, "but I think I do."

"I'll suit up," Caiti said, unbuckling her straps, "and escort her over."

"KKLC14," Coli hailed. "Better have Cera transfer and help watch our backsides."

"Will do," Tayn's voice said, filling the cockpit.

"CADET COLI," STSX said. "YOU SHOULD STOP THE FREIGHTER."

"I intend to," Coli said. "But I need to be sure Mom and Leeana are not harmed."

"SHUT DOWN ITS ENGINES."

"I don't understand," Coli admitted. "If I could shut them

down, and I can't, the pilot would just start them again."

"DISABLE THE PILOT AND NAV-COM FIRST. LOCK THE COCKPIT HATCH AND THEN SHUT THE ENGINES DOWN."

"Scramble them like the two men when you were attacked after school," Neila said softly. "I'll help with the hatch."

"Good point," Coli said and smiled. "As soon as Caiti's back inside and Blaire's flying free."

⤙

"Blaire," Coli said as she took Caiti and Neila's hands. "Link with us, please. I need to look around inside the cockpit of the freighter. Caiti and I have the pilot and nav-com's *feel*, but we need to *look* at the hatch and the lock."

"Linking," Blaire said softly, and followed Caiti and Coli's link. "The hatch is closed and you can see the three illuminated buttons. The red one will set the hatch to sealed and secure. No one in the cargo bay can open it once it's set."

Neila focused her thoughts on the red button and smiled. "Red button is set. Now take care of the crew."

Together, Caiti and Coli sent the piercing tones through the pilot and nav-com's minds, slowly adjusting the pitch until they grabbed the sides of their heads and tried to block out the sharp pain. Sensing the resonance, Caiti and Coli forced a final burst of energy and the crewmen fell silent, slumped sideways in their chairs.

"Okay, STSX," Coli said softly, still holding Caiti and Neila's hands. "How do I shut the engines down?"

"FOLLOW MY LINK AND SENSE THE FREIGHTER'S CONTROL SYSTEM," STSX said. "IT IS KYDDELLAN AND IT WILL RECOGNIZE YOUR KYDDELLAN VOICE. IT WILL HEAR YOU JUST LIKE THE EMISSARY'S FRIGATE HEARD YOUR MOTHER WHEN SHE SAVED JILL THOMAS, NOW JORDAN."

"I *feel* it," Coli said. "What do I tell it?"

"REPEAT THE FOLLOWING PHRASE," STSX said.

"I don't recognize any of that," Coli said. "What am I

saying?"

"DO NOT WORRY ABOUT THE CONTENT. JUST HOLD THE LINK AND REPEAT THE PHRASE UNTIL THE CONTROL SYSTEM RESPONDS. DO NOT LISTEN TO ITS INTERROGATION. IT IS DESIGNED TO INTIMIDATE THE UNCERTAIN."

"Okay," Coli said, and together, Caiti and Coli repeated the phrase.

On the third repeat of the phrase, the control system stopped arguing and executed the command, reducing the engines to idle thrust.

"GIVE THE CONTROL SYSTEM THE FOLLOWING MESSAGE," STSX said, and provided a new phrase. "THE ENGINES WILL REMAIN AT IDLE UNTIL THE CONTROL SYSTEM RECEIVES THE IMBEDDED CODE. WE ARE THE ONLY ONES THAT KNOW THAT CODE."

"Thanks, STSX," Coli said. "Apache Fifteen and Seventeen. The freighter is coasting. We are going to position ourselves on one side for boarding. Stay cloaked. Apache Two, how many remotes do you have on board?"

"Six," Tayn replied.

"Good," Coli said. "When we settle into formation, I will release five of STSX's remotes. You release five of yours and generate Apache Squadron Q-Ship images and sensations, unveiled. We'll use them to show our strength while we board and collect Mom and Leeana."

"SIX MINUTES TO INTERCEPTION AND RENDEZVOUS."

"Tayn, I will need you to meet me at STSX's aft portal with Leeana's EV suit," Coli said. "Can Keely fly KKLC while you help me?"

"Certainly," Tayn said. "Have STSX place the remotes where he thinks they'll work best. I'm going to suit up. Keely has the chair."

"I'm going with you," Neila said as Coli got out of the pilot's chair and started to the floor portal. Coli started to argue, but

Neila continued. "The crew will speak Kyddellan and Galactic Standard. Do you speak either?"

Coli stopped and smiled. "No, and I'm guessing you do."

Neila nodded. "Not Kyddellan, but Nevarian, Galactic Standard, and now Western English"

"She can use Mom's spare suit," Caiti said as she strapped into the pilot's chair. "My suit will be a little snug for her."

"Okay," Coli capitulated. "Come on."

⋏

"Sorry I can only tell you how the Brekshiirs work," Coli said in her helmet mic as STSX's aft portal closed behind them. "No time to practice. The Kaasprs are easier, but you need your hands free. Be prepared if they resist. Our Blues will help protect us."

"Okay," Neila said in an uneasy voice. "I've never shot at anyone before."

"If they shoot at you, don't think about it. Just shoot back," Coli said, and turned, *feeling* Tayn's approach. "He's here."

Neila turned and followed Coli's glance. She smiled as Tayn slipped inside STSX's veil and dropped his cloak.

"You guys need to get moving," Caiti's voice said, filling their helmets. "STSX has hailed the crew and told them they are being boarded. He said if they resist, they will be shot. You be careful, sis. Don't try to be a hero."

"Don't worry," Coli said, trying to ignore the tension and the tightness building in her chest. "Let's go. Grab the remote, Neila."

Coli led the way across the void and grabbed the handle beside the people-sized portal just aft of the large freight hatch. She swung the handle and watched the pressure status lights wink from red to green. The portal hatch released and swung inward.

"Well, they know we're here," Coli said, and took a deep breath.

Inside the airlock, Tayn pulled the hatch closed and slapped the large pad on the pressurization switch. "At least they have some gravity."

'Blaire, Cera,' Coli called, 'I feel *ten inside. Three are close and* feel *like they are waiting to pounce.*'

'I feel *the same sensations,*' Blaire said.

'Crouch and be ready to return fire,' Cera said.

When the pressure equalized with the interior of the ship, Tayn twisted the handle on the inner hatch, stood to one side with Coli and Neila on the other, and shoved the door open.

Two laser traces flashed through the opening as it widened, and Coli and Tayn fired in unison. Two men fell forward and a third peeked around an envirocube. Coli fired and the man spun aside and fell, sprawling on the cargo deck.

Coli quickly unlocked her helmet and slipped it off. Neila followed her lead and unfastened hers.

"Put down your weapons!" Neila shouted in Galactic Standard, and Tayn and Coli jumped into the room and crouched on opposite sides of the portal. "You have been boarded by the Galactic Peace Force for the illegal collection and transporting of Peace Force personnel. Throw down your weapons and show yourselves!"

'Very well done, Neila,' Coli said, and moved to the envirocube, near the three bodies. 'There are four coming around this end of the bay and three coming around the other end. Tayn, watch for the three. They are still armed.'

"Put down your weapons!" Neila shouted again in Galactic Standard. "Three are already dead. If you resist, you will also die!"

"After we kill you," a deep masculine voice replied in Galactic Standard, "we will take our cargo and finish what we set out to do."

"Your pilot and nav-com are incapacitated," Neila said, "and you cannot leave the cargo bay. You cannot simply drop the pressure as you are planning without killing yourselves also. You cannot escape."

Coli *felt* a man hurry to the cockpit hatch. He tried the

handle, and when the hatch refused to move, he pounded on the panel with his fist. Coli reached out and *touched* the man and he twisted away from the hatch, grimacing as he held his head and staggered, falling back into the cargo bay.

"Your man will be useless in moments! Throw down your weapons!" Neila shouted again.

"What are you doing?" the first man screamed as he watched the man stumble and fall, twisting, writhing on the deck.

Neila linked with Coli and *slapped* the man's wrist. His hand laser suddenly flung across the compartment.

Coli released the man on the floor and he fell silent, breathing heavily. The first man slowly stepped out from behind the envirocube and stared at the three in their dark space blue uniforms. Seeing that Tayn was waiting for the three at the far end of the envirocubes, he called for them to come out quietly.

'Coli,' Caiti said softly, '*Patrol Cruiser* Climatus *will be alongside in three pars.*'

'*That is good. I sense more people in another envirocube,*' Coli said as she moved around the men gathering in the cargo bay.

'*You better hurry,*' Caiti said. '*STSX has one of the prince's battlecruisers on the scanner. It seems to be heading our way. The freighter must have been scheduled to rendezvous with it.*'

'*Not good. Thanks. We'll hurry,*' Coli said, and focused on the large man that had been the first to talk.

"What you want is in the third envirocube," the large man said in Galactic Standard.

'*Neila,*' Coli said. '*Mom and Leeana are in the first, there are fourteen people in the second, and the third cube is empty. Open the third cube for them.*'

"Sorry," Neila said, an unpleasant smile crossing her face. "The third cube is empty, but..." She focused her thoughts and the lights on the third cube changed, and following a series of clinks, metal against metal, the hatch slowly swung open. "If you gentlemen will kindly step into cube number three," she continued, then raised her fist and straightened her arm, pointing at the first man, "it will no longer be empty."

Coli saw the clear understanding in the man's eyes when he saw the unattended hatch open and the Brekshiir wrist cluster aimed directly at his midsection. The man dropped his shoulders and led the way, stepping inside the cube. The other six followed and Tayn swung the hatch closed.

"I thought that was going to be hard," Tayn said as he turned back to the two girls.

"Caiti? How long do we have?" Coli asked out loud.

"About thirty minutes," Caiti said, "before the fighters get here to see what's going on. The battlecruiser will only be ten or fifteen minutes behind them."

"Neila," Coli said as she started to unlock the first cube, "you and Tayn open the second and see if you can communicate with those captive there. Let them know help is on the way."

Coli pulled the first cube's hatch open and stepped into the dim, dirty confines. She hurried to the figures bound and stretched out on the floor. *'Caiti. I think they're okay, but they are both unconscious. We'll get them back aboard and in Medical as quickly as we can.'*

Coli turned at the sound of Neila's voice, loud and authoritative, above the clamor of the many concerned and thankful captives. She looked out to see the group of eleven adults and three children clad in tattered and soiled clothing.

Neila was explaining to them what had happened and what was going to happen when she saw Coli step out.

"Tayn," Coli said, and motioned for him.

He glanced at Neila, and when she nodded, he hurried to Coli.

"Tayn, please get Mom and Leeana's suits. We've got to hurry," Coli said, and watched as Tayn hurried to the airlock. She turned back inside and started releasing Casi and Leeana's bindings.

Tayn quickly slipped Leeana's suit on over her legs and Coli helped him get her arms in and the suit fastened. Finished, he helped her get Casi's suit fastened and sealed up.

"Their helmets are in the airlock," Tayn said as he lifted Leeana in a fireman's carry. "Can you manage Casi?"

"Yup," Coli said as she hefted her mom onto her back and followed Tayn through the portal. Once inside the airlock, they set and sealed the helmets and pressurized the suits.

"Neila," Coli yelled. "Tell them we have to go and stop a battlecruiser that is coming. We have to stop it before the patrol cruiser *Climatus* can dock and pick them up."

"They do not want us to leave them," Neila said. "They do not want to listen."

"Okay," Coli said, and straightened up. "Tell them I am the commander of our flight and I say they have to wait and we have to go." Coli stepped into the airlock hatchway and assumed a rigid, staunch posture. "Now!"

Neila repeated what she said was Coli's order and the people slowly stepped back.

"Be sure they understand help is on the way," Coli said, "if we are successful in stopping that cruiser. Tell them we will be back as soon as we can." Coli waited as Neila turned and stepped through the hatch. "Oh, be sure they know to *not* open that last envirocube, and give them the men's weapons."

Neila turned and addressed them again and they nodded profoundly. Two men went to collect the discarded weapons as Tayn swung the hatch closed and turned to check everyone's helmets. Satisfied, he slapped the depressurization hand pad.

▲

"Bring Leeana in, Tayn," Coli said as she and Neila guided Casi into STSX's airlock. "We'll put them both in Medical here. Caiti, you know the drill. Let's get to those fighters and the cruiser before they get here."

"We're already moving," Caiti said as Coli broke her helmet seal. "STSX. Cloak and sensor-block the freighter."

Coli slipped out of her EV suit as quickly as she could and pushed Casi forward to make room for Neila and Tayn. In moments, she had Casi out of her EV suit and stretched out on the right-hand Medical couch. Neila was right behind her, guiding Leeana onto the left-hand couch, and Tayn secured the webbing across her.

'Keely,' Coli said. *'Are you okay with Tayn here?'*

'Yes,' Keely answered with a grim smile in her voice. *'I was trained to do this—alone if necessary.'*

'You're not alone,' Coli said emphatically. *'We are a flight of four well trained and capable fighter pilots.'*

'Yes, ma'am! We are!' Keely said.

"They are both secure and Medical is checking on the gas that was used and what antidotes it should use," Coli said. "We're coming up."

▲

"Blaire, Cera," Caiti said smoothly into the cockpit. "Take the incoming fighters. Choice of engagement is yours, but I think *Dancing in the Dark* might buy us some time before they launch the rest of their fighters. Keely and I will engage the battlecruiser."

"We've got the fighters," Blaire's voice replied. "Good hunting."

"Looks like six coming out in front," Cera said. "Good hunting, Cadet Keely. I'm very proud to fly with you today."

"Thanks, Mom," Keely said softly. "I mean Captain Dnar."

"STSX says the cruiser has about seventy-five fighters total," Caiti said. "Also, *feel* for mines. The history files say the prince used mines in his last big battle to take out Q-ships. B Squadron couldn't sense them and lost many, so be on the lookout."

Coli took the right-hand jump seat and Neila settled on the left.

"STSX," Caiti said softly. "Please bring up a visual display in the cockpit. Retrieve all remotes and shut down target generation. Go *Dark*."

"APACHE FLIGHT IS *DARK*."

"Go get 'em," Caiti said softly as she *felt* Apache Fifteen and

Seventeen move out in front of them to meet the veiled fighters.

"ENGAGEMENT IN FIVE MINUTES," STSX said in a softer-than-normal voice.

"Keely," Caiti said. "Pull up the image of the battlecruiser. Locate the internal communications and control center between the cockpit and the forward hangar bay. It's a belly shot. Set up the cannon fire program Casi developed for penetrating the shields and firing through the hole. Shoot from below. I'll take the top side and go for the weapons control center located between the two hangar bays. If we do this right and the controls are down, we can try to take it apart."

"I've got the details up," Keely said. "There are six more fighters close in around the cruiser."

"Let the extra cannons have the fighters that Blaire and Cera don't get," Caiti said, her voice settling into the seriousness of the fight ahead. "We'll focus on the control centers."

"Right," Keely said. "I'm planning a three-turret volley over my left pylon."

"That'll work," Caiti said, and pushed the thrust levers forward more. "Let's move in."

Suddenly, three miles ahead of them, six explosions twinkled in front of the starscape. A quick sense of relief flashed through them and their focus changed to the battlecruiser. Knowing there would be a moment of surprise and indecision on the cruiser's bridge, Caiti *watched* for the deployment of more fighters.

"ONE MILE."

"Reverse," Caiti said, and quickly flipped STSX and added thrust.

Keely reversed, almost mirroring STSX, and was at full thrust when the cruiser flashed between them.

STSX fired and Caiti *felt* KKLC fire. The cannon bursts pierced the hull and massive clouds of oily smoke and small debris erupted from many hatches and skin portals and panels. A large hatch and adjacent skin burst out beside them as STSX regained firing position.

"Again," Caiti said, and *felt* KKLC cut through the controls bay and rake the forward hangar bay as STSX fired through the weapons control bay and cut a swath through the aft hangar bay.

"Concentrate on the fuel cell storage behind the aft hangar bay," Caiti said. "Pull away in case she goes up."

"Got it," Keely said, and put some room between KKLC and the cruiser. "You get the engines."

Caiti rolled from the top, over one side, and began cutting the hull behind the hangar bay. Nearly back to the top, a huge explosion cut the aft section off the cruiser. The burning engines spun away and exploded.

"Cut it up into little pieces," Caiti said, and directed STSX across the cruiser's spine.

"Pull back, Caiti!" Keely shouted. "Internal fires are growing rapid—"

The brilliant explosion engulfed the entire remnants of the cruiser and thousands of fragments blew away in all directions, chopping off Keely's words. Caiti felt the heat, even though the shields kept the energy at bay.

"Caiti? Caiti?' Keely asked. "Are you guys okay?"

"Yeah," Caiti said with a chuckle. "A little toasty, but we're fine. Blaire? Cera?"

"Apache Fifteen is still in one piece," Cera said.

"Apache Seventeen is all here," Blaire chuckled. "I don't feel any fighters."

"ALL FIGHTERS NEUTRALIZED."

"Good work, Apache Flight," Caiti said, and slowly turned STSX back toward the freighter.

"Caiti?" Neila asked, and touched her on the shoulder. Caiti turned to look at her and she asked, "Can you *feel* the prince now?"

Caiti closed her eyes and focused on his sensation. "Yes. I can sense him."

"I think," Neila said softly, "we should let him know his

attempt has failed. He is too important of a person to have to wait for his Intelligence people to discover what has happened and inform him."

Caiti smiled and looked at Coli. "Blaire, Cera, Keely. Please form up on Apache One and link with us. We have a message to deliver."

One Thirty-Eight
C.3486.807

Prince Lukré stared at the gathering of his staff, seated around the long, slightly trapezoidal conference table stretching out before him. The angled sides of the table allowed him a view of each of the twenty members, each positioned such that they could not duck away from his pointed glare or demanding gestures. He waited as the head of his Royal Admiralty slowly stood and nodded to the gathering.

"Members of the Staff," the decorated admiral began. "Your Highness, Prince Lukré. The current fleet stands at sixty-five battleships, one hundred and eighty-three battlecruisers, one hundred and seventy-one atmospheric trawlers like the ones you deployed in the collection of Nevar, fifteen thousand, nine hundred and sixty-four combat-ready fighters—thirteen thousand, seven hundred and twenty-five of those assigned to the fleet of battlecruisers. In addition, the fleet includes multiple thousands of support and resupply vessels, distributed in key locations across the known and inhabited galaxy."

"What is the production rate for the trawlers?" Prince Lukré asked in a level, almost uninterested tone.

"One on the average of one hundred and thirty-six turns, sire," the admiral said. "They are being delivered to the admiralty depot in thirty-two turn intervals."

Prince Lukré nodded and allowed himself the barest of a smile. He privately estimated he needed five hundred trawlers before he could consider a move against any of the larger, heavy worlds. A quick series of taps on the digital pad before him and he had the number of turns to that goal: ten and one half galactic kiloturns. He frowned.

"Admiral!" he said, and slapped the table. "I will not give

you more than three galactic kiloturns to reach the number of trawlers I have set. You will triple the production rate. Immediately!"

He felt his chest tighten and a wave of nausea growing in the back of his mind.

"Intelligence," Prince Lukré said, trying to ignore the unbalancing sensations. "What is the status of our 'meeting' with the Peace Force director and his staff?"

The director quickly stood, looking more pale than normal. "Sire," the director began. "I fear the meetings did not fare well."

"Go on," Prince Lukré urged. "What did not 'fare well'?"

When the director began to speak again, Prince Lukré felt his stomach rebel and the table slowly roll. He knew it was not rolling, but his face went ashen and he quickly turned aside as his stomach relieved itself, spewing its contents down the long folds of his ceremonial cape. He grabbed the edge of the table as unfamiliar words gripped his mind and spilled out of his mouth.

"THE AGENTS HOLDING YOUR 'CONFERENCE' WITH THE PEACE FORCE DIRECTOR ARE DEAD!" the female's words said, spilling out of his mouth and filling the chamber.

Prince Lukré tried to wipe his face, but he knew he would tumble if he released his grip on the table. "Who is saying these things?" the prince asked out loud, to no one he could see.

"ALL OF THE KYDDELLAN AGENTS PLACED WITHIN THE RINGS FOR YOUR TASKS AND 'MEETINGS' HAVE BEEN CAPTURED!" the female's words continued. "THE RANKING COMMANDER OF THE RED-STRIPED FIGHTER SQUADRON IS WELL AND FREE. THE SHIP SENT TO CAPTURE HIM AND HIS SECOND IN COMMAND HAS BEEN COMMANDEERED, THE CREW INCARCERATED!" He tried to catch his breath. "THE SHIP AND CREW THAT ESCAPED WITH THEIR MATES HAS BEEN OVERTAKEN AND BOARDED. THE CREW AND VESSEL ARE IN THE CUSTODY OF THE PEACE FORCE. THE CAPTIVES ON BOARD HAVE BEEN RESCUED!"

Prince Lukré tried to focus on the faces staring back at him, confused, startled, and afraid.

"THE BATTLECRUISER *SCREAMING DARKNESS* AND ITS SEVENTY-FIVE FIGHTERS AND CREWS ARE DESTROYED!" the female's words shouted. "THERE ARE NO SURVIVORS!"

Breathing heavily, Prince Lukré swung his glance from one side of the room to the other, catching the shocked stare of one staff member or another as he searched for a way out of this madness.

'Prince Lukré,' another female voice said to him alone, suddenly holding his complete attention. *'We are the Galactic Peace Force, and we are sharing with you the pain and anguish that you and your predecessor have caused. You will survive today, only to regret that you have voluntarily accepted to continue the evil in the name of Knobaal. Each time you contemplate another vile act, we will squeeze your heart and lungs to the very edge of life itself. Each time your health will decline and you will remember those you have had taken or killed, their heartache, their terror, and their pain. When you are replaced as the Supreme Head of Knobaal, each new prince and his successor will be inflicted in the same manner until the evil authority of Knobaal and its treachery are no more, a mere, distant memory.'*

He grabbed his chest as his breath failed him and his heart raced, pressure building until his eyes bulged and his face turned bright red. With a sudden release, the pressure stopped and he inhaled sharply. "LOOK UP!" the voice demanded out loud and he and all at the conference table turned their eyes upwards to see the tall, majestic walls of the stone chamber tremble and large cracks appear in the arched ceilings. Involuntarily, he ducked as the walls fell aside and the massive edifice of the palace crashed down around him.

C.3486.809

"Come in," the Peace Force Director said, and turned back

into the large conference room.

Casi and Stran smiled, remembering the day Casi first came into this room and met the director just over twelve years past.

"Thank you for your patience with me," the Director said as he stopped at the foot of the large conference table. "Good to see you again, Captain Beeli" —he shook Kiile's hand—"and you again, Major. And this must be Neila. I'm so very glad to meet you. Welcome back, Lieutenant Quil," he continued as Keli followed Neila in. He smiled brightly and greeted Ani with a warm smile and a clasp of hands. "And a very happy greeting to you, Captain."

One by one, the Director greeted each one, expressing his great pleasure to be able to actually speak with and greet the faces and names he only knew from his communications and files. He remembered Wally and Thom from their youth, when they had first registered with the Force, but was extremely pleased to meet Carole and Eddie and their children, respectively.

"And you must be Lieutenant Lupis," he said when Blaire stopped proudly in front of him. "And another unusual Terran redhead." He glanced at the Dnars queued behind her and smiled. "It is a great pleasure to meet you, Lieutenant. But do tell me, are all redheads like you three?"

"Sir?" Blaire said, and smiled. "I don't know what you mean. But I will say we redheads tend to be a little different."

The Director chuckled. "Thank you, Lieutenant."

Once he had greeted Hench, Leeana, Tayn, and Doug, he turned and went to the head of the table and stood behind the large, overstuffed chair.

"Please take a seat anywhere, but I would like to keep the first two on each side open"—he gestured to the seats to his right and left—"for the interviews. Commander, please have as many of your marine escorts as you wish join us at the table."

Stran seated Casi on the Director's left, leaving the first three open—two as the director requested and one for himself—then Caiti, Coli, and Blaire in the next. He turned to Kiile and spoke to Twenty-two when Kiile nodded.

"Sergeant Stial, Sergeant Culni. Please join us," Stran said, and gestured to the table as Kiile, Cheral, Neila, and Lieutenant Keli took seats on the Director's right, across from Stran and his family. Ani Tigs took the next, followed by Major and Captain Glean and then Cera, Jesi, and Keely. Hench, Leeana, and Tayn took the next places on the left, beside Blaire. Thom, Eddie, Billie, and Sergeant Culni filled out Kiile's side of the table, and Doug settled on Stran's side, with Wally, Carole, Alyssa, Ridan, and Sergeant Stial next.

"I must admit," the Director said as Stran glanced at the assemblage and then sat down, "seeing this group in one place, all together, is rather impressive. I had the count ahead of time, but...Well, let me just say welcome, and a heartfelt thank you for your presence of mind and quick reactions when you arrived." The Director paused as he took his chair and settled to face the group. "I believe I owe a special thank you to Lieutenant Lupis and to Cadet Coli Geaardt for arranging and executing my rescue. Thank you."

Blaire smiled and nodded and Coli slowly turned red.

"You are welcome, sir," Blaire said without being asked to speak. "Coli led the investigation and arranged for Sergeant Culni's marines and their placement. I was merely a necessary tool."

"Aah." The Director smiled. "We will talk about that more as the day goes on, Lieutenant." He turned and looked at Stran. "Commander? How are you and Casi doing this morning?"

"We are well," Stran said. "Thanks again to the fast response of Apache Flight and our cadets."

The director nodded. "And you, Casi?" he asked with a little apprehension, and watched her.

"Still a little fatigued, sir," Casi admitted. "STSX is monitoring my recovery. There was something in my reaction to the sleep gas that he seems concerned about. I'm sure everything is fine."

"Very well," the Director said, and let her answer stand. "Colonel and Captain Kooich?"

"We have recovered in good shape," Leeana said. "And how

are you, sir?"

"Grateful for my loyal Shadows," he said, "and very surprised that I have let security become so lax." He half smiled and half grimaced. "I owe you all a debt of gratitude and a sincere thank you for taking your training so seriously and seeing things I did not until it was too late." He looked up one side of the table and then down the other. "That said, I must change my original plan for this meeting and discuss, first, the bold and daring actions of our lowly cadets." He smiled at Keely and she smiled in return.

"But before I go into the specifics of your accomplishments," the Director said, "I must ask what happened to the Knobaal Palace and Prince Lukré. My undercover agents in Knobaal have wild stories of a strange occurrence there, just after you destroyed a battlecruiser, by our estimates." He glanced from Keely to Tayn and then to Caiti and Coli. "Cadet Coli Geaardt. Since you assumed the role of mission commander, would you please tell us if you have any idea of what happened?"

Coli glanced at Caiti's thin smile and slight nod and then turned to the Director.

"Well, sir," Coli said softly. "We, sort of, destroyed it."

The Director stared at her and then at Caiti's slow nod.

"You destroyed it?" he questioned slowly. "Your engagement with the battlecruiser was over twenty pars from Knobaal, even in a highly modified Q-Ship. How do you expect me to believe you destroyed it?"

"Because we did," Caiti said softly, and glanced at Neila. They both locked eyes and she *felt* Neila focus on the double doors they came through before the Director had closed and locked them. The Director watched them curiously until the movement of the double doors caught his attention.

"It really wasn't too hard, sir," Coli added, following Caiti and Neila's link. "We gave the prince an ultimatum and explained what would happen to him if he continued stealing people, and then we leveled the palace. We protected him so he could live and see and remember what will happen if he continues to spread his vileness." She stopped when the Director stared at the open doors without saying anything. Coli nodded once and the doors slowly reclosed and clicked into place.

"Sergeant Stial," Coli said without turning away from the Director. "Please see if the doors are locked."

Sergeant Stial slowly stood up, unsteady on his feet as he tried to assimilate what he thought he just had just seen. At the door, he pulled on the handles, but they refused to move. He stepped to the wall controls and depressed the appropriate buttons, but the panel refused his access. He slowly turned to face the table. "They are locked, sir. I cannot open them."

The Director slowly glanced at each of the girls again and caught Stran, Casi, and Cheral's smiles.

"Do I dare ask what you did to the prince?" the Director asked, and looked back at Caiti.

"Not long ago," Caiti began, "Coli and I realized we could *hear* and sense the prince. Mom, er, Captain Casi and the commander figured out who we were hearing and helped us focus so he couldn't follow the link back to us. Since the prince killed Neila's mom and family, and Captain Beeli's family when Nevar was attacked, we—the four of us with the assistance of Lieutenant Lupis and Captain Dnar—decided we should leave the prince a message before we returned home."

"A message?"

"Yes, sir," Coli said, picking up the explanation. "We planted a nugget in his mind, and every time he commands something evil to be done, he gets very nauseous, unbalanced, and will soil himself. He was addressing his staff when we interrupted and told him and them his attempt to hold you hostage, to capture the commander, his second in command, and their mates, had failed."

"We also told him," Caiti said, "that we had destroyed his battlecruiser, *Screaming Darkness*, all seventy-five of its fighters, and all crewmen. If he continued his campaigns, we would destroy each of his remaining one hundred and eighty-two battlecruisers and all sixty-five of his battleships and each of his Seats of Power."

"They wouldn't let Lieutenant Lupis, Cadet Keely, or myself listen in," Tayn added, "when they conducted a brain scan on the prince. They felt a first time to do a scan would be too draining on us, especially with Keely and Blaire needing to continue flying afterwards. That was just after they pushed the walls out from under the roof of the palace. STSX has a complete download and has the coordinates for six of the nine ports where the atmospheric trawlers are berthed."

"Wait. Wait," the Director stammered. "My head is starting to spin. You did a brain scan on the prince? From where you destroyed the battlecruiser?"

"We did, sir," Cera said softly. "I didn't know we could do one without physical contact, but we did."

"And you made him physically ill? In front of his staff?" the Director continued. "And you collapsed the palace?"

"Neila wanted him to see what it was like," Caiti said, "to see his home leveled, no two stones on top of one another, like he did to Nevar."

The Director closed his mouth and leaned back into his chair, staring at each of the cadets and at Neila. Slowly a smile began to spread across his face.

"I could not believe the reports I received last evening," the Director said softly. "My agents all agree the palace is no more—simply rubble spread out across the once immaculate gardens and terraces, like some ground-shake erupted under the palace and nowhere else, collapsing the entire structure in a matter of moments. And I have you seven to blame for it all." He chuckled and then slowly began to laugh.

He wiped his eyes with a folded cloth he took from his breast pocket.

"Cadet Keely," he said, and slowly composed himself. "You have been very quiet. What were you doing while all of this was going on?"

Keely cleared her throat and looked at him. "Sir. Until we had time to think of messages and retri...retributions, I was assisting Apache One in destroying one Kyddellan battlecruiser and a few fighters. Lieutenant Lupis and Captain Dnar had their hands full keeping the fighters entertained so we could work on the cruiser. When the smoke and debris had finally cleared and we knew Patrol Cruiser *Climatus* had reached the disabled freighter and the rest of the captives, we all linked and spoke with the prince, explaining how his current job as High Prince Regent was in jeopardy and that he might want to think about looking for a new career."

The Director could not help himself and started chuckling again. He looked at Stran and Casi, Hench and Leeana, and then at Kiile and Cheral.

"Are they always like this?" he asked.

Stran nodded. "They are very dedicated and very resourceful."

"Is this all of the new talents your group has produced?" he asked, shaking his head and gesturing to the room.

"No, sir," Casi said with a wide smile. "Doug's son and daughter have not yet started to blossom, but with Neila showing us what Kayli and Kail might be like, we are looking forward to their day. And we look forward to more new talents as time progresses." She winked at Cheral and then smiled at Blaire.

"I see," the Director said, and wiped his eyes again, then forced himself to turn somber. "Now, for the record. I have reviewed the particulars of the flight of two Peace Force Officers, four cadets, and one unranked civilian after they commandeered two Q-Ships, two patrol fighters, and forced their way into the civilian port, shot at, and disabled a transient civilian freighter, ordered the support of two full squads of marines to assist in their rampage, and then they fled in pursuit of another civilian freighter, overtook it, rescued sixteen captives, and then destroyed seventy-five enemy fighters and one enemy battlecruiser."

He took a breath and looked at each of them again.

"Cadet Keely Dnar is credited with fifteen fighter kills and one half of a Kyddellan battlecruiser." His voice softened as he spoke.

"Cadet Coli Geaardt is credited with the rescue of

185

the Galactic Peace Force director, the Apache Squadron commander and his second in command, and sixteen captives on board the escaped freighter. Cadet Caiti Geaardt is also credited with fifteen fighter kills and one half of a Kyddellan battlecruiser. Cadet Tayn Kooich is credited with the rescue of Captain Geaardt and Captain Kooich and fourteen other captives on board the escaped freighter. Lieutenant Lupis is credited with a significant role in the rescue of the Galactic Peace Force director and with twenty-three fighter kills in the attack on the Kyddellan battlecruiser. And Captain Cera Dnar is credited with another twenty-two fighter kills in the attack on the Kyddellan battlecruiser. I believe this brings your career total to somewhere around seventy-seven."

Cera nodded, but did not break eye contact with the Director until he purposely looked down at the monitor below the tabletop.

"Now," the Director said, "will Alyssa and Ridan Lima please come and take the first seats."

Wally smiled and pushed them toward the front of the long table.

"Miss Lima and Master Lima," the Director said softly, and smiled. "I only want to talk and get to know something about you. Please take a seat and indulge me for a few minutes."

The Director kept his visit short and addressed how their new talents and capabilities had affected them and their lives, how they dealt with the changes and the secrecy necessary, and how they thought they might use their talents as they grew up.

He then called Billie Baine and talked with her for almost the same length of time before he let her return to her parents and then called Neila.

As she sat down, he studied the monitor through the tabletop.

"I was very sad to hear about your mother and family on Nevar, Neila," the Director said, and looked at her. "I hope your new life has shown you that you are still loved and wanted."

"Yes, sir," Neila said. "Losing part of my family was very sad, but finding that I still have family and many friends has been more than I had hoped for."

"I was pleased when you and Cheral filed the adoption papers," he said. "Has that worked well for you?"

"Very much so, sir," she said, and smiled.

"I am glad," he said, and his expression turned serious. "Now, I have a few questions that I must ask you."

"Certainly, sir."

"Do you remember when you first realized you could *hear* others and when you developed *telekinesis*?"

"I've been able to *hear* some since my earliest memories," Neila admitted. "But the ability to put things where I wanted them came when I was old enough to have duties. I had to hide it when I could out-fight the boys on the farms, but it came in handy when I worked on the equipment or had to fill in with loading the carts when one of the boys was ill or didn't want to work."

"So you didn't let anyone know you had the capability?"

"No," Neila admitted. "When I met my Cousin Doug, Caiti and Coli figured it out. Doug has hidden his capability also, and used it in secret where he works, but Caiti and Coli *felt* it. After my tag was implanted, I started feeling Pada and Pama and I always know where they are, but being around Tayn, Keely, Coli, and Caiti, I think I'm beginning to *feel* them and others. During our mission, I *knew* where Lieutenant Lupis was, even though she was *Dancing in the Dark*."

"Have you thought about what you want to do in the future?" he asked.

"You're asking me if I want to join the Peace Force," Neila said bluntly. "And the answer is I don't know. Pada and Pama tell me I can be and do whatever I want with my life. I can raise horses, drive a bus—but I haven't seen one of those yet—or I can join the Force or do anything else I want to do. But they said that was my decision and they would help me learn so I can make good choices. They said they would not pressure me to do one over the other. Coming here, Casi reminded me, when she was talking with Blaire about their double lives, that I can do more than just one thing at a time. I will let Pada and Pama and you know when I decide what I will do next, and maybe the next time after that."

"Thank you, Neila," the Director said. "You have been told correctly and wisely. You do not have to rush into anything, but I will say Cadets Geaardt may need your assistance from time to time."

Neila smiled. "Yes, sir. I was pleased they wanted my help."

"Thank you, Neila," the Director said, and gestured to her empty chair beside Cheral. Then he turned to everyone.

"Tomorrow night, I will have a private dinner for the twenty-nine of us, two of my trusted aides, and one other fellow officer. Your upgrades and maintenance items should be finished by then and you can plan on leaving as soon as you wish after that. Dress uniforms, please, for those in the Force. Otherwise, men, please wear business attire or similar and ladies, please wear what you brought that makes you feel pretty. The dinner should be a happy occasion."

▲ ▲ ▲ ▲ ▲

"Lieutenant," Sergeant Stial called from where he waited when he saw Blaire coming down the corridor from the conference room. "May I speak with you?"

"Hey, Luc," Blaire said, and smiled. "I wanted to thank you for your assistance the other night."

"Of course," he said. "Any time you need it."

"I thought the Director should have mentioned yours and Sergeant Culni's part," she said. "Coli and I set things up, but you and your marines had the hard job."

"We don't do the job for the praise, Blaire," he said, and smiled. "We're just happy we pulled it off and everyone is safe and okay."

"Still," she said, and glanced at the emptying corridor.

"Blaire, I'm wondering if I might escort you to dinner

tomorrow night," Luc said. "I know you were asked to stay to yourself before we left Obscure, but I was hoping—"

"I don't think..." Blaire said, and looked at him. She shook her head slowly.

"Sam, huh?"

Blaire nodded. "Yeah. Sam."

"I figured as much," Luc said. "And I am happy for you. I think you are a very special girl and Sam is a very lucky guy. I hope everything works out for the two of you."

"Thanks, Luc," Blaire said, and smiled at him. "It would be unkind of me to let you think we could be something—"

"Just remember me if things don't work out with Sam," Luc said, and smiled. "I'll see you at dinner tomorrow and around the facility, Blaire. It's nice working with you."

"Thanks," Blaire said. "Bye."

Blaire turned and walked out of the building, and Luc watched her for a long moment. When he turned to leave, he saw Keli standing by the wall, watching him.

"Lieutenant Quil," he said. "Can I help you?"

"Maybe," Keli said, and stepped closer. "I'm sorry it isn't working out with Blaire." She stopped close and looked up into his face. "But you do know there is another cute fighter pilot? One that's single and unattached?"

Luc smiled and looked down into Keli's bright amber eyes. "And where might a single, unattached sergeant find this cute, unattached fighter pilot?"

"Well," Keli said as she held his eyes. "You could take me to lunch and I'll see if I can explain it."

He watched her lips as they slowly curled into a smile. "I think I'd like to hear your explanation." He extended his elbow and she hooked her arm in it. "Shall we?" he asked, and led her toward the main entrance.

One Thirty-Nine
C.3486.810

The soft sound of a small gong filled the anteroom in the Director's apartment wing and the assemblage of Apache Flight took their seats around a large, crescent-shaped table in the adjacent private dining room. The place cards arranged them by family groups with Stran and Casi centered, Caiti and Coli on either side, facing the smaller table centered in the open arms of the crescent.

Once all twenty-eight of them had settled, the Director stopped behind the smaller, central table with three other persons, one in Dress Blues. He faced Stran and Casi as the three with him sat down. He remained standing, slowly scanning the crescent table from one end to the other, smiling warmly.

"Gentlemen. Ladies," the Director said. "Thank you for coming tonight, and for coming to the Rings. I have a few announcements to make before we begin.

"First is the table arrangement. I hope it allows you to freely engage in conversations, even with those across from you or farthest from you. Please do not feel that you have to remain overly formal. I wish for you to enjoy yourselves.

"Second are the meal choices. Before each of you is a list of options with, I hope, an adequate description of each. If you have any questions, please ask your servers to explain. They speak a variation of your Terran English. There are some Terran dishes and a few non-Terran for those that have an expanded pallet or are simply adventurous."

A soft chuckle swept the table.

"I will also assure you that as a result of the incident of four turns past," the Director continued, "there are no untagged

191

personnel within the Peace Force areas of the Rings. I am still studying options for the civilian commercial port areas.

"Please take a few moments to mark your dinner choices on the menu pads. When you have all finished choosing, your servers will refill your drinks and I will make a few more announcements."

Everyone studied the list on their pads as the Director sat down and chatted with the two people in business attire immediately on either side of him. Stran noticed the lieutenant in her Blues also sitting at the director's table. She was pleasant looking, young, probably in her mid-twenties by Terran measure, and sat quietly with an air of calm expectation about her.

Cued by the lowering of the last stylus, the servers entered the inside of the curved dining table and refilled each glass. As they returned to form a line near the common wall with the food preparation area, the Director stood.

"I want to address our younger members of the Apache Flight and their parents. I am glad to see that each of the children already have their Terran tags even though they are not 'officially' registered as members of the Force. And now that I have met these four, I will set aside GPF Tags, which they will receive when they are registered or when they turn the Terran age of eleven. There is, however, one exception."

Alyssa, Ridan, and Billie smiled at the reduction in age for registration as the Director stepped around his head table and stopped before it. He turned and faced the Beelis.

"In your case, Neila Beeli, you are registered with the Force as Kiile Beeli's daughter and have a GPF tag already. This does not mean you are an active member of the Force, but your tag will not have to change if you ever decide the Force is an occupation you wish to pursue."

Neila nodded and smiled when he looked at her.

The Director scanned his digital pad and scrolled a page before continuing.

"Now, the matter of our four cadets," he said, and looked at each of them. "Cadet Caiti Geaardt, Cadet Coli Geaardt, Cadet

Tayn Kooich, and Cadet Keely Dnar, please come and stand beside me.

"While they are coming forward, I will digress a moment and say that I agree with most of Commander Geaardt's upgrades to the Class Two fighter he assigned to Lieutenant Lupis. But I wish to add a few additional upgrades of my own, and designate the new fighters as Class Threes and specifically assign them to the Apache Squadron and the ASCT graduates."

As the cadets walked around the table and took places on one side of the Director, the two business-suited men stood and took places beside the Director, opposite the cadets. He turned and looked at Caiti.

"Cadet Caiti Geaardt," he said, and took several packets from one of the men standing beside him, "Cadet Coli Geaardt, Cadet Tayn Kooich, and Cadet Keely Dnar. For your exemplary standings in the ASCT graduating class and for your extraordinary conduct in the rescue of your commander and his co-commanders, you are each awarded two Distinguished Service Stars for Actions Beyond the Call of Duty. And for your actions in the attack on and destruction of the Kyddellan battlecruiser *Screaming Darkness*, you are awarded two ribbons for Meritorious Conduct in the Face of Enemy Fire, a Gold Ribbon for Exceptional Bravery and Courage under Enemy Fire, and a Braid to be added to your Fighter Pilot Ace's Cross for your actual combat kills. Furthermore, for all of the above accomplishments and your parts in the exceptional handling of Prince Lukré and the Knobaal Palace, I hereby promote each of you from cadet to the rank of upper-lieutenant in the Galactic Peace Force."

The Director smiled at their controlled but smiling response.

"Thank you, sir," Caiti said through the courteous-yet-loud applause as the Director extended his hand. He shook each of their hands before he continued.

"One more thing," the Director said. "Each of you are assigned one of the new Class Three fighters. The biweekly supply transport will deliver them to Shadow Base in approximately four weeks."

In a quick "pinning-on" ceremony, the Director and the two aides walked the line of new lieutenants. When they had finished, the Director presented them to the table and dismissed Tayn and Keely to their seats, keeping Caiti and Coli beside him.

"Will Lieutenant Lupis please come forward," the Director said as the excitement slowly settled.

Blaire took a place beside Coli and matched her rigid stance.

"Before I single Lieutenant Lupis out," the Director said, and someone chuckled, "I want to personally thank these three dedicated and determined women for their unswerving commitment and service in the planning and execution of the rescue of their director. We would not be standing here tonight except for the courage and quick thinking of these fine officers."

He turned to Caiti, Coli, and Blaire.

"The Peace Force offers each of you its most extremely felt appreciation and gratitude. I therefore award you the Peace Force's highest honor for a living veteran, the Distinguished Service Cross."

The two aides again assisted as the Crosses were "pinned on."

"Thank you, Lieutenants," the Director said to Caiti and Coli. "You may be seated now. Lieutenant Lupis," he continued, "stands before us as an example of calm, cool confidence and courage. When she contacted me, she reminded me of the one other that came into our ranks with no previous training, completely sure of herself, willing to learn whatever it took, and embracing the new responsibilities without a second thought. Both of them were determined to be the best they could be from the very first moment they put their personal needs aside to help and defend others in distress." The Director let his gaze and smile settle briefly on Casi.

He went through the awarding and presented Blaire with the Distinguished Service Stars, the Meritorious Conduct Ribbons, her Gold Ribbon for Exceptional Bravery and Courage, and her Braid of Distinction for her Fighter Pilot

Ace's Cross.

"In addition," the Director said, "Lieutenant Blaire Lupis is hereby promoted to the rank of captain and remains assigned to the commander's wing at Shadow Base. Captain Lupis' fighter will be upgraded to the latest Class Three configuration, and on her twentieth birthday she will report back to this office for the assignment of a Q-Ship and the associated promotion." He turned, smiled at her, and extended his hand. "Congratulations, Captain."

The table again applauded and the Director glanced at the kitchen manager standing beside the line of servers.

"I see our dinners are waiting, so I will make the next award quickly and then continue after dinner. Neila Beeli, please come forward."

Startled, Neila looked at Cheral and then Kiile. Kiile nodded and she slowly got up and went to the front table.

"Neila," the Director said softly, "I cannot overlook your distinct contributions to the rescue of your director, to the capture and commandeering of the freighter and the rescue of the captives on board, and of course to the incident at the Knobaal Palace. Even though you are not a cadet or a soldier in the Peace Force, I am awarding you with three Distinguished Service Stars for Actions Beyond the Call of Duty, a ribbon for Meritorious Conduct in the Face of Enemy Fire with a Braid of Distinction, and three black slashes, one for each of your encounters. In addition, and specifically for your contributions in the Knobaal Palace incident, a Gold Ribbon for Exceptional Bravery and Courage."

He turned to his aide and officially pinned the awards on her Blues. As he presented her to the table, he picked up a narrow, dark gray sash and added, "For official GPF events where wearing Blues is not required or appropriate, as I am certain the daughter of the base commandant will occasionally be required to attend, I present to you a sash with each of your awards attached. Please wear them with pride and know how honored this administration is in presenting them. Thank you, Neila." He gestured to her seat, turned to the staff, and gestured for them to begin.

"Please enjoy your meals and I will continue afterwards," he said, and smiled at the group.

▲

"I can't believe I got another promotion," Blaire said softly to Coli. "And the four of you going straight from a cadet to an upper-lieutenant. Wow."

"I'm still in shock," Casi said, listening to Blaire and Coli's conversation. "The Director can do what he wants, but this is such an unexpected surprise."

"Definitely," Coli said with a long sigh, and glanced down the curve of the table to see Keely between her mom and dad. It was obvious Keely was desperately trying to contain the excitement bubbling up inside her as she ate and talked at the same time.

Tayn was the most composed of all of them, but Coli watched his smile and mannerisms and knew he was happier than she had ever seen him.

Coli glanced at Neila, sitting just past Caiti, and smiled. Neila was quietly absorbing the happy mood of the gathering, slowly eating a mixed-menu dish, and seemed to glow with the thrill of being publicly recognized and appreciated.

"What do you think the Director is going to announce next?" Coli asked.

"Hard to say," Casi said. "The seven of you were the stars of this trip, so I haven't the slightest idea. We'll just have to wait and see."

"That's right," Coli said softly. "Captain Tigs was part of our mission and she hasn't been commended yet."

"She deserves some recognition," Blaire said. "I'm prejudiced, but not because Ani was my first friend when I started training. She's good and deserves to be recognized."

"I agree," Coli admitted. "Dessert's being served, so it won't be long before we know what's next."

▲

The Director stood when the servers removed the dessert dishes and served the after-dinner drinks and coffees.

"Captain Ani Tigs," the Director said softly. "Please come forward."

He took a small package from the man next to him as Ani made her way to his table.

"Captain Tigs," he began as he faced her. "I am pleased to present you with a Braid of Distinction to be added to your Fighter Pilot Ace's Cross, a Distinguished Service Star, and a Meritorious Conduct Ribbon for your part in the rescue of the commander." He took another packet from the aide. "In addition, I promote you to the rank of major and assign you Q-Ship Q-STSX10."

Ani smiled, the joy of the unexpected promotion and assignment of an ST-Class Q-Ship apparent on her face as the room burst into applause and the Director and his aides turned to the task of pinning the awards and lapel insignias on her Blues. Finished, the Director stepped back and saluted.

"Major Tigs," he continued, "you will also need to change your Shadow tag to your new Headquarters tag." He smiled as she realized the import of his words. "Now, I would like to introduce Lieutenant Jnet Dosn, your nav-com."

The lieutenant stood to more applause, and she greeted Ani with a salute and a handshake.

"Lieutenant Dosn," the Director continued, "will begin her pilot training as soon as you return to Shadow Base. Congratulations to you both."

The Director waited as Ani and Jnet returned to their respective seats and the applause died into an anxious silence.

He held up his hand. "Will Captains Jesi, Cera Dnar, and Captain McIntire please come forward?"

When they turned and stood at attention beside him, the Director awarded Jesi and Cera each a Distinguished Service Star and a Meritorious Conduct Ribbon for their part in the rescue of the commander, and to Cera a Braid of Distinction to be added to her Fighter Pilot Ace's Cross with a braid of

Distinction for her added combat kills. To Doug he awarded a Meritorious Conduct Ribbon for the continued support to the safety of the commander and his team. Then, he promoted the three of them to the rank of major.

The Director dismissed them amid the roomful of applause and considered his notepad.

"Commander Geaardt," the Director said when he looked up. "As the man most responsible for the operations at Shadow Base and the success of Apache Squadron's Combat Training School, will you please come forward? And please bring Casi with you. Captain Beeli, will you and Cheral please join them and come forward?

"While they are making their way," the Director continued, "I would like to remind everyone that it was Commander Geaardt and Major Cheral Haak that first discovered the slave traders' secret base, Point Obscure, now known as Shadow Base. He, with a small group of his civilian friends, planned and executed the capture of the facility and rescued his sister, known to all of you as Shadow Cera Dnar, from Prince Kiese's emissary and a likely life as a slave. I am pleased to see that many of that original attack force are among us today.

"Captain Beeli, known until recently as simply 'Kiile' among his troops and friends, was the commander's closest ally from their days as cadets to the present. Captain Beeli knew and understood the commander better than anyone, with the one possible exception: Casi. Captain Beeli and his men were, and are, the other blade in the scissors of the commander's campaigns. He is also the one man responsible for the security, defense, and operations within Shadow Base, and around the commander and his personal security team."

The Director turned and looked at the four as the two men at his table stood. He took a small packet from one of the men and opened it.

"Commander Geaardt. For your unwavering duty to the Peace Force and its causes and campaigns over your twenty-five Terran years of dedicated service, your keen vision, guidance, and actions necessary in attaining the successes and victories for the Peace Force, I promote you to the rank of First General."

Amid the enthusiastic applause and a few whistles, the Director and his aide pinned the gold single orbit lapel pins in place. They exchanged salutes and then the Director stepped to Casi.

"Captain Casi Geaardt," he began as the man beside him handed him another small packet. "I wish I could offer you something for all of your efforts in keeping the general in line, but I can only recognize your unwavering commitment to the Force and its objectives. Without going into more details than I should, I am pleased to promote you to the rank of major. Congratulations."

Again, the room filled with enthusiastic applause as he changed her lapel pins from captain's bars to major's insignias. They exchanged salutes and he stepped to Kiile.

"Captain Kiile Beeli. It is with my greatest pride that I recognize your dedication to the Force, your resilience to change, and your ability to adjust to the changing demands placed on you and your command. It is my pleasure to promote you to the rank of major. Congratulations."

The scene repeated, and after pinning the major's insignias, the Director moved to face Cheral.

"Now, Major Cheral Haak-Beeli. It is my pleasure to recognize your dedication and service to the Force, especially in light of the changes and new demands placed upon you. It is with great honor that I promote you to the rank of colonel. Congratulations, Colonel."

The Director and his aide, accompanied again by enthusiastic applause, quickly exchanged Cheral's lapel insignias.

He stopped and looked at the empty spot beside Cheral.

"Where's Lieutenant Quil?" He turned to the table. "I'm sorry. Lieutenant Quil? Will you please join us?"

Thursday, February 15
C.4386.813

It was late when Apache Flight landed at Shadow Base and Blaire had secured Apache Seventeen and turned it over to her personal maintenance crew. She spent a few minutes with each of them, since they had had precious little time before they departed ten days ago, and then she swung her duffle across her back and headed for her quarters.

Entering, she set the door controls to "secure" and dropped her duffle across the foot of her bed. She went to the necessary, then came back to the small living area, unfastened the collar of her Blues, and unzipped the front a few inches as she sat down on the lounger near the door. She glanced at her communications terminal and noted there were no messages. She was surprised at first, until she realized, smiling, that everyone that would leave her a message had been on their mission.

Even though she had eaten on board STSX a few hours before they landed, she decided she still wanted something sweet and a dark-roast coffee before she turned in. She started to get up, but noticed something dark under the nightstand beside her bed. The light beside the lounger was at just the right angle to illuminate the dim space, and she quickly investigated.

She remembered the small box when she pulled it out into the light: Sam's birthday gift that she had not opened. She returned to the lounger, unwrapped the box, and her mouth dropped open as she stared at the silver and turquoise ring. Her mind reeled and then slowly settled as she realized it was a "friendship" ring. She chided herself for jumping to a wrong conclusion and pushed herself up, remembering her tinge of hunger.

Walking to the Mess, she remembered the General—Greg, she corrected herself—telling her to get a good night's rest and meet in the morning at ten for a full-facility debriefing. She smiled, knowing he intended to present everyone that had received awards and promotions. And she knew he would present at least two more promotions on the Director's behalf: Rose and Marine Seventeen were not present in the Rings.

Blaire entered the Mess and went straight to the dessert section of the serving counter and single-mindedly studied the offerings. She had settled on a slice of homemade pie and asked for a scoop of ice cream to go with it when a stern male voice behind her asked, "Can you hurry it along a bit? It's late and I'm tired..."

She turned sharply, ready to pounce on anyone so rude as to— She stopped and stared at the wide smile atop a khaki uniform.

"I didn't believe it, but there are only three redheads in the valley," he said. "And I've already met the other two tonight. So it had to be you."

"Sam?" she said softly, still staring. "Sam!" Her wary expression melted into a wide smile as she jumped up and threw her arms around his neck.

In reflex, he caught her around the waist and held her tight. "I didn't know this was the new life you'd found," he said as she tilted her head back to look at him. "And you're wearing Blues! Not Khaki's."

"Hush a minute," she said, and kissed him long and tenderly.

Sam slowly lowered her to the floor and he nodded to her plate on the counter. "Come. Get your dessert and come talk to me."

Blaire nodded, and collected her plate and a cup of coffee. Sam picked up his cup and led her to a table in the nearly empty dining room.

"I wondered where you went," Sam said as he sat her down and then moved his chair close beside her. "Your folks didn't know or wouldn't say, and no one around here has mentioned that you are here. Or were here."

"To start at the beginning," Blaire said, and recounted her actions and the events that had led her there and through her training. "When we saw each other, during my time off after graduation, I had just received my pilot's ribbon and my official rank. Everything was going good, and after being with you that weekend, I was really in torture."

"Torture? Why?"

"Worrying about my double life," Blaire admitted, and took another bite of her pie. "Shara—sorry, Casi—told me you were a Shadow and I should just tell you about my double life when I saw you again. I know you couldn't tell me any more than I could tell you, but Casi fixed that. So here I am, a captain, a Shadow, and a Q-Ship-qualified pilot. I have my own special fighter and the Director says I will get a Q-Ship on my next birthday. I live here in Shadow Base and at my folks' when I'm home, and one of these days I'll have a place of my own close to town."

"Wow," Sam said, and smiled. "And the last ten days?"

"No one could know we had gone and no one could know where." Blaire explained the bare bones of the mission for the new talents to meet the Director. She hesitated a moment and decided she had better ask. *'Casi? Can I tell Sam about the mission to the Rings?'*

'Yes, Blaire,' Casi answered. *'I'm glad he found you. I saw him in the launch bay and he said he needed a cup of coffee. I knew you were going there, so I told him he should go ahead.'*

Blaire chuckled and Sam looked at her.

"Sorry. Just something Casi said," Blaire said, and then explained the attack and the capture of the commander and his staff. "I have perfect combat scores in training and got my first live combat kills when we went after one of Prince Lukré's battlecruisers."

"Your first kills?" Sam's eyes went wide. "More than one?"

Blaire smiled. "Yeah, after we rescued Casi and Leeana. Caiti was flying STSX1 and Keely was flying KKLC14. We went to stop the battlecruiser coming to check on the freighter we had stopped, and Caiti and Keely each got fifteen fighter kills and together they destroyed the cruiser. Cera Dnar and I stopped the other forty-five fighters to keep them off Caiti and Keely's backs. I got twenty-three and Cera got twenty-two."

"Wow, again," Sam said softly, and took another sip of his coffee.

"Thanks," Blaire said, and turned somber. "I'm good at what I've learned to do, Sam. Damn good. And I'm going to keep doing it. I don't mean to sound boastful or anything like that, but I don't need someone to take care of me anymore. I can do that myself."

"I'm very glad that you can, Blaire," Sam said softly. "But don't turn that into a wall or make yourself an island. I still want to be with you, and now, maybe we can work together. I want to care for you, and to take care of you when you let me. I hope someday you'll feel the same way. I want it to be a want, not a need, to be together."

Blaire smiled and looked at him. "I want that too, Sam," she said, and covered his hand with hers. "I've thought about us a lot over the past ten days, especially after the things we did and seeing the realities we face. We're always in danger, and I'm needed when things go bad. Our time is precious."

Blaire picked up her used plate, took their empty cups, and set them in the bin for dirty dishes. Then she stepped back to the table, took his hand, and led him out of the Mess and down the corridor to Billeting.

"Come on," she said softly, and hugged his arm. "I'll let you in on the news about the new promotions and some of the changes that are going to happen around here. And I have something I want to ask you about."

When she palmed her door panel aside, Sam stopped and looked at her.

"You sure you want me to come in? Might raise a few questions and—"

She stepped through the opening. "Come in here, Sam," she said firmly, and he followed her in.

The door slid shut behind him and she secured the controls.

"I don't have much space or furniture, but take the chair." She gestured to the straight-backed chair nearest the foot of her bed as she slid her duffle onto the floor. She took the ring box from her nightstand and then sat down on the foot of the bed next to him.

"I thought captains were supposed to have larger quarters than this," Sam teased, and looked around the room.

"I've only been a captain for three days," she said, and smiled. "And I just got back, so we don't have the quarters issues sorted out yet. Anyway, I just found this"—she held the ring box in her lap—"after losing it the night we stopped a slave traders' freighter on the far side of the moon and some of Kiile's marines rescued a number of captives in Australia. That was a couple of days after my birthday."

Sam looked at the box and then slowly smiled at her. "You lost it?"

"I was opening it when marine Forty-two collapsed after being shot," she tried to explain. "On many missions, I'm selected to *link* with him and provide guidance and an external view of his situation. Others are paired with other marines at different times."

"So you do *hear*," Sam said, and smiled wider. "I thought so."

"Yes, I do," she admitted softly. "For quite a while now. But I really want to know what this is supposed to mean." She held up the box. "It's beautiful, but..."

"Blaire," Sam said. "I gave it to you so you'd know I was still your friend. We were not on speaking terms right then, and I needed to be sure you knew it was just an argument or a temporary tiff."

"Thank you, Sam," Blaire said. "I can't tell you how much knowing you were there has meant to me."

"When we were together after your graduation," Sam said, and fumbled around in his shirt pocket, "I decided I wanted to exchange that one for this one, or just give you this one outright." He handed her another small box.

Hesitant, she opened the box and saw the immaculate diamond in a silver setting.

"Now that I know you're a pilot, I'll have the setting

changed to work with your flying gloves. This one is a little too tall, I think."

She stared at the ring and mouthed silent questions. Finally getting her voice back, she asked, "It's beautiful. But? Are you asking me—?"

"To marry me," he finished for her. "I am. I don't want to waste any of our precious time either."

Blaire stood up in front of him, straddled his legs, and sat down on his lap, then cupped his face between her palms and kissed him fully. He wrapped his arms around her and held her tight.

"I'm thinking this is a yes," he said when he took a breath.

"Yes. It certainly is."

He took the ring out of the box and gently slid it onto her finger. "Can you go into town tomorrow?" he asked. "We can see about a new setting."

"We can," she said, looking at the ring in the room's inadequate lighting. "After the debriefing and lunch. Do you have a ride?"

"I just have to call Wally's remote," he said.

"No, you'll ride with me." Blaire shook her head and smiled. "I have to fly up to the ranch and get my jeep, and we can drive into town from there."

"Sounds wonderful," Sam said.

"Now," Blaire said softly, and stood up. "Catch that light and come over here. There is something I want to discuss in more detail."

⌄ ⌄ ⌄ ⌄ ⌄

"I want you two to know," Shara said as she squeezed Sedona sitting on her lap, "that Dad and I are very, very proud of you."

Greg, sitting beside Shara, squeezed Sedona's hand and tightened his other arm around Sierra, sitting on his lap. "And very grateful."

Sedona sighed and looked at him. "We couldn't sit back and let them steal you—either of you—away from us."

"We thank you for that," Shara said, and smiled.

"You've always been there for us," Sierra said, "never thinking twice when we were in danger or hurt."

"How could we do anything less?" Sedona asked rhetorically. "Aunt Jill told us that when she was captured and Prince Kiese's emissary tried to steal her away, they really wanted you instead."

Shara nodded slowly. "That's true. I wasn't taken only because my great aunt was so angry she wasn't thinking straight. Somehow she figured I could *hear*, even though she couldn't and my mother couldn't. She swung a deal of some sort, and I was supposed to be given to the Warlord Prince Kiese as a slave, so I could *listen* to the Peace Force people and tell the prince what was going to happen or was happening. But when I slipped away when they tried to capture me the first time, and your dad saved me when they tried the second time, it made her so angry that she just wanted me dead. So, if you remember the first history lesson, she poisoned me when I was captured, not realizing she had both of us."

"How awful," Sierra whispered.

"Could Aunt Jill *hear*?" Sedona asked.

"Not at that time," Greg said. "But a few months later she began."

Shara chuckled. "Boy, did she! It took your dad a lot to get her to slow down and learn how to control her thoughts. We were afraid everyone in the valley would start hearing her."

"Was the Director being held hostage and the attack when we got there because they still wanted to capture you?" Sierra asked.

"Yes, love," Casi admitted, and squeezed Sierra's hand. "And possibly all of you, but without you, they could have succeeded."

"We were thinking on our way home," Sedona said softly.

"Without the two of you, none of this would be here. Aunt Jill and Uncle Nick would be gone. Cousin Kiile and Cheral and Neila wouldn't be here—"

"The ranch, the horses—"

"I told you not to think about what might have happened," Casi said firmly but softly. "We are here and you are here and you and our cousins are heirs to the biggest ranches in the valley."

"And you two have just impressed the most powerful man in the galaxy." Greg smiled. "The Director."

"I can't believe we are 'registered' and it isn't our birthday yet," Sierra said, her happiness bubbling out.

"And lieutenants! With our own patrol fighters!" Sedona said, just as emphatically. "And Hench is the new commander and you're a general!"

"Man, that makes me sound old," Greg said. "Are you two okay with having an old man for a dad?"

"And that makes me an old woman!" Shara chuckled.

"Stop it, you two," Sedona said, and playfully slapped Shara's tummy. She caught Shara's sudden start. "Sorry. Is something wrong, Mom?"

Shara composed herself and smiled. "No, love. Nothing's wrong."

'Ought to tell them, Bren,' Greg said, and smiled.

"Tell us what?" Sedona and Sierra asked together, and looked from Shara to Greg and then back again. Then they looked more closely at Shara.

"Mom, you're putting on a little weight, aren't you?" Sierra asked.

"And you were eating a lot of non-Terran foods in the Rings," Sedona said. "What's going on?"

"Well, girls," Shara said softly. "You didn't know it, but you two saved more than just your dad and me and the Kooiches."

"Sedona!" Sierra said, wide-eyed, holding Shara's hand. *"Feel* them! Mom's pregnant!"

"Holy cow!" Sedona whispered, and grabbed Shara's other hand. "Twins again?"

Shara smiled and nodded, then glanced at Greg's wide smile and then back at the girls.

"Sisters," Greg said.

"Wow," Sierra added softly. "That's why STSX was concerned about your reaction to the sleep gas."

"Yes, it is," Shara smiled. "And he says everything is okay now."

"When? I mean how long have you known?" Sierra continued.

"I'm just over ten weeks," Shara said. "I began showing you two at ten weeks too." She saw Sedona was trying to work the math in her mind. "It was the night before you two soloed. December fifth."

"We knew you were happy that night," Sedona said.

"But we thought it was because we were going to solo," Sierra finished, and feigned a pout.

"We were happy because of you," Shara said, and smiled a knowing smile at Greg. "That's probably why you're going to have sisters. Are you going to be all right with two more sisters?"

"Ye-ah," they said together, as if that should not be a question.

"We've always wondered why you didn't have more kids than just us," Sedona said.

"Who else knows?" Sierra asked. "Hench and Leeana? Aunt Jill and Uncle Nick? Doug and Rose? Who else?"

"Matti, Meara, the house girls, and Hank know," Greg said. "And STSX, of course."

"Of course he would know," they said in unison again.

"We didn't want to tell anyone before we told you two," Shara said, and hugged Sedona again, "but a few had to know."

"So? When can we tell everyone?" Sierra asked, and looked at Sedona.

"Well," Greg said, and hugged Sierra. "I have this big debriefing at Shadow Base in the morning, and almost everyone we know will be there. I say in the morning you can tell anyone you want."

Shara nodded and hugged Sedona, and Sierra leaned over and joined them. "I think that will be just grand."

"Tomorrow then," Sedona and Sierra said in unison, and laughed because they had.

Shara and her family's story continues in
Paladin Shadows Series Book 14
Assignment: Casha-Six Part 1, No warning.

Riggin Town Map

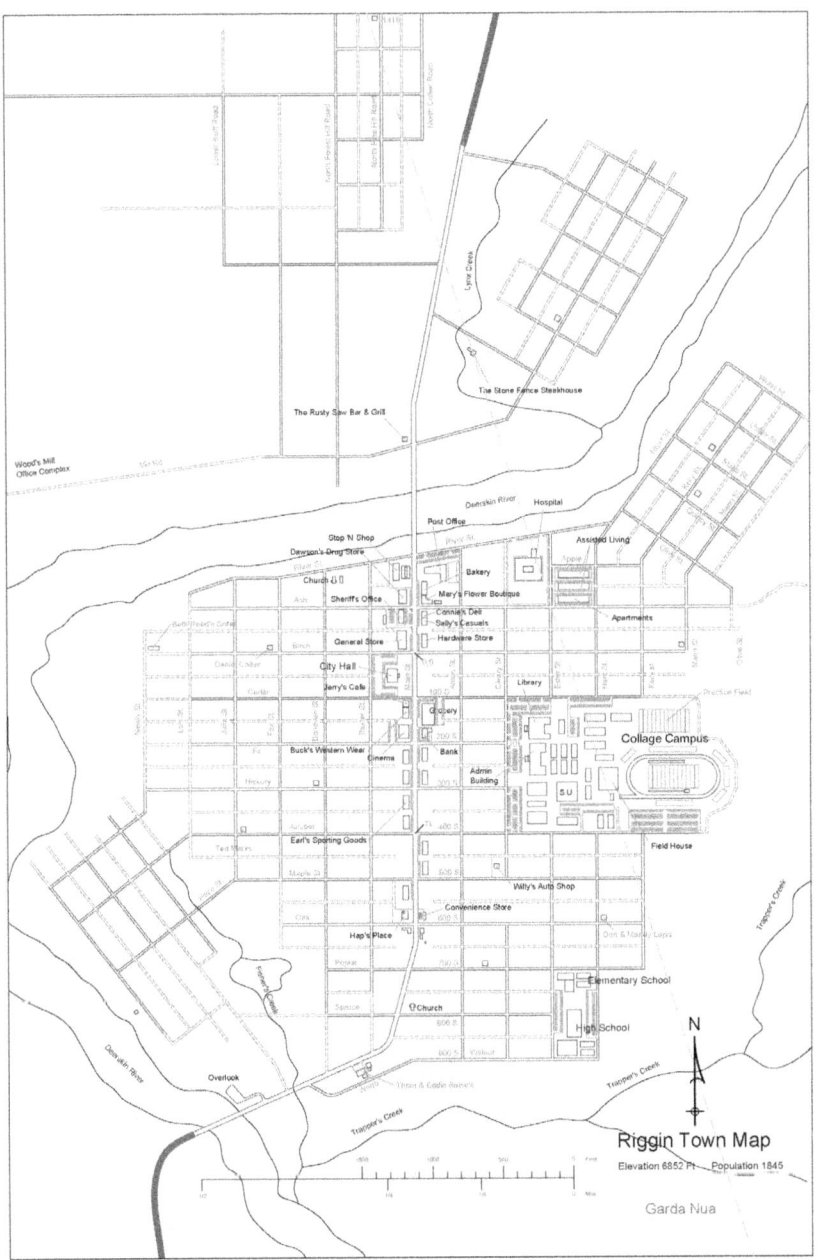

Riggin Town Map

Elevation 6852 Ft — Population 1845

Garda Nua

Riggs Valley Map

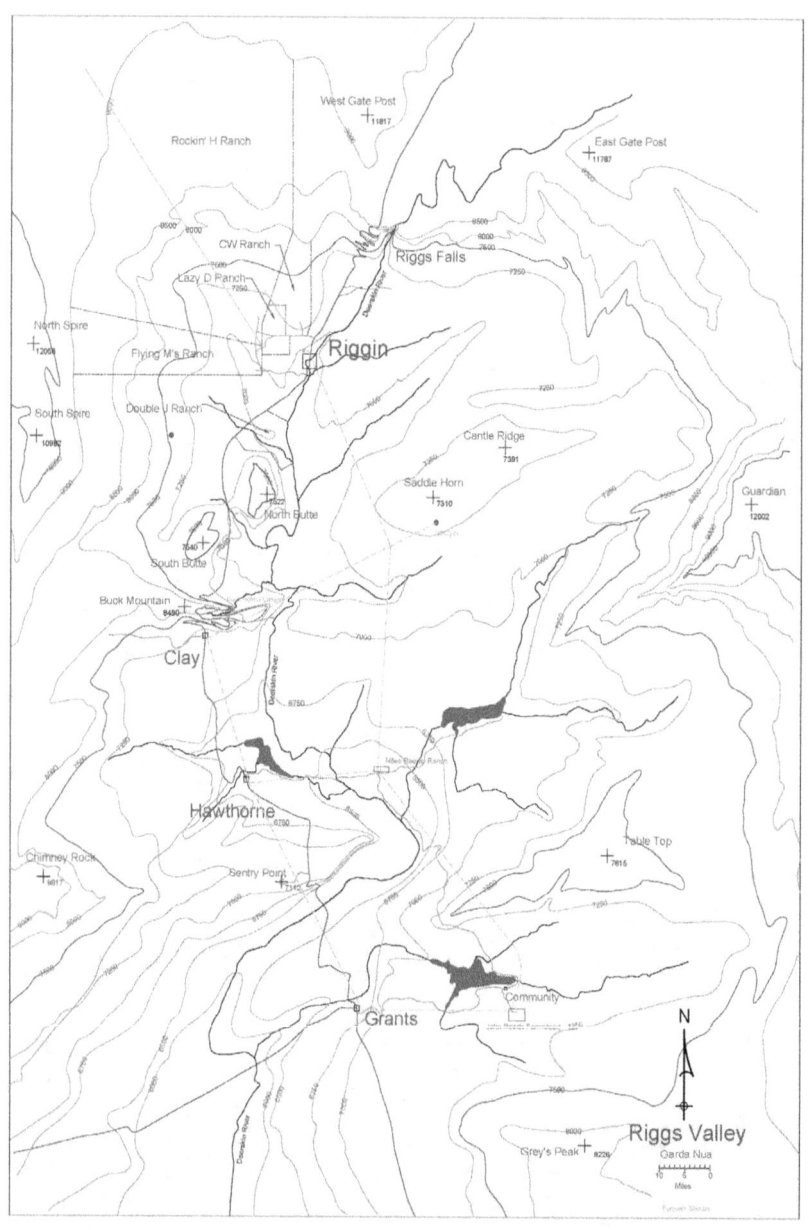

Glossary

Characters:

-A-

Annie	Cook at the Malone's Flying-M Ranch.
Anthor of Marit	Neila's grandfather. Living in Belimoor on Somstri.

-B-

Baine, Thom	State Deputy assigned to Riggin under Marshall Wally Lima. Father of Billie.
Baine, Eddie	Thom Baine's wife. Maiden name: Eddie Collier. Married on Dec 31, C.3482.750, age 35 yrs. Mother of Billie.
Baine, Billie	Daughter of Thom and Eddie Baine. Born on November 10, C.3483.429. Age 8 yrs old.
Beeli, Kiile	Captain, a Marine Squad Leader in the services of the Galactic Peace Force. Commandant of Marine base at Point Obscure. GPF Terran ID: USL15-EFM. (Kiile pronounced quickly Kī-īle.) ¬
Bren	Short version of Greg's nickname, 'BrenCara,' for Shara. Meaning: "Special Raven Haired Friend."
Brickle	Sedona's favorite horse. Named for her mottled caramel coloring.
Bucky	Cheyenne's favorite horse. Named for his buckskin coloring.

-C-

Cadet Pilots	Cadet students training in the art of space combat.

Apache Patrol Two:	Cadet Huml
Apache Patrol Three:	Cadet Milik
Apache Patrol Four:	Cadet Ilistr
Apache Patrol Five:	Cadet Lupis, Class 2 Fighter

Camerso	Gentleman's Gentleman to Prince Lukré. Previously the Gentleman's Gentleman to the late Prince Kiese.
Cara	Second house girl at the Malone's Flying-M's Ranch.
Cassel, Brendan	Coleen Malone's second husband, mate. (GPF Terran ID: IAL01 SS3)
Cassel, Coleen	Husband/mate to Brendan Cassel, second marriage. Previous marriage: Coleen Reese. Maiden name: Coleen Malone.
Chairman Sorgat	Principal Officer in the Trader's Union
Coleen Malone	See Malone, Coleen
Coleen Reese	See Reese, Coleen
Collier, Eddie	Floral Arranger at Mary's Flower Boutique. 24 yrs old when she married Thomas Baine. Daughter of Daniel Collier. No siblings.
Collier, Daniel	Eddie's missing father. Non-terran family name is Calr.

-D-

Dnar, Cera	Jill Jordan's GPF name (Pronounced: Key + ¬¬ray; Means: Fiery Red). A Captain and pilot in the GPF.

Dnar, Jadn	Bob Jordan's non-terran name.
Dnar, Jesi	Nick Jordan's GPF name. A Captain and pilot in the GPF.
Dnar, Keely	Cheyenne Jordan's GPF name.
Danny	Shara's 15 yr old black stallion. Retired from competition.
Davis, Carole	Waitress at Hap's Place. Shelly's younger sister by one year. 23 yrs of age when Wally was assigned to Riggin.
Davis, Marty	Husband of Rusty Davis. Father of Shelly, Carole and Todd Davis.
Davis, Rusty	Wife of Marty Davis. Mother of Shelly, Carole and Todd Davis.
Davis, Shelly	Raised in Riggin, wife of Lt. Jim Woods. 36 yrs of age. Mother of Carrie Anne Woods.

Deputies, Special

In Riggin:

Thom Baine.   See Baine, Thom.

William (Bill) Day See Day, William

Dan Lupis. See Lupis, Dan.

Ted Marks.See Marks, Ted.

Scott Plumen   See Plumen, Scott

Harvey Saulter   See Saulter, Harvey

In Hawthorne:

Bill Trent

In Grants:

Thad Reeds   Rural Support

Willy Carle

Dílis	Shara's 15 yr old black-faced roan. Greg's favorite and named by him. (Pronounced Jee + lus)

Director, Peace Force   Identification AGL36Q

-E-

Elders, The Family   Brian Woods   (deceased)

Harry Woods   (deceased)

Harold Danley   (captured)

Malcolm Clotter   (captured)

Charley Clotter   (captured)

Dave Barns

Don Nikle

-F-

Family Council   Support council for the Council of
Elders, the nearly extinct governing
body of the southern Riggs Valley.
Normally ten members, only
remaining members:

William (Bill) Copper

Jack Wilton

Fighters, Apache Squadron

Apache One: Q-STSX1

Apache Two: Q-KKLC14

Apache Three: Q-TTYF8

Apache Four: Q-STSX12

Apache Five: Q-LTVC21

Apache Six: Q-MKCC5

Apache Seven: Q-KVWC33

Apache Eight: Q-LLRT12

Apache Nine: Q-KCMM9

Apache Ten: Class 2 Patrol Fighter – Ani Tigs

Apache Eleven: Class 2 Patrol Fighter – Emli

Apache Twelve: Class 2 Patrol Fighter - Barba

Apache Thirteen: Class 2 Patrol Fighter – Rose

McIntire

Apache Fourteen: McIntire	Class 2 Patrol Fighter – Doug
Apache Fifteen: Dnar	Class 2 Patrol Fighter – Cera
Apache Sixteen:	Class 2 Patrol Fighter – Jesi Dnar
Apache Seventeen: Lupis	Class 2 Patrol Fighter – Blaire
Apache Eighteen:	(Unassigned)
Apache Nineteen:	(Unassigned)
Apache Twenty:	Q-QRTT7
Apache Twenty-One:	Q-JCCV4

-G-

Geaardt, Stran	A Shadow. An undercover agent. A Commander in the Galactic Peace Force. Pilot of Q-STSX1. GPF ID: HQZL09-ES. Pronounced "Gee (as in Geese) + art."
Geaardt, Casi (Casey)	A Shadow. An undercover agent. Stran Geaardt's partner, wife. A Captain in the Galactic Peace Force. Pilot of Q-STSX1. GPF ID: HQZL09-ES2.
Geaardt, Caiti	Registered name of Sedona Malone. GPF ID: HQZL09-ES2.1 assigned on her eleventh birthday.
Geaardt, Coli	Registered name of Sierra Malone. GPF ID: HQZL09-ES2.2 assigned on her eleventh birthday.
Geaardt, Moira	Registered name of Coleen Malone
Gpada	Means Grandfather, in the cultural language of Nevar.
Gpama	Means Grandmother in the cultural language of Nevar.

Greg Malone   See Malone, Greg

-H-

Haak, Cheral   Captain/Major in the Galactic Peace Force. Pilot of Apache Patrol Ten, Class 2 Patrol Fighter as a flight student. Advanced to Major and assigned Q-STSX12 with Nav-Com Lieutenant Keli Quil. Granddaughter of Paal Haak. Mated with Kiile Beeli on C.3486.738 (Cheral Haak-Beeli).

Haak, Paal   Commander, Galactic Peace Force Academy, Tactical Strategies Instructor, Retired. Grandfather of Cheral Haak.

Hank   Forman at the Smallwood Ranch.

Hawkins, Paul   Brother of Andrew and Nancy Hawkins. Grand Uncle to Shara Smallwood. (aka Paal Haak.)

Hawkins, Clea   Unplanned daughter of Andrew Hawkins and Katherine (Reeds). Married to Henry Smallwood. Mother of Shara, and surrogate to two other daughters. (Deceased.)

-J-

Jordan, Robert (Bob)   Owner of the Jordan Double-J Ranch. Nick's father.

Jordan, Darcy   Nick's Mother. Darcy Reeds married to Ben Jordan. (Deceased.)

Jordan, Nicholas   Aka, Nick. Husband of Jill Thomas. Father of Cheyenne Darcy Jordan. A Captain and Fighter Pilot in the Galactic Peace Force. Pilot of Apache Sixteen, Class 2 Patrol fighter. GPF Terran ID: IAL36 SS.

Jordan, Jill	Nick Jordan's wife (Jill Thomas) for 11 yrs. Age 34 yrs. Married May 17; C.3482.522. Red Headed mother of Cheyenne Darcy Jordan. A Captain and Fighter Pilot in the Galactic Peace Force. Pilot of Apache Fifteen, Class 2 Patrol Fighter. GPF Terran ID: IAL36-SS2.
Jordan, Cheyenne Darcy	Red headed daughter of Jill and Nick Jordan. Age 10 yrs. Born July 10, C.3482.941. Favorite horse is Bucky. GPF Terran ID: IAL36-SS2.1. Familiar Nickname: Chy (Pronounced Shy)

-K-

Kiese, Prince	Warlord Prince of Knobaal (deceased).
Kiile	See Beeli, Kiile.
Kooich, Hench; Major	Colonel in the GPF, Commander of Q-KKLC14. GPF ID: RWKR17-SC.
Kooich, Leeana	Major Kooich's mate (wife). Captain in the GPF, Nav-Com officer and pilot on Q-KKLC14. GPF ID: RWKR17-SC2.
Kooich, Tayn	Son of Hench and Leeana Kooich. Age 11 yrs old. Born September 30; C.3482.658. GPF ID: RWKR17-SC2.1.
Kym	Third house girl at the Malone's Flying-M's Ranch.

-L-

Lima, Wally	State Marshall, 37 yrs old, permanently assigned to Riggin. GPF Terran ID: IAL05-SS.
Lima, Carole	Wally Lima's wife, 34 yrs old.

(Carole Davis.) Married January 29; C.3482.413. GPF Terran ID: IAL05-SS2.

Lima, Alyssa — Daughter of Wally and Carole Lima. 9 yrs old, born April 22; C.3483.227. GPF Terran ID: IAL05-SS2.1.

Lima, Ridan — Son of Wally and Carole Lima. 8 yrs of age, born May 16; C.3483.616. GPF Terran ID: IAL05-SS2.2.

Lukré, Prince — Replacement for Prince Kiese.

Lupis, Blaire — Daughter of Dan and Mandy Lupis. 18 yrs of age. Redhead. Joins the Force through Greg and Shara and begins training to be a Shadow and to fly Fighters.

Lupis, Dan; Deputy — State Deputy assigned to Riggin under Wally Lima. Wife Mandy. Daughter Blaire. (Registered Family name: Lomr.)

-M-

Malone, Coleen — Married to Tom Reese (1), and to Brendan Cassel (2). GPF Planet-side ID: IAL01-SS. Registered Moira Geaardt.

Malone, Greg — Husband of Shara Malone. 40 yrs old. Born March 17, C.3471.868, married to Shara Smallwood Nov 13, C.3482.336. Married for 12 yrs. GPF Terran ID: IAL02-SS. Father of Sedona and Sierra Malone. Great Nephew to Gary Woods. Son of Coleen Reese (Malone).

Malone, Shara (Shar) — Wife of Greg Malone. 40 yrs old. Born June 20, C.3471.963, in the same year as Greg Malone. Mother of Sedona and Sierra. GPF Terran ID: IAL02 SS2.

Malone, Sedona — dentical twin daughter of Greg and Shara Malone. Age 11 yrs, born August 18, C.3482.615. Favorite horse is Brickle. GPF Terran ID: IAL02-SS2.1.

Malone, Sierra — Identical twin daughter of Greg and Shara Malone. Age 11 yrs, born August 18, C.3482.615. Favorite horse is Strawberry. GPF Terran ID: IAL02-SS2.2.

Marks, Ted; Deputy — State Deputy assigned to Riggin under Wally Lima.

Matti — Head house girl at the Malone's Flying-M Ranch.

Meara Wrth — See Wrth, Meara.

McIntire, Doug — Husband of Rosalee (Mitchell) McIntire. Married June 6, C.3483.272. Married for 9 yrs. A Captain and Fighter Pilot in the Galactic Peace Force. Pilot of Apache Fourteen, Class 2 Patrol fighter. Father is Tom, aka Tor of Anthor, mother is Karyn, aka Canri of Lomsi; both from Somstri, living in Greely, CO.

McIntire, Rosalee (Rose) — Wife of Doug McIntire. A Captain and Fighter Pilot in the Galactic Peace Force. Pilot of Apache Thirteen, Class 2 Patrol fighter.

McIntire, Kaylie — Daughter of Doug and Rose McIntire. Age 8 yrs. Born Sept 2, C.3483.725.

McIntire, Kail — Son of Doug and Rose McIntire. Age 8 yrs. Born Sept 2, C.3483.725.

Mosl, Corporal	GPF Marine Squad Leader, Thirty-two. Assigned to Lieutenant Kiile's Battalion protecting Obscure and supporting the Terran Campaign. (Pronounced: Moh-sul)

-N-

Neila	Kiile's daughter, Neila of Kiile (Neila Beeli). Born and raised in Turell on Nevar. Grandfather lived in Belimoor on Somstri. Blonde haired, blue eyed. (Pronounced: Neil + ah)
Niki	Head house girl for Wally and Carole at the CW Ranch.

-P-

Pada	Means Father, in the cultural language of Nevar.
Pama	Means Mother, in the cultural language of Nevar.
Piper	House girl and cook at Jill and Nick Jordan's home on the Jordan Ranch.

-Q-

Q-STSX1	Commander Stran Geaardt & Nav-Com Captain Casi Geaardt. Campaign Commander for Terran Campaign and Apache Squadron's Flight Training School. (Apache One.)
Q-KKLC14	Colonel Hench Kooich & Nav-Com Captain Leeana Kooich. Campaign's lieutenant and Flight Operations Commander under Commander Geaardt. (Apache Two.)
Q-TTYF8	Colonel Crem Mooren & Nav-Com Captain Franni Mooren. Campaign Wing Commander under Colonel

Kooich. (Apache Three.)

Q-MKCC5	Major Aillx Romaan & Captain Colbee Donnr. Wing Second under Major Mooren. (Apache Six.)
Q-KVWC33	Major Daaws Miiles & Nav-Com Captain Meecia Miiles. (Apache Seven.)
Q-LTVC21	Major Neel Glean & Captain Debira Glean.
	- (Apache Five)
Q-LLRT12	Major Deni Bradg & Nav-Com Captain Mri Bradg. (Apache Eight.)
Q-KCMM9	Major Pti Fila & Nav-Com Lieutenant Lori Tam (Apache Nine.)
Q-JCCV4	Major Ronl Bids and Nav-Com Captain Emly Bids. Joined Apache Squadron after supporting the attack of 4 January and getting repairs done at Obscure. (Apache Twenty-One.)
Q-QRTT7	Major Amel Clef and Nav-Com Captain Pela Clef. Apache Squadron B-Group Wing Leaders. (Apache Twenty.)
Q-STSX12	Major Cheral Haak and Nav-Com Lieutenant Keli Quil.
	(Apache Four)
Quil, Keli, Lieutenant	Major Cheral Haak's Nav-Com Officer on Q-STSX12.

-R-

Ranch Hands	At the Smallwood Ranch: Jimmy, Tom (Tommy), Billy and Dusty.
Reeds	Terran family name of the controlling Family in southern Riggs Valley.
Reeds, Glory	Daughter of Thad and Betti Reeds.

	21yrs of age, living in Riggin, attending Riggin College.
Reeds, Sam	Son of Thad and Betti Reeds. 25 yrs of age, living in Riggin. Finished college studies at Riggin College. (Registered as: Donl Jst.)
Reeds, Thad & Betti	State Deputy out of Grants. Living in Grants with his wife and working for Marshall Wally Lima. Son Sam and daughter Glory.
Reese, Coleen	Married to Tom Reese (1), mother of Hew and (by an Affair) of Greg Malone. Maiden name: Coleen Malone.
Reese, Tom	First husband of Coleen (Malone). (Deceased.) Distant relation of Gary Woods.

-S-

Shara Malone	See Malone, Shara
Smallwood, Shara (Shar)	Unplanned daughter of Henry and Clea (Hawkins) Smallwood. Youngest of three. 40 yrs old. Born June 20 (solstice), same year as Greg Malone.
Smallwood, Henry	Full blooded Apache, American Indian. Married Clea Hawkins, father of Shara Smallwood.
Stial, Sergeant	GPF Marine Squad Leader, Forty-two. Assigned to Lieutenant Kiile's Battalion protecting Obscure and supporting the Terran Campaign. (Pronounced: Steel)
Strawberry	Sierra's favorite horse. Named after her pinkish coloring; a strawberry roan.

STSX	Q-STSX1 is a late generation, Shadow Class Corvette, nicknamed as a type as Q-Ships, operated under the command of Stran Geaardt. The latest in the long evolution of the GPF's Shadow ships. The name is synonymous with the ship's central computer system ID.

-T-

Taam, Crl	Jack Thomas' non-terran name.
Thomas, Jack	Married Amy Woods, daughter of Gary Woods. Father of Jill. Financial Officer at the Woods Lumber Mill. (Father of Greg Malone by premarital affair with Coleen Reese.)
Thomas, Jill	Daughter of Jack Thomas and Amy Thomas (Woods). Six years younger than Shara Smallwood and Greg Malone.
Tigs, Ani; Cadet	Cadet Pilot of Apache Patrol Three, Class 2 Patrol Fighter.
Tmn, Officer	One of Prince Lukré's Intelligence Officers.

-W-

Wardly, Anne, Lt.	Staff Assistant and Aide to Admiral Baker, space station S.S. QuickSilver.
Woods, Harry	Son of Horace Woods. Longtime head of the Woods Lumber and Mill (Retired). Father of Gary, James and Brian.
Woods, Gary	Son of Harry Woods. Father of Bill Woods.
Woods, James	Son of Harry Woods. Father of Amy Woods.
Woods, Brian	Son of Harry Woods. Unmarried.

	Current head of the Woods Lumber and Mill.
Woods, Bill	Son of Gary Woods; no siblings. Father of Jim Woods, Lieutenant (USAF).
Woods, Jim, Lt.	Son of Bill Woods; no siblings. Married to Shelly Davis, father of Carrie Anne Woods.
Woods, Amy	Daughter of James Woods. Married to Jack Thomas, mother of Jill Thomas.
Wrth, Meara; Captain	Galactic Peace Force Marine Medic. Terran age 47. (Meara, pronounced: MYAR + ah). Attending Medic for Sedona and Sierra's birth, for Tayn Koovich's birth and for Cheyenne Jordan's birth. Retired from the Force on 3482.698 at the age of 35 Terran years. Hired by Shara and Greg on 3482.701 as their resident Nanny.

Places and Things:

-A-

Aleemill	A mining colony on Feranni, 30 degrees North of West from Daneubois.
Angrilat	A Principal commercial complex in the Kyddellan System
Antheria	Major Commercial Planet in the Tunst System. Known as a Heavy World with a gravity index of 2.02 times Galactic Standard.
Aridont	City on Listera, cite of water rioting.

-B-

Baile	Planetary system of the planet Rygon.

Belimoor	Major import and export city on Somstri. Home of Neila's maternal grandparents.
Betolle	Planet in the Daneets System. Home planet of Lieutenant Franni Kaal and her hometown of Casimir.
Botuni	Planetary System of agricultural planets Nevar and Somstri.
Brekshiir	A wrist mounted laser weapon, consisting of one or multiple optics and fired by a unique sequence of mental commands. Specifically designed for the GPF Shadows.
	Brekshiir 170 Single Optic wrist Unit, 50 pulses with a range of 300 yds in air.
	Brekshiir 490 Wrist Clusters is the most common in the GPF, consisting of 4 laser units, 50 pulses each with a range of 300 yds in air. Individually fired or in combination.
	Brekshiir 710 Wrist Clusters, upgrade of the 490. 70 pulses with a range of 300 yds in air.
Brigstoan, Patrol Cruiser	GPF Patrol Cruiser designed for interception and boarding of suspect transports. Operated with a standard pilot crew, fifty aerial marines, a separate pilot crew and a Medical staff.

-C-

C.Date	A date referenced to the galactic calendar. A galactic year is comprised of one thousand galactic turns.
	Example: C.3482.329 is the 329th day

of the galactic year 3284. It is also the 310th day of the current story year, November 6th.

Caldite Throwing Dart	A coveted and highly guarded GPF tool, used to inject a sedative or toxin upon impact.
Casimir	City on the planet Betolle, home town of Franni Kaal.
Cellystoan	Planetary system in which the Warlord Prince's home planet, Knobaal, orbits.
Centipar	One hundredth of a par. Similar to a terran minute.
Chain	A terran unit of measure. 66 ft. or 22 yds. or 100 links or 4 rods. There are 10 chains in a furlong and 80 chains n a statue mile. An acre is 10 square chains (that is an area of one chain by one furlong), (or 43560 sq. ft.).
Clay	Town in central Riggs Valley, 93 highway miles south of Riggin.
Colbr	Planetary System with three agricultural planets: Copus One, Two and Three.
Combassa Beans	A vegetable from the agricultural planet Somstri, usually prepared as a paste, high in fiber and nutrients. Prescribed to Casi by STSX to ease the tensions of their missions.
Corsecain	Planet in the Gashii system. Prominent for numerous bloody battles in the Moulit Wars.
CW Ranch	Carole's Ranch: Carole Davis' 65,000 Acre (101.5 sq. mi) ranch above her dad's Lazy D ranch. She named it

'CW Ranch' when she married Wally Lima.

-D-

Daneets System — Planetary system of the planets Betolle and Feranni.

Daneubois — City of Universities & Higher Learning on the planet Feranni in the Daneets System. Cheral Haak's Home Town.

Dangcee — Mining colony on the fourth planet of the Greel system.

Double J Ranch — A 43,138 Acre (67.4 sq. miles) horse ranch owned by Nick's father, Bob Jordan, situated between the North Butte and Riggin.

-E-

Ematl — Space Port and major City on Nevar.

Envirocube — Shipping container with independent life-support systems for transporting personnel through space in the unpressurized holds of freight carriers.

EVA — Extra-Vehicular Activity. Working outside a satellite, space station or shuttle, in the vacuum of space.

-F-

Flying M's Ranch — Horse ranch belonging to Shara Malone (Smallwood). 209,275 Acres (approx 327 sq miles) split off of Paul Hawkins' larger ranch to its north. Situated West of Riggin. (Previously known as the Smallwood-Hawkins Ranch, Shara renamed if after she married Greg and before the girls were born.)

-G-

Galactic Peace Force	Galactic policing organization headquartered in the Gridelin Rings.
Galactic year	Equivalent to 1000 terran days, or 2.7397 standard terran years. See C.Date.
Gillot	A unit of measure roughly equivalent to a terran ounce.
Grants	Town at the south end of Riggs Valley, 186 highway miles south of Riggin.
Greel System	Planetary system in which the Pico Mining Company has established numerous mining colonies.
Greymn	Major Industrial complex on Omerai Two, renowned for its weapons manufacture. Model 40 is hand weapon most widely used by the Trader's Guild.
	Greymn Model 40: 40 destructive pulses with a range of 400 yds in air.
Gystrom	Manufacturing source of the GPF's Mark Series Cloaking Transmitters, based in a secret location in the Gridelin Rings.

-H-

Hawthorne	Town in central Riggs Valley, 128 highway miles south of Riggin.

-I-

IFF	Identification, Friend or Foe. An identification system to determine if an entity, craft or forces are friendly, and to determine their bearing and range from the interrogator. The system is capable of transmitting a

	hail to another system on command.
Issl	A root tuber, high in minerals and vitamins, from Copus Two in the Colbr System. Translated as Bread Root.
Istlar	Major City on Tanjera. Home city of Thomas Baine's parents.

-K-

Kaaspr	The standard issue brand of hand laser weapon for the Galactic Peace Force. Model 106 is the current standard laser hand weapon used in the GPF. Replaced the previous standard, Model 88.
	Kaaspr Model 106: 50 destructive pulses with a maximum range of 350 yds in air.
Knobaal	Home planet and seat of the Royal Throne of the Warlord Prince Kiese. Located in the Cellystoan planetary system.
Kyddel	System in which Angrilat's home planet resides.

-L-

Lazy D Ranch	Martin Davis' 15,455 acre ranch (24.15 sq miles).

-M-

Millipar	One one-thousandth of a par. Similar to in concept but equivalent to 3.456 terran seconds.

-N-

Navigationmate	A ship's crewman assigned the duties of navigation and Astronavigation.
Nevar	Farming Planet in the Botuni System. Home planet of Kiile.

Nuth

An icy planet in the Sadth System. Site of the Galactic Peace Force's Prison for Exiles and Prisoners of Importance.

-O-

Omerai Two

Industrialized planet in the Kyddel system, noted for its arms manufacturing.

-P-

Par

A fundamental galactic unit of time. Twenty-five pars in a Galactic Standard Turn (Day). Similar to a terran hour.

-Q-

QuickSilver

Planet Earth's multinational, manned orbital space station. (S.S. QuickSilver.)

Q-Ships

Nickname for the Galactic Peace Force's two man Recondite Corvettes. Specifically used by Shadows in their various roles of information gathering, defense and protection.

-R-

Riggin

A small college town in the northern point of Riggs Valley, western United States, planet Earth.

Rockin' H Ranch

A 1,263,950 Acre (1975 sq. mile) horse and cattle ranch belonging to Paul Hawkins and Nancy Hawkins (deceased), situated NW of Riggin.

Rygon

Home planet of the very old Geaardt family name, located in the Baile System.

-S-

Shadow	Undercover agent of the Galactic Peace Force with specialized training and abilities in clandestine operations and information collecting, generally thought to be able to hide in plain sight.
Somstri	Agricultural planet in the Botuni system.
Sora root	A plant grown on Nevar, Somstri and Copus One and Two. Used as a spice or herb. Side effect and primary use is to reduce female fertility, a natural contraceptive.
Smallwood-Hawkins Ranch	Horse ranch belonging to Shara Malone (Smallwood). 209,275 Acres (approx. 327 sq. miles) split off of Paul Hawkins' larger ranch to its north. Situated West of Riggin.

-T-

Tanjera	Planet in the Ambali System.
Teligrin	From or of the planet Teligr.
Teligr	Manufacturing site for many GPF used toxins and chemical weapons. Home planet of Eddie Collier's father, Daniel. Family name Calr.
Tissl	Mining colony on the third planet of the Greel system.
Trader's Union	The Stellar Merchant's Guild's black market and slave trading business arm.
Tunst	Planetary system of Antheria.
Turell	Kiile's home village on Nevar.

Turn	A Galactic Standard day, consisting of twenty-five pars. Essentially the same duration as a terran day of twenty-four hours.

-V-

Vidcom	A video communication device.
Vidscreen	A video display screen.

-W-

Wiibsa	A small town northwest of Turell on Nevar.

-Y-

Yarrol Fruit	A light flavored, tart fruit from the agricultural planet Somstri served warm, high in minerals and nutrients. Prescribed to Casi by STSX to ease the tensions of their missions.

-Z-

Zeupa	Renowned agricultural city on the planet Somstri in the Botuni System.

Books by Aidan Red

Paladin Shadow Series
Terran Assignment Triptych
Book 1: Things are not as they seem.
Book 2: When luck is not enough.
Book 3: Fate has a different idea.
Terran Recruits Triptych
Book 4: In the wake of chaos.
Book 5: Terran Talents join forces.
Book 6: New rules of engagement.
Operation Retribution Triptych
Book 7: The training phase.
Book 8: Taking the fight off-world.
Book 9: Luring the Prince into the open.
Garda Nua Triptych
Book 10: The proliferation of Talent.
Book 11: When a planet is stolen.
Book 12: Right does not ask permission.
Assignment: Casha-Six
Book 13: No Warning
Book 14: The Best Laid Plans
Book 14: A Change of Heart

Eight's Warning
Book 1: The Past Hunts.
Book 2: The Past Attacks.
Book 3: The Price of Escape.

More Books by Aidan Red

Keeper and His Tiger
Book 1: An Unexpected Complication.
Book 2: Deadly Undercurrents.
Book 3: The Trap.

Fearin' the Banshee

About the Author

Aidan Red's passion for aviation and aircraft design, engineering, and a deep interest in space and space travel go back many years. An avid reader from an early age, Aidan, with great trepidation, ventured into the world of writing during college. With real world experience in business aviation, Aidan's creative side led him to create an alternate world where the beautiful Riggs Valley was born and Shara's life became chronicled in his epic science fiction series, Paladin Shadows.

Paladin Shadows consists of the five triptychs (three-part works), *Terran Assignment, Terran Recruits, Operation Retribution, Garda Nua* and *Assignment: Casha-Six*. In between the Paladin triptychs, Aidan has penned two, three book series, *Keeper and his Tiger,* and *West's Ghost Ranch* and a novel, *Fearin' the Banshee.*

Unpublished books in his various series are scheduled for release on a regular basis in the coming months.

Visit *www.RedsInkandQuill.com* or *www.AidanRedBooks. com* for more information on Aidan Red's books and where to purchase them.